MAIL ORDER BRIDE

Montana Hearts

Echo Canyon Brides

Book 6

LINDA BRIDEY

Dedication

This book is dedicated to all of my faithful readers, without whom I would be nothing. I thank you for the support, reviews, love, and friendship you have shown me as we have gone through this journey together. I am truly blessed to have such a wonderful readership.

Contents

Author's Note

Dear Readers,

Originally named Multiple Personality Disorder, Dissociative Identity Disorder (DID) has been documented as far back as 1646. In the 19th Century, there were approximately 100 cases of the mental disorder reported by various physicians around the globe, although there were most likely many more cases that were misdiagnosed as other disorders. This disorder is usually caused by severe emotion and/or physical trauma that has occurred during childhood or adolescence. Because DID is such a complex and mysterious disorder, research continues to find exact causes and to search for better treatment and a cure.

Chapter One

The buck moved cautiously across the glade, constantly testing the wind, searching for any hint of danger. Slowly, Wild Wind, a Cheyenne brave, pulled back his bow string and took careful aim, making sure to make no sound as he moved. Before the buck decided to scamper off, Wild Wind released his arrow, which flew swiftly, accurately hitting its mark. The buck dropped and Wild Wind hurried out of his hiding place.

Quickly, he field dressed the deer and hefted it across his shoulders. As he carried it through the woods to his new home, he smiled as he thought about how his friend, Billy Two Moons, couldn't stand the sight of blood. This was a rare trait in an Indian, but Billy had been raised in white society by his foster parents, Remus and Arlene Decker, instead of with a tribe.

It didn't take long for Wild Wind to reach his new cabin on the old Mercer land. His good friend, Lucky Quinn, who was really more brother than friend, owned a sheep farm on another tract of land. The farm was booming and they now needed more room for the sheep. Originally, Travis Desmond, Billy, Winslow Wu, and Ross Ryder had gone into business with Lucky. However, Travis, who worked for Marvin Earnest, had pulled out of the operation because Marvin had not only given him a pay raise, but also a share of the ranch profits. The deal was too good for the newly single father to pass up

Lucky had asked Wild Wind if he wanted to take over Travis' share and the brave had jumped at the chance, knowing that the steady income would afford him a good life. He'd already been helping them, so he knew the business and was good at it. Once it became clear that the herd had to be split, Lucky had asked Wild Wind if he wanted to oversee the herd on the Mercer land. Wild Wind had agreed, proud that Lucky felt he was competent enough to take on the responsibility.

The bitter February wind carried snowflakes and bits of ice on it and Wild Wind was glad that he would be home before the storm grew stronger. As his farm came into view, his two sheepdogs, Rafe and Bubba, barked at him in welcome, coming to meet him. Rafe was not a typical sheepdog—he was half coyote, half collie. He looked like a shorter haired collie, but his eyes were amber in color. Bubba was a huge, gray-and-white Old English Sheepdog. He was only a year old, but was good at his job.

They jumped up, trying to reach the deer, but Wild Wind made them stay down. He would give each of them some meat once he'd butchered it. Sending the dogs back to the herd, he took the deer to a shed and made quick work of it. He hung some of the meet to dry and some he carried outside. He threw the dogs each a steak and continued on to his cabin. Snow now fell in earnest and the fire he'd started before going hunting felt good.

He was putting on some tea when someone knocked on his door.

"Come!" he said.

Lucky Quinn came through the door, shutting it quickly behind him. "Good mornin'," he said, smiling. "Did ya have luck today?"

"Aye," Wild Wind said, mimicking Lucky's Irish accent. "A nice buck. That'll keep me in meat all week. I'll make some wasna, too."

Lucky nodded. "Good. If ya need anything, let us know. I brought your mail since I was in town."

Wild Wind took the two letters from Lucky and frowned at them. "I can guess what they say." He sighed and tossed them on the table in the kitchen area.

"Aren't ya gonna read them?" Lucky asked.

"Later. Do you want some tea?" Wild Wind asked.

"Sure," Lucky said, taking off his coat and sitting down.

Wild Wind sat two mugs of tea on the table and joined his friend. "Are you checking up on me?" he asked, his dark eyes smiling.

"Not about the job, just missed ya the last couple of days. I'm used to seein' and workin' with ya every day," Lucky said.

Wild Wind replied, "I would think you have enough to do with a pregnant wife, a son, and an Arliss on your hands."

Lucky groaned. "Don't remind me. I feel so bad for him, but I don't know what to do about him. It must be terrible to not know anything about yerself."

"Yeah," Wild Wind agreed.

Arliss Jackson had showed up at the sheep farm last November. He was a friend of Lucky's from when Lucky had spent some time in Alabama five years back. Lucky hadn't seen him since then. When Arliss had arrived, the only thing he'd known about himself was that he could play fiddle and that Lucky was a friend—he'd had a letter from Lucky in his coat pocket when he'd been discovered in an alley almost beaten to death.

"Yer really not gonna open those letters?"

Wild Wind smiled at Lucky's curiosity. "Go ahead. I don't mind. I'm going to do the milking. If there's anything interesting, let me know."

He left the cabin, heading for the barn that housed fifteen Nubian goats that needed to be milked.

Lucky opened the letters and read them. Putting them back in the envelopes, he laid them aside with a sigh. More Christian women. While this was certainly not a problem for Lucky, who was a devout Christian man, it was for Wild Wind, who was just as devout to his Cheyenne religion.

Lucky found Wild Wind in the barn. "Lad, don't give up. Ye'll find someone."

"Who, Lucky? Do you understand what it's like to give up almost everything about your old life? I've had to learn a new language, wear white man's clothing for the most part, live in a house, and do work that has nothing to do with the culture I grew up in. Listen to the way I talk. I almost sound like a white man, except for a little bit of an accent. Where am I going to find a woman who can accept my religion and who doesn't expect me to convert to Christianity? Nowhere." Wild Wind laughed.

"I sound like Billy used to, but now I understand his frustration. When I first came back with you and him, all I cared about was having my freedom to live the way I wanted to. I didn't think through the problem of finding a wife. I could have had one by now if I would convert, but I just can't."

Lucky knew that Wild Wind was talking about Echo's new, young pastor, Andi Thatcher. She was a six-foot-tall beauty with golden brown hair and lively brown eyes. She had a poise and authoritative air that was rare for someone of her age. She was also kind, fun, and had some sort of psychic power. She and Wild Wind had flirted with the possibility of a romance, but because he couldn't accept Jesus as his personal savior, it had quickly become apparent that it wouldn't work out. As a pastor, Andi needed a spouse who shared her beliefs, and while there were some similarities in the two religions, there were a lot of differences, too.

That's when Wild Wind had decided to advertise for a mail-order bride. So far he hadn't found anyone who was willing to accept his religious beliefs.

"I'm not asking a woman to convert, I'm just asking for my beliefs to be respected. It works for Win and Erin," Wild Wind said.

Lucky nodded. Winslow Wu, Win to his friends, was an atheist while his wife, Dr. Erin Avery, was a Christian. However, they were able to respect each other's views and agree to disagree. Their eleven-month-old baby, Mia, had been christened and Win had participated in the ceremony even though he wasn't a believer. He had done it for Erin's sake and he was fine with Erin teaching Mia the Christian religion.

"Don't get down about it. I'll keep prayin' for ya."

"No. I won't get down. I'm just frustrated. I appreciate it. At least I can hunt and go where I like instead of being forced to rely on the military for whatever scraps they decide to give us. I'm grateful to you for letting me come with you," Wild Wind said.

"I owed ya for saving me from those Pawnee and takin' me in like ya did. Ya taught me all about bein' a Cheyenne and helped me get married. I wouldn't have Otto if it weren't for you."

Wild Wind said, "I guess that makes us even."

"Aye, it does. Well, I'm off to home to do some work of my own. It's strange havin' Otto in school now instead of home all day. I miss him," Lucky said.

"Just think; soon you'll have another little Quinn running around."

Lucky's handsome face split in a wide grin, his gray eyes gleaming with happiness. "I can't wait for July to get here."

Wild Wind chuckled as he moved to another goat. "I'll bet."

"All right then, lad. Will we see ya tonight?"

"It's Tuesday, isn't it? Of course you'll see me. I'm not missing your mutton stew," the brave said.

"Good. See ya then," Lucky said, leaving the barn.

In town later that afternoon, Wild Wind stopped in at Temples' General Store to pick up a few things. He rounded the one aisle and collided with another body. His quick reflexes allowed him to grab the person before they ended up on the floor. He found himself staring down into the wide hazel eyes of Roxie Ryder, Ross' sister.

"Sorry about that," he said. "Are you all right?"

She nodded and smiled, but couldn't speak at first.

"Are you sure?"

"Y-yes. Thank you."

He let her go and retrieved her basket from the floor where she'd dropped it. He handed it to her and went on his way, oblivious to the appreciative way Roxie watched him walk away. Roxie's sister-in-law, Callie, came up beside her.

"When are you going to stop mooning over the man and do something about it?" Callie asked in her Mississippi accent. "I've never known you to be shy around men since I came to Echo. You have all sorts of men tripping over themselves trying to snag you."

Roxie said, "I know, but they're not him. I've never seen a more beautiful man. All that gorgeous black hair, muscles, and those piercing dark eyes!"

Callie giggled. "Don't swoon on me, Roxie. I can't pick you back up if you fall," she said, patting her growing tummy.

Smiling, Roxie said, "I can't wait to be an aunt. You and Ross didn't waste any time."

Callie wasn't a bit bashful. "No, ma'am. Ross is quite a beautiful man himself."

Ross was a big man with dark brown hair and brown eyes. His muscles came in handy since he was the town butcher and had to have plenty of strength for carrying around carcasses and chopping them up.

"Yes, my brother is a very handsome man," Roxie said.

"You need to do something about this crush you have on Wild Wind. He's a good man with a steady income. You could certainly do worse," Callie said.

"I know, but what will people think?"

"Roxie, how can you admire the man and still be prejudiced?"

Roxie's pretty face registered her offense. "I am not! I don't care what they think about me; I only care for his sake! You know that people aren't always fond of Indians, and I wouldn't want to cause him any trouble."

"I think he can take care of himself," Callie said. "I wouldn't worry about that."

"But maybe he's still pining for Andi," Roxie said.

It was common knowledge that things hadn't worked out between the pastor and the brave. Of course, in a town of Echo's size, almost everything was common knowledge.

Her blue eyes twinkling, Callie said, "There's only one sure way to get a man over that; give him something else to think about. You need to do something so that he has no trouble understanding that you're interested in him."

Roxie smiled as an idea came to her. "Hmm. I think you're right. It can't hurt to try."

"Now you're talking," Callie said.

Chapter Two

"It was nice of Callie to invite me to dinner along with you and Leah and Billy and Nina," Wild Wind said as they rode along in Lucky's wagon a few nights later.

"Of course she'd invite ya. Yer their friend, too," Lucky said.

"I know. I guess there are still times when it surprises me that people accept me."

Leah, Lucky's wife, was deaf, but she read lips very well and could speak as well as sign, although she preferred signing. She was self-conscious about the way she sounded even though Lucky and Leah's sister, Sofia, were always telling her that there was nothing wrong with the way she sounded.

She had been reading Lucky and Wild Wind's lips. She sat half-turned on the wagon seat so she could see what Wild Wind was saying even though he also signed while he spoke.

She said aloud, "People are used to you now and are getting to know that you're a good man, not a savage like most people think Indians are."

"Listen to my wife. She's a wise woman," Lucky said. "I know it's been hard, but ye've caught on to things quick and most people like ya. The ones who don't can go to blazes."

Wild Wind laughed. "Thanks. I just stay away from them."

Arliss was also attending the dinner. "I like you just fine. I don't care if you're an Indian. I don't know if I liked Indians before or not, but I do now. Lucky, did I like Indians?"

Lucky shook his head. "I don't know. It never came up."

"Ok. It's not really important," Arliss replied.

Wild Wind said, "I appreciate that, Arliss."

Arliss said, "I wonder what Callie's making for supper. Ross has himself a good-looking woman."

Leah said, "She didn't say what she was cooking. Callie is a very pretty woman. One day, you'll find a pretty woman."

"Not until I find out who I am," Arliss said. "I don't want some poor woman to take a chance on me and find out I'm some sort of gangster or something."

Lucky said, "Yer not a gangster. Ya just picked pockets now and then. I never heard of ya robbin' a store or anything."

"You said it's been five years since you saw me. I could have become anything. I was someone that somebody wanted dead for some reason. People don't just want people dead for no reason," he said, his brows knitted over his blue eyes.

Wild Wind smiled. "Maybe you stole someone's woman."

Arliss laughed. "Well, Lucky did say that I was popular with the ladies. That's a possibility."

Leah said, "No wonder you and Lucky got along with the way you both flirt with women."

Arliss just grinned.

"I don't know what yer talkin' about," Lucky said.

Otto, who had blond hair like Lucky, but dark eyes like his Cheyenne mother, Avasa, said, "I flirt, too, but no one's gonna catch me for a long time."

Leah stroked his silky hair. "That's good. Don't grow up too fast."

Otto was in his girls-are-yucky phase even though he was friends with several girls, one being Julia Taft, the two-year-old daughter of Evan and

Josie Taft. The sheriff, his wife, and Aunt Edna were very good friends with the Quinns and Wild Wind and had also befriended Arliss.

"I won't."

The dinner of roasted chicken, green beans, parsley potatoes, and shoofly cake was enjoyed by all. Although business was discussed for a little while, the conversation mainly resolved around funny stories and jokes.

Callie said, "Lucky, you must have so many interesting stories about living with Wild Wind's tribe, especially about him."

Lucky grinned. "Aye. Like the time he decided to hunt a bear by himself."

Ross asked, "You were gonna take on a bear all alone?"

"Yeah. It was a show of either bravery or stupidity. Take your pick," Wild Wind said.

"What happened?" Roxie asked Lucky.

"There were several of us there with him, but he wanted to do it alone. Just him facing the bear with a knife," Lucky replied.

Arliss said, "Fightin' a bear with only a knife. I'll go with stupidity."

Wild Wind laughed. "It wasn't too hard since it was fall. The bear was almost asleep."

"Which was why he had the rest of us wake it up some so it would be a fair fight," Lucky said.

Callie asked, "Why on Earth wouldn't you want it to be easy?"

"Because I respected the bear and I wanted it to be a fair fight," Wild Wind said. "And it wouldn't have been as fun if I was able to make an easy kill."

Roxie asked, "You respected the bear?"

"Yes. The Cheyenne respect all life; the animals are our friends since we depend on them for survival. The Great Spirit created the animals to feed us and also to aid us in our everyday lives," Wild Wind said.

"How do they help you?" Ross asked. "I've never really asked you, Lucky, or Billy about this before."

Wild Wind took a drink before saying, "The buffalo are our most sacred animal because we use every part of the animal for survival. I won't go into that right now because we're eating and some people are, um, not offended, but ..."

"Squeamish?" Callie supplied.

"Yes. Squeamish. Thank you. Deer, rabbits, pheasants—there are many animals we rely on for food and we also use almost every part of them," Wild Wind said.

Ross said, "A lot of people eat all of those, including bears. Did you kill the bear?"

Wild Wind smiled. "Yes, but I bear scars from the fight. They are badges of honor and I received much coup for my victory."

"Coup?" Roxie asked.

"It's a sort of game that many Indian tribes play. Sort of like points in baseball. In battle, if you can get close enough to an enemy to touch them, either with your hands or with an arrow or something, without getting injured or killed, you can count coup. You also count coup for stealing ponies and other acts of bravery, including fighting and killing a bear by yourself," Wild Wind explained.

Ross shook his head. "I can't imagine playing a game while you're killing someone or fighting for your life."

"It's just a difference in how our cultures view things, that's all," Wild Wind said. "But there are things that are alike, too."

"What's that?" Arliss asked.

"The way we treat our women," Wild Wind replied.

Roxie perked up even more at that.

"Our women are treated with great respect and there is nothing we won't do to protect them and our children. Your culture is much the same," Wild Wind said. "We believe that the family is the most important part of life, but also that we are all family. But we do not scold our children. We are much like the Lakota that way, and our tribes are very close. There has been much intermarriage between us, too. The Arapaho are also allies and there have been marriages," Wild Wind said.

"That's fascinating," Roxie said. "If you don't scold your children, how do you make them behave?"

"You need only to watch Lucky and Leah with Otto for your answer," Wild Wind said. "They are a good example of how we raise our children, and when I have children, I will do the same."

Roxie thought about that as the conversation turned to something else. She had seen the way that the Quinns dealt with Otto and he was mostly well behaved, even though she'd never heard them raise their voices to him. She remembered the way her and Ross' parents had scolded and yelled at them sometimes. Occasionally they'd been spanked, but it didn't sound as though the Cheyenne believed in such punishment. She thought that sounded very nice.

As dinner concluded, everyone helped clean up, carrying their dishes into the kitchen. Otto carried his own dishes there, just like he did at home, and he was tall enough now to put them up on the counter. Wild Wind smiled at the way Otto seemed to take this duty very seriously.

When the brave passed the pantry, Roxie called to him.

"Will you help me a moment?" she asked.

"Of course," he said, stepping inside with her.

"I can't reach that dish up there." She pointed at it.

Wild Wind reached it easily and handed it to her. "There you go. Is there anything else you need?"

"No, thank you. I was wondering ..." Roxie lost her train of thought as she got lost in his eyes.

"Yes?" he prompted her.

"Um, what do you do with bears once you kill them?" This wasn't her original question, but she couldn't go through with asking him to dinner. It frustrated her because normally Roxie didn't have any trouble dealing with the opposite sex at all.

He smiled. "We use their hides, of course, but we also render their fat for different uses and their meat is very tasty."

"Sometime you'll have to tell me more about that. I've never had bear meat," she said.

"If I ever kill one again, you'll have to try some," he said.

"Hey, Wild Wind, you ready to go?" Arliss called from the kitchen. "Train's movin' out."

Wild Wind rolled his eyes a little. "Thank you for a nice dinner," he said to Roxie and left the pantry.

Roxie wanted to bang her head against the wall in frustration because the moment had slipped away.

Wondering along the main street in Echo Canyon, Montana, Arliss nodded to people he was coming to know and exchanged pleasantries with them. Since coming to find Lucky, he'd helped out on the sheep farm, but he wasn't really needed much of the time since Lucky and Win also employed a boy from town, Adam Harris. He knew that his friend was just trying to be helpful, but Arliss didn't want to keep taking charity. He needed work.

The problem was that even though the town was starting to bounce back a little bit from dire economic hard times, there was still a job shortage. Arliss had no idea what he was good at since he remembered nothing from his past. When he'd known Lucky, the Irishman had said he'd mainly played fiddle and picked pockets for money to live on.

He was on his way to Spike's, the more reputable saloon in town, to see about possibly playing there a few nights a week. Even if Spike couldn't pay him, maybe he'd let him play for tips. His travels took him behind the church, where he heard the sounds of someone chopping wood. He found Andi dressed in men's trousers and shirt swinging an ax. He had to admit that the lady pastor had a fine figure.

"Here, now, Pastor," he said, going over to her. "You shouldn't be doin' that sorta work. Ain't fittin' for a lady."

She halted her work and said, "Good morning, Arliss. How are you?"

"Fine, ma'am. And yourself?"

"I'm well, thank you."

He reached for the ax. "Let me take care of that for you."

"I'm fine, Arliss. I'm used to doing this sort of thing," she said, smiling.

"You mean you ain't got no man to help you and Miss Bea out?" he asked, his brown eyes meeting hers.

Andi bristled a little. "I don't need one, as you can see. I'm quite capable."

Arliss backed down a little. "I didn't mean no offense, Pastor. I can see that you're strong. Ain't a question of you being able, it's just that it ain't right for a man not to offer to help you. You got more important things to do than this, like writin' sermons and such. You can't do that if you're out here choppin' wood and all. Now how 'bout you let me help you out so you can get to your other work? Besides, I ain't got anything else to do and this'll keep me busy. Idle hands and all that."

Andi smiled. "So you're being gentlemanly and trying to stay out of trouble."

"I reckon so, ma'am," he said, holding out his hand for the ax.

"Well, since you put it that way, I'll take you up on your kind offer," she said, handing it over.

"Stand back, Pastor. We're gonna find out if I know how to do this," Arliss said. He hefted the ax and prepared to swing.

"Wait! You don't know how chop wood?" Andi asked.

Arliss chuckled. "I don't know what I can or can't do or what I do or don't know how to do, ma'am. I ain't tried to chop wood yet, so I'm gonna give it a whirl. If I chop off my foot, well, we'll know I don't know how."

Before Andi could stop him, Arliss swung and split the large log on the stump neatly in half. "Whooo! Look at that! I know how," he said, grinning.

Andi laughed in relief and at his devil-may-care attitude about the situation. "It looks like I don't have to worry about you chopping your foot off."

"Looks like. You go on and tend to your flock and I'll take care of this for you," Arliss said.

"Thank you, Arliss. I appreciate it," Andi said.

"You're welcome," he said and started to split the rest of the log. She'd walked a few feet away. "Pastor?"

"Yes?"

"I ain't sure if this is proper or not, but I just gotta tell you that I don't think it's every woman who could wear pants as well as you do," he said as he set up the next log.

She laughed. "Since it's one of the nicest compliments I've ever had about it, I'll look the other way."

"I better do the same if I don't wanna get in trouble," Andi said.

Andi blushed. "Do you always flirt like that?"

"No, ma'am. Only when there's a woman around worth flirtin' with," he said.

When he winked at her, she chuckled and walked into the church.

Chapter Three

Once Roxie had finished helping Ross with the morning chores in the butcher shop, she went on her way, knowing that Ross would be fine for a while. She wanted to go to Temple's to buy some canned cherries to make a pie. It had been a week since the dinner they'd had at their house, and she was going to try the old method of getting to a man through his stomach.

Just his name was enough to conjure up romantic images of him riding across the plains, his hair whipping in the wind, his spear at the ready. She knew that there was much more to him than that, but a woman could be forgiven her fanciful notions once in a while. As she walked along the street, several men smiled and nodded to her in the hopes of currying favor with the beautiful blonde.

Not only was Roxie a very pleasing woman to the eye, but she was one of the few single women in Echo. Over the past few years, Mayor Jerry Belker's plan to increase the population of Echo by men obtaining mail-order brides had been working, but there were still more single men than women. Callie had originally come to Echo to marry Billy Two Moons, but when Billy had gone with Lucky to the Cheyenne reservation in Oklahoma, he'd met his wife, Nina, and they'd fallen in love.

It had worked out because while Billy had been gone, Callie and Ross had met and had developed feelings for one another even though they hadn't meant for it to happen. However, both Callie and Billy had wound up with the person they each were meant to. Nina was a white woman who'd been kidnapped by the Kiowa as a child and later traded to the Cheyenne. Billy had been fostered by white parents. Each knew what it was like to be of one race and raised by another, giving them a powerful common ground.

Callie and Ross were opposites that made a perfect whole. Callie was vivacious and quick witted while Ross was quieter and more grounded. Their strengths and weaknesses complemented each other and they'd developed a deep love for one another.

"Ah, Miss Ryder, how fortunate that I should run into you."

Roxie was startled to hear her name and looked up to see Marvin Earnest smiling at her.

"Oh, Mr. Earnest. How are you?" she asked.

Although there was something different about Marvin these days, he still made Roxie nervous. Marvin had been feared in Echo for many years, known for his cruelty and coldness. As one of the few people in Echo who'd retained wealth after the collapse of the mining industry, Earnest was one of the two largest employers in the town. He'd held that over the head of his employees for a long time, paying them a pittance for their hard work. But with jobs so hard to come by, his workers knew it was better than nothing.

"I'm very well, thank you. And yourself?" Marvin asked, his beautiful features enhanced further by his smile.

"I'm good. Was there something you wanted to talk to me about?" she asked.

"Yes. Actually, I was wondering if you knew if either Lucky or Wild Wind were butchering today or tomorrow."

"I'm not sure. I know we have some mutton in the shop," she said.

"Actually, I wanted a whole sheep," Marvin said. "I would just take one of ours, but I know that Lucky and company are giving us their older sheep and they're just not as tasty or tender."

Roxie hadn't known that Marvin was aware of that fact and she didn't know what to say about it. An idea came to her. "I can let Wild Wind know that you'd like one. I'm sure he's home."

"Would you be so kind? I wasn't planning on going to the sheep farm today since I have a few meetings here in town," Marvin said.

"I'd be happy to," she said.

"I'm grateful to you, Roxie."

She smiled at him and hurried off to pay for her purchases. Marvin watched her go with a bemused expression. There was a perverse part of him that enjoyed the fact that he still made people leery of him. Well, most people, anyway. Others who were coming to know him weren't intimidated by him any longer, which was refreshing. Putting that out of his mind, Marvin continued on his way to the bank for his next meeting.

"Wild Wind?" Roxie called out as she neared the barn on the Mercer property.

There had been no answer at his cabin, so she'd decided to look in the barn. Before reaching the barn, she stopped to look out over the land, thinking it beautiful. Unlike Lucky's farm, this one was a little flatter and had fewer trees, allowing the viewer an unobstructed view of the panorama.

A stream flowed through the property, far enough away to only be a threat to the buildings if a major flood occurred. Trees grew close to it, but there were also some around the buildings. The trees were bare and the grass brown, but the creek sparkled in the sunlight and what snow was left over from the week before was pristine, almost blinding in its intensity—a very pretty picture indeed.

"Roxie?"

It was the second time she'd been startled out of daydreaming that day.

"Hello," she said.

Wild Wind smiled. "Hello. What are you doing all the way out here? It's cold for a ride."

"Mr. Earnest wanted to know if you were going to butcher today or if you could possibly take him a young sheep—a whole one," Roxie said.

Wild Wind stretched his shoulders. He'd been cutting some boards to make another pen and his muscles were tight from the work. "He sent you out here to ask me that?"

"No, he asked me if I might know and I offered to come ask since I was coming over anyway," Roxie said with a sly smile.

Wild Wind frowned. "You were?"

"Yes. I brought you a little gift," she said.

"A gift? For me?" He was perplexed. "Why?"

"Must there be a reason?" she asked.

His smile made her breath catch in her throat. "I guess not. What is it?"

"Come and see," she coaxed, leading him to his cabin where a basket sat on the porch.

Jumping up onto it, he picked the basket up and looked under the cloth that covered it. "Cherry pie! I love cherry pie." As she joined him on the porch, he asked, "Will you join me for a piece? After all, you should get a reward for making it."

"I'd love to."

"Come," he said, motioning her inside. "Good. It's still warm in here. It's cold for you to ride all the way out here," he said, making sure the fire in the cook stove was still strong. "Please have a seat."

Roxie took off her cloak and hung it by the door. Smoothing out her skirt, she carefully sat down at the kitchen table and gazed around at his cabin. A large, decorated bearskin covered most of the wall behind a long, mahogany missionary sofa with blue cushions. A matching chair sat in one corner and a mahogany coffee table stood between them. In the other corner, a sitting mat had been placed on the floor.

Wild Wind put on coffee and cut them each a piece of pie, which he placed on simple white-and-blue dishes. Remembering that Roxie wasn't used to eating with her hands, he took out silverware, turned around to serve the pie, and almost dropped it when he saw what Roxie was wearing.

While the rose-and-white dress wasn't overly fancy, the tight bodice was a little low, revealing the fact that she had been blessed in the bosom department. His eyes trailed upward over her pretty shoulders and neck to her face, which was in profile at the moment. He'd always thought that Roxie was a pretty woman, but had never really paid attention to her before.

This was due to the fact that he'd been mainly concerned with setting up a life for himself and not on finding a wife. It hadn't been until last fall that he'd thought it was time to look for one. He'd hoped that things could work out with Andi, but there was just no way to bridge the gap between their two faiths. Andi had assured him that it had nothing to do with race, but as a pastor, it was important that she marry someone who embraced the same beliefs she did. Even though he'd understood, it had still been hard ending something that had never really had a chance.

Wild Wind was paying attention now, though. Roxie's peaches-and-cream complexion and honey blonde hair were an attractive combination. Forcing himself to stop staring, Wild Wind put the pie on the table and retrieved their coffee before sitting down.

"Is that the hide from the bear you killed?" Roxie asked.

"Yes. It was one of the few things I brought with me from the reservation."

"I'm sorry. You shouldn't have had to leave your way of life. It's not right," she said.

Wild Wind shrugged as he chewed the tart-sweet bite of pie. "There are many things that should not happen to people. Disease, killing, betrayal. I learned early in life that we have to deal with things as they come and change what we can. All the rest of it simply has to be accepted or we'll go mad."

Roxie smiled. "I'm sure I must seem very naïve to you."

Wild Wind frowned. "How so?"

"I've never had to endure anything like you have, so how could I possibly understand what it's truly like? I've never gone hungry, I've always had a warm place to sleep, and I've always been protected. I've never had to fight for my life or live in poverty."

"I'm glad," he said. "Women should be protected and cared for. That's what men are for. We're supposed to provide because truthfully, we're not good for much else."

Her mouth opened in surprise. "Well, of course you are. Why would you say such a thing?"

He grinned, enjoying her reaction. "Think about it. Men can't bear children or feed them with our own bodies. Most of us aren't good at keeping a home or knowing how to nurse a sick child. Unless you're Evan, we're not good at making clothing or cooking."

"You're wrong," Roxie challenged him.

"I am?" He arched a brow at her.

"Yes. There are many chefs who are men and make superb meals. I've seen you with Otto, and Lucky is a very doting father. He helped nurse Otto when he was sick with the flu. I've seen Lucky's lodge and it's very nice. It's different than what I live in, but it's nice, nonetheless. And your home is very nice. It's true that you can't bear children, but women can't have children without men. I don't think it's a case of men not being able to do those things, it's just that they don't want to or are told that it's not their place to do it."

While she'd been talking, Wild Wind had finished his treat. He was amused by her defense of the male species and was caught up in the fire from her hazel eyes and the way her pretty mouth moved.

"In Cheyenne culture, women are very territorial over their roles and don't like it when the men interfere," Wild Wind said. "They make it very clear that men are not to do domestic chores. It is a sense of pride for them and men are not taught how to tan hides or do more cooking than necessary when they're out on a hunt or raid."

"Lucky tans hides and cooks. How did he learn?"

"He's very convincing and he conned Avasa into teaching him how to do all sorts of things that only women do," he said. "However, I have learned how to do some cooking, so I guess I'm teachable."

She smiled. "Do you sew?"

"No. You wouldn't want me repairing any of your clothing. I'd ruin it," he said. "You're right about a couple of things."

"And what would those be?"

"I don't want to learn how to do those things and I've been taught that it's not my place."

Roxie laughed. "At least you're honest."

"I was taught to be and I prefer it. Why get caught in a lie and make things worse? No, the truth is always best," Wild Wind said.

"So if I ask you a question, you'll be truthful about it?"

He nodded. "Or refrain from answering if I don't want to talk about it."

"I see. Well, I'll take my chances. If you choose to answer, I won't talk about it to anyone, but I have a reason for asking. Why didn't things work out with you and Andi?"

Her direct question caught him off guard and he didn't know what to say for a moment. Then he figured that there was no reason not to tell her. He was sure there were many people curious as to the reason, just ready to spread gossip. However, Roxie had said she had a reason for asking.

For a moment, Roxie thought he wasn't going to answer as his midnight eyes stared back at her.

"Andi and I couldn't agree on our religious beliefs. I can't—won't—convert, and she needs someone who believes as she does."

Roxie digested this for a moment as she took a sip of coffee. "So it wasn't because of race?"

"No."

"Did you expect her to convert to your religion?"

"No. Just to respect it," he said.

"I'm sure it must have been difficult for you both," Roxie said. "You seemed to like one another."

He smiled slightly. "Yes and yes. You said you had a reason for asking?"

"Let's say, hypothetically, if a man of a different faith should come calling on me, I would be able to respect his religion as long as he respected mine," she responded, meeting his eyes without flinching.

Suddenly it all came together in his mind: the pie, the way she was dressed, and now this announcement. She was letting him know that she was receptive to him as a man, not just as a friend of her brother's.

Admiring her courage and cunning, Wild Wind saw Roxie in a new light. Would they make a good match? Would Ross be open to such a relationship? Being friends with an Indian was one thing; one possibly marrying your sister was another. There was also the fact that he and Ross were business partners to consider. If he offended Ross, who sold their meat, goats' milk, and cheese for them, would Ross pull out of the operation?

Deciding to tread carefully, he said, "It's good to know that there are women in the world like you who can respect a man's religion, no matter what it might be. It's no wonder you're such a desirable woman."

Roxie smiled and stood. Wild Wind stood as well. "I'll make myself very clear: there's only one man's religion I'm speaking about and I just had a very nice time with him. Have a nice day, Wild Wind."

"You do the same, Roxie. Thank you for the pie. It's very good," he said, walking her to her horse.

She mounted and smiled down at him for a moment before riding away as Wild Wind watched her go.

Chapter Four

"Oh, God, it's you."

Marvin smiled at Thad when he opened the door. "I always enjoy your witty greetings, Mr. McIntyre."

Thad moved back from the front door. "C'mon in. What do you want?"

"I'm here to see Mrs. Watson," Marvin said as he entered. "Is she at home?"

It still didn't seem possible to Thad that the girl who'd become his stepdaughter had become a married woman all before a year had passed. She'd barely had time to take his name before she'd taken Keith's. He still couldn't believe that she was married at the age of sixteen, but she and Keith were happy.

They entered what the McIntyre/Watson household called the Everything Room because that's what they did in it. Thad's office space was sectioned off from the rest of the room by some bookcases. Mismatched furniture, including a large dining room table and chairs, occupied the rest of the room. It had a homey feel that Marvin liked. His own parlor at home now had the same sort of ambiance. The McIntyres' original parlor and dining room had been converted into a small apartment for Keith and Molly when they'd married.

"Look who's here, everybody. Echo's number one pain in the ass," Thad said, sitting down in a chair.

His wife, Jessie, who was eight months pregnant, gave him a disapproving look for cussing, but he just smiled at her. Marvin saw Jessie fight a smile of her own. Thad waved at the other pieces of furniture. "Plant yourself somewhere."

J.J. McIntyre, who was now nine, said, "Here, Marvy. You can sit with me."

"I would love to sit with you," Marvin said, lowering himself onto the sofa by her. "And what are you doing?"

"I'm doing math. I hate it," she said.

"Why do you hate it?"

"Because I stink at it," she said.

Marvin smiled into her blue eyes. "You're a bright girl. I'm sure you don't stink at it."

Her sister, Liz, said, "No, she really does stink at it."

Thad said, "Liz, that's not nice."

"Sorry," Liz replied. "But she does." A hard glare from Thad made Liz look away.

"Have you tried visual aids?" Marvin asked.

J.J. gave him a confused look. "What's that?"

"Come, I'll show you," Marvin said.

Thad and Jessie exchanged glances but remained quiet to see what Marvin was up to. He had J.J. sit at the table and sat next to her. "What are you having trouble with?"

"Fractions." J.J. said.

"Mmm, yes, they can be tricky," Marvin said. "Where's your book?"

J.J. rummaged through a pile of books on the table and pulled one out. "Here." She handed it to Marvin, a couple of pages falling out of it.

Marvin took the book and looked at it, putting the pages back where they went. He noticed that some of the problems were faded and unreadable. "How do they expect the children to learn with books like this?" he said aloud. "Are all of your books like this?"

"Some of them. We don't have books for all subjects since we ain't got the money for them," she said.

Thad and Jessie smiled at each other and Thad winked at his wife. She barely suppressed a laugh.

"Don't have—how can you study properly if you don't—well, no matter. I'll figure that out. Anyway, I'll help you with your fractions for now," Marvin said.

For the next twenty minutes Marvin walked J.J. through fraction problems. He drew a picture of a pie, using it to show her various fractions and how to add them. This helped J.J.'s mind grasp the concept and Marvin made up problems for her, using drawings of various fruits and animals as aids. "Do you understand better now?" he asked as they finished the last problem together.

J.J. smiled. "Yeah. Thanks."

Thad and Jessie were impressed. They wouldn't have thought to have drawn pictures for J.J. the way Marvin had. Liz had even become interested and Marvin also added humor to the lesson. "You're quite welcome."

"You should have been a teacher, Marvin," Jessie said.

He smiled at her. "Well, I was to Shadow, growing up. This is how I taught him. But I wasn't interested in it as a profession. Now, I must go see our favorite reporter. You never did answer me as to whether she's at home, Thad."

"Oh, didn't I? Yeah. Just knock on their door," Thad said.

"Jessie, how are you feeling?" Marvin asked.

"Tired," Jessie said. "Having a baby at my age is harder than when I had Allie and Molly."

When Thad and Jessie had married the previous year, the last thing on either of their minds was having a baby, but her unexpected pregnancy was one of the things that had made Thad decide that it was time to retire from being a bounty hunter. Not only was Jessie pregnant, but Thad had a lot of other people counting on him, too. Jessie's daughters, Allie and Molly, who were from Jessie's previous marriage, had quickly become daughters to Thad. There were also the three children he'd adopted before he and Jessie had married.

Their mother, Darlene Daughtry, had been a prostitute who'd mainly worked at the Burgundy House, the other saloon in Echo. Thad had rented a room from her, but there hadn't been any romantic relationship between them. Darlene had been a terrible mother, leaving the kids to fend for themselves much of the time. Shortly after moving in with them, Thad had begun taking care of the kids whenever he was in town.

He'd fallen in love with them, and when Darlene had been murdered, he'd decided to adopt them rather than letting them go to an orphanage since there wasn't any other family to take them in. That's what had prompted Thad to look for a wife: he'd needed someone to be with the kids when he'd had to leave Echo on a job and might be gone for two or more weeks at a time.

Since retiring, he'd become one of Echo's two deputies—Marvin's brother, Shadow, being the other one. Once in a while, Thad felt the itch to go out hunting criminals, but he liked working for his best friend, Evan, and whenever that itch came, he'd just look at his wife or one of his kids and the itch would go away.

"I'm sure you'll be very glad when the babe comes along," Marvin said. "Well, I'll not intrude on your family time any longer. Have a pleasant evening."

When he'd gone from the room, Jessie asked, "Do you think he has any idea what everyone's doing?"

"It's hard tellin' with him," Thad said. "If he don't, he'll catch on eventually, but we'll get as much out of him as we can until then."

Jessie stifled a laugh while Thad grinned.

A few nights later, Wild Wind had joined the Quinns and Arliss for dinner. Halfway through the meal, someone knocked on the door. Lucky answered it and found himself staring into a revolver barrel.

"Back up, mister," said a strange man. "Back up and no one gets hurt."

Lucky did, putting himself between the man and Leah and Otto. "What's this about?"

Wild Wind pulled Leah and Otto behind him and together he and Lucky protected them.

The man's gaze found Arliss. "Well, well. Just the man I'm lookin' for. How are you, Arliss, you piece of crap?"

Arliss asked, "Do I know you?"

The man with dirty, long, gray hair and blue eyes laughed. "Do you know me? I guess you ought to. Come with me and no one here has to get hurt."

Arliss nodded. "Sure. Don't hurt my friends. I'll come with you."

"Arliss," Lucky objected. "Don't."

Arliss said, "I'm not gonna let y'all get hurt. I'll just go with this gentleman peaceful-like and you won't get in any trouble."

Suddenly, the man jerked and let out a short cry of pain. Looking down at his stomach, he saw a small knife protruding from it. Arliss, who was closest to the man, took advantage of the distraction. He swiftly disarmed the man with efficient moves that few people, outside of trained fighters, would know. Then he pointed the gun at the man's head and fired. Blood and brain matter sprayed the kitchen door and walls behind the man. His body dropped to the floor as Leah screamed.

All of this had happened in the matter of a few seconds. Arliss looked down at the body and said, "Damn it! I still don't know who I am."

Lucky and Wild Wind looked at each other as Lucky put an arm around Leah and looked around for Otto. The boy stood right in front of Wild Wind with a satisfied smile on his face. Looking at the small knife, Lucky saw that it was Otto's. Cheyenne boys were taught fighting skills very early in life, so it wasn't unusual for a boy of Otto's five years to have a knife.

"I saved us, Da," Otto said.

"Get over here," Lucky said. "You were supposed to stay behind me."

Arliss had set the gun down and was going through the man's pockets, hoping for a clue as to his own identity.

Lucky said, "Arliss, stop that. We'll have to get Evan and he'll do that."

Arliss flicked a glance at Lucky and said, "I don't need to wait for a sheriff to go through the man's pockets. We know how he died, so you don't have to try to figure out who killed him or why. I killed him so that he didn't kill any of us."

Wild Wind said, "I'll help get him out of here so we can clean up."

Win ran up onto their porch and saw the bloody hole in the glass and saw his friends inside. The brave noticed him and motioned for him to stay back. Arliss saw his movement and looked out the door window. Seeing Win, he smiled a little and opened the door.

"This one's a goner, but we better make sure he was alone," he said.

Win's dark eyes widened when he saw the dead man on the floor. "What happened? I heard a gunshot."

"Well, this fella came lookin' for me, but I don't know who he is. He had us at gunpoint and wanted me to go with him. I was willin' to so nobody got hurt, but Otto helped save the day. He threw his knife and got the guy in the gut. So I disarmed him and shot him. I'm tryin' to figure out who he is and why he came after me. I'd also like to know who I am," Arliss said.

Win looked at Lucky as he listened to Arliss' matter-of-fact recounting of the situation. He spoke like someone in law enforcement, the military, or in a gang of some sort might. There was something about Arliss that was off, but no one could put a finger on it. Most of the time, they just thought it was because of his previous head trauma, but right at that moment, none of them were sure that was the case.

Remaining calm, Win said, "Well, why don't you come with me for now and Evan can help sort things out. Right now, you need to let Erin see to Leah. It's not good for her to be frightened like this in her condition."

Arliss said, "You're right. I'm real sorry about this, everyone. I don't know who this guy is." Something clicked in Arliss' mind and his disposition changed. "Oh, Lord. Y'all might have been killed because of me. I have to leave here before someone else comes lookin' for me. I won't be a part of any of y'all gettin' killed."

He pushed his way past Win and ran off into the night.

When Andi worked on her sermons, she often lost track of time. Such was the case that night, so when the church door was flung open with a bang, she jumped in her desk chair. She heard someone wearing boots stomp across the wooden floor and head into the sanctuary. Curious about who it was, she left her office, which was located off the narthex, and went into the sanctuary. The only light in the sanctuary was the eternal flame near the altar and one of the wall sconces, but she could make out the back of a man where he sat in the left side of a pew near the front.

His head was down, resting on his forearms, which were propped up on the pew in front of him. As she neared him, a wave of torment, anger, and sorrow hit Andi so hard that it stopped her progress for a few moments. Steeling herself against the torrent of emotion, she pressed onward until she reached him.

"Sir, can I help you?" she asked.

When he raised his head, she recognized Arliss and saw that he was crying. He wiped his face on a shirt sleeve. "No one can help me, Andi. I'm beyond that."

It looked like there was blood on his shirt. "Arliss, are you hurt?"

"No, ma'am, only in my heart."

"Whose blood is that on your shirt? Is someone else hurt?"

"Nope. He's dead and I killed him."

Andi's sharp intake of breath made Arliss look at her and she saw the agony in his eyes.

"I didn't mean to do it. It happened so fast. I didn't know I knew how to do such a thing," he said.

Andi sat down by him. "Why don't you tell me what happened?"

Arliss nodded and told her about the situation at the sheep farm. "It was like I changed into some other person who knew how to disarm someone and kill them. It was so easy, like I'd done it before. I probably have. How many people have I killed, Andi? How many have I hurt? It's not safe for anyone to be around me. I have to leave Echo so that no one gets hurt because of me."

Although shocked and worried, Andi had no fear of Arliss. "It's not your fault that this man came looking for you. You don't control the actions of others. I know you're worried about your friends, and you're right to, but running isn't the solution. You need to find out who you are so that we can figure out how to prevent anyone else from following you."

"We?"

"Arliss, you're not alone. You have people who care about you now. You don't have to do this by yourself," she said. "May I have your hand?"

"My hand? Why?"

"You may not believe me, but I have a gift, given to me by God. When I was twelve, I drowned and died. I was dead for over an hour. My parents prayed over me all that time, but they'd eventually given up. Dad said that as soon as they'd stopped praying, I woke up. I've been to Heaven, Arliss. I've seen the wonderful things that await us there. Ever since then, I can feel things about people, and sometimes I'm able to see things and to receive messages from God about things that will happen. Will you let me try to help you?"

In her eyes, Arliss saw her sincerity and felt some sort of power emanating from her. It seemed to reach out to him and the hair on the back of his neck rose in response. He nodded and held out his hand to her. Andi slipped hers into his strong, calloused hand and was instantly swamped by the sight of blood. So much that it was a river of red flowing around her.

Putting aside her fear, she waited for it to clear so that other images or feelings could come to her. Gunshots and the sound of punches landing on flesh came to her along with fiddle music. Moving through that, she saw Arliss in a hospital bed, bruised and battered. Knowing that wasn't what they needed to know, she tried to force her mind beyond that, but butted up against a wall. Calling for more strength, she heaved herself over it, sensing secretive actions on Arliss' part. A name rose in her mind and she latched onto it as she was flung back into herself.

She slumped against the back of the pew and Arliss put an arm around her.

"Andi, are you all right?"

Catching her breath, Andi nodded. "Yes. I just need to rest a moment."

"Ok." He stayed quiet until she regained her strength and sat up straight again.

"Arliss, who is William Daniels?" she asked.

Arliss closed his eyes and concentrated hard, but the name meant nothing to him. "I don't know."

Taking a breath, Andi explained to him what she had seen. "Arliss, I think you're right. There has been a lot of killing around you, but sometimes what I see is symbolic, not literal. Maybe you killed people, but we don't know why. Or maybe a lot of people around you were killed, but by someone else. I think we need Sheriff Taft's help. You can't run. You have to stand your ground and help figure this out." She held his trembling hands and stared into his brown eyes. "Promise me you won't leave Echo."

Arliss' jaw set. "Why do you care so much?"

Andi said, "Because I have a driving need to help others. Also because you're the only one who's ever complimented me on how I look in pants."

Arliss let out a short laugh. "I can't believe some man hasn't by now. Andi, I'm dangerous. I feel it inside of me, but I don't know why. A person doesn't do what I just did unless they're dangerous."

She nodded in agreement. "I know, but you aren't dangerous to the people you care about. You saved your friends. You shouldn't have killed that man, but you were acting in the best interests of the rest."

"I'm going to Hell, aren't I? Who knows what all I've done? I doubt I'm gonna get past those pearly gates."

Andi took his handsome, angular face in her hands. "Arliss, everyone deserves forgiveness. You only have to ask for it and be sincere."

Arliss wanted to believe her, but he couldn't reconcile it in his heart. Maybe someday, but not now. "I appreciate what you're trying to do, but I'm not worthy of it."

She gave him a small smile. "None of us are. That's what grace is all about."

He took one of her hands and kissed the back of it. "You're a special woman, Andi. You're worthy or God wouldn't have sent you back so you could do great things. I have to go. I won't leave town, but I'm gonna be somewhere no one will ever find me."

Andi's hand tingled where he'd kissed it. "Will you come see me so I know you're all right? Please?"

In the light from the eternal flame, Andi's eyes looked amber and Arliss thought they were the most beautiful eyes in the world. In them he saw concern for him and he was humbled. He couldn't refuse her request. "Yeah. I'll come see you."

"Do you promise?"

"I promise," he said. "I better go. I'll come see you sometime tomorrow. I'll have to come talk to Evan anyway, so I'll stop in."

Her smile captivated him. "Good. Where will you stay tonight?"

"I know a place. I'll be ok."

Acting on impulse, he quickly kissed her cheek and then hurried from the church. Andi sat rooted to her seat, her fingertips touching the place he'd kissed her. Her pulse was a little rapid from the contact. She'd been kissed chastely by Wild Wind and a boy in her past, but those kisses hadn't made her feel the way Arliss' kiss had.

She left the church, blowing out the wall sconce and the lamp in her office before she did. In the parsonage, she fixed a cup of tea and took it upstairs to bed. She drank her tea as she read a few chapters from her Bible, but her turbulent thoughts kept her from really concentrating on what she was reading. Giving up, she set her Bible aside and lay down, her mind going over the evening's events. Closing her eyes, she prayed for Arliss, asking God to keep him safe and warm wherever he was.

Chapter Five

Sheriff Evan Taft looked at the array of personal possessions laid out on the table in the sheriff's office, trying to fit the pieces of the puzzle into a whole picture. He'd become a sheriff at the young age of twenty-two because he'd had a great closed case record and he was fearless in his pursuit of justice. He often came up with unorthodox theories that panned out. He liked to brainstorm even if whatever he came up with seemed crazy. He kept circling the table, his brain whirling with possibilities.

Shadow Earnest, a.k.a. Deputy Mayhem, was about to say something, but Thad, who sat on a chair by Shadow's desk, put his hand over Shadow's mouth and shook his head. He knew Evan's investigative style better than anyone and could tell when Evan was onto something. He didn't want Evan's train of thought disrupted.

Evan's green eyes kept going back and forth from the table to the tablet on which he made notes. He shoved coal-black hair out of his eyes, thinking that he needed Win to cut it again even as he worked.

Thad lit a cigarette, much to Shadow's dislike, and leaned back in his chair a little. "Whatcha got, Sheriff?"

In sign language, which many of their friends now knew, Shadow asked, "I thought you didn't want him to be disturbed."

Thad's sign language was a little shaky, but he was able to get his point across. "I know how to help him work it out."

"We need Arliss to look at this stuff and see if anything triggers a memory. This matchbook from this saloon could be a place where Arliss and this guy's paths crossed. I don't know what the letters on the inside mean though. There's five—too many to be initials. I had Dan make a bunch of copies of the pictures he took of all of these things to send out to various sheriff and police departments in Alabama. Maybe this William Daniels is wanted somewhere and we can get more information about him, which would help us figure out who Arliss is.

"This knife is probably stolen since it has a different name on it. Casey Marlin might be someone this guy killed or he could've won it in a poker game. I wish we didn't have to go to Dickensville to send telegrams. It would be great to be able to communicate right away with law enforcement. It would help keep things safer around here to have a head's up about criminals in the area. Plus, it would help Molly at the newspaper, too.

"Anyway, this hanky doesn't really help us any. This money clip might help identify him because it has initials on it and someone might recognize it. The money doesn't help us, either, since it's not a big amount. This key, though, goes to a bank deposit box. I might actually have to go to Alabama to find the bank and see what's in that box."

"Nope. If someone's watching for Daniels to come there, they'll make you for a sheriff in ten seconds, Evan. You can't help it. It's in the way you carry yourself," Thad said. "I'd go, but with Jess about to give birth, there's no way I'm leavin' town."

"I'll go," Shadow said.

Evan smiled. "We need someone with some tact who can schmooze people if necessary. That's not you. You'll just kill them and wind up in jail."

Shadow smiled. "You're probably right."

"So who's gonna go?" Thad asked. "If someone's watching that bank to see who shows up, it needs to be someone no one would suspect as being out of place."

Evan said, "The problem is that we don't know who would be out of place. Wait!" He picked up the key and read the bank name. "Mobile Trust Company Bank. We need to find out what kind of bank this is."

"What do you mean?" Shadow asked. "Isn't a bank just a bank?"

"You got a lot to learn, son," Thad said. "Some banks only deal with certain types of clientele. We need to find out if this bank serves mostly uppity snobs or just everyday folks. That way, we can decide who to send."

Evan sighed. "The problem is that we don't have anyone around here who's trained to do that sort of thing. It's not like we have some sort of detective living here."

Shadow said, "Send Marvin. He would pass any test if the bank is more upscale, and who else would be devious enough to get the job done? After all, he kept me a secret for almost two decades. He's a master at subterfuge and manipulation and has no problem causing people pain."

Evan said, "Not a bad idea, but what if it's a lowbrow place? Could he pull that off?"

"I think Earnest could pull off just about anything he put his mind to. The question is if he's willing to go. He's a new father. This could be dangerous. He shouldn't go alone."

Shadow said, "Don't let Marvy fool you. Who do you think used to spar with me? I was always careful with his hernia area, but he's no lightweight, especially with a garret or a knife. Since his surgery, he's worked hard to strengthen that area and he's much more lethal than before. What he lacks in brawn, he makes up for in speed and cunning."

Thad and Evan looked at each other in surprise.

"Earnest can fight?" Thad asked. "He doesn't look the type."

Shadow said, "As I said, don't underestimate him."

"This I gotta see," Thad said.

Evan said, "We still need someone to go with him if he's willing. Well, let's find out what kind of bank this is and go from there."

"Good idea, Sheriff," Thad said. "Lucky said that Arliss didn't come back this morning. No one knows where he is. He might have left Echo."

Shaking his head, Evan said, "I don't think so. He's hiding out somewhere, but I think he's still around."

"Will you arrest him?" Shadow asked.

"Nope. He killed in defense of others. We can't be sure Daniels wouldn't have shot everyone else there, even if Arliss had gone with him," Evan said.

Thad chuckled. "Our little Irish Indian helped save the day. He might only be five, but he's got balls."

Evan and Shadow agreed and laughed.

The sheriff said, "Well, I'm gonna see if Dan has those photos done and head to Dickensville to send telegrams. I'll see you two later. Hold down the fort."

Thad saluted him. "Yes, sir!"

"Shut up," Evan said and left the office.

Shadow asked, "How much would it cost to run telegraph lines here?"

Thad shrugged even as he smiled inwardly. "Beats the heck out of me."

"Hmm," Shadow said and fell silent.

Hiding a grin, Thad stood up and said, "I'm off to patrol. See ya later."

Wild Wind walked towards the post office, his mind full of thoughts of the previous night. He'd helped Win clean up the Quinns' house while Erin had made sure Leah and Otto were all right. Leah had calmed down and Otto didn't understand why Lucky and Leah were upset with him. Wild Wind didn't, either. He'd only been protecting his family and home. In his mind, Otto should be awarded coup. However, he'd refrained from mentioning that, knowing that it would only anger Otto's parents and confuse the boy.

He was so preoccupied that he jumped when someone slipped a hand under his arm.

"Wild Wind," Roxie said.

Stopping he looked down at her. "Hi, Roxie."

"Are you all right? I just heard about what happened." Her hazel eyes looked him over.

"I'm fine, thanks to Otto and Arliss. Don't tell anyone I said that about Otto, though. I don't think that's something his parents want to hear," Wild Wind said.

Roxie said, "It has to be hard. On one hand, I'm sure they're proud of him, but on the other, he has to understand that he can't go around throwing knives at people."

"You're right, but in that situation, what he did was right. It wasn't anything I wouldn't have done," he said, waiting to see how she would react to that.

Roxie said, "Do all Cheyenne boys learn those skills at such a young age?"

"Yes. By the time I was only a little older than Otto, I could throw a knife and shoot a bow and arrow with great accuracy. Otto is young, but he knew what he was doing. He was only trying to wound Daniels. If he had wanted to, he could have killed him."

It was hard to imagine sweet little Otto being that calculating, but Roxie thought about Otto being raised by the Cheyenne before meeting Lucky and coming to Echo. With Lucky also having lived with the Cheyenne and Wild Wind around, his training was sure to have continued.

"I'm sure they'll get it figured out so that there can be a balance."

Wild Wind liked her diplomatic answer and thought it wise for him to also be diplomatic. "I agree. What were you doing?"

"Going to the post office, the same as you. Walk with me?" she asked.

"Sure. The street is a little icy. I wouldn't want you to slip," he said, offering his arm.

"How very gentlemanly of you," she said.

As he helped her across, he noticed that most people didn't make anything of the fact that he was walking with a white woman. It had been different with Andi, most likely because she was the pastor, a prominent person in the town. A few people spoke with either him or Roxie, but other than that, no one paid them much mind.

They both collected their mail and Wild Wind noticed that Roxie took his arm again.

"Where are we going?" he asked.

Roxie gave him a coy smile. "Does it matter? I know; let me buy you a cup of coffee."

"Ok," he said.

He was surprised to see that Leah had opened her cobbler shop. "Do you mind if we stop in?"

"No, of course not," Roxie said. "I'd like to see how she's doing. I wouldn't have thought she would open."

"Me, neither."

He held the door for Roxie and they entered the store. Leah and Keith Watson, the former pastor's eldest son who worked for Leah, stood at a work bench going over something. They looked up and smiled. There were dark smudges underneath Leah's eyes—a sign that she hadn't slept much the night before.

Roxie went to Leah and hugged her. "Are you all right? I heard what happened. You should be resting, and not here."

Leah smiled. "I'm fine," she signed. "I couldn't stay there today and keep thinking about it. I needed to be busy. Besides, it's cold in the house since Lucky is replacing the glass in the kitchen door. He wanted to get it done right away so we could sort of get back to normal."

Keith, who at nineteen stood six-foot-four and weighed around two hundred pounds, said, "I'm watching out for her." He was on his way to reaching his father's six-foot-seven height, although Keith hoped that he was done growing. He'd grown almost an inch in the last year and he felt that he was tall enough. "I won't let her overdo it."

Smiling at him, Leah said, "My protector."

Keith flexed his biceps. "That's right."

"And a very handsome protector you are," Roxie said.

Keith's brown eyes shone with good humor. "Thanks. My wife thinks so, too."

Roxie said, "I can't believe you're both married at such young ages."

Keith wasn't going to enlighten her about one of the reasons they'd gotten married. It was true that he and Molly had fallen in love, but they hadn't been able to control their passion for each other and Molly had wound up pregnant outside of wedlock. However, she'd lost the baby during a time of great stress, which had devastated the young couple. They'd gotten married anyway because they loved each other and had wanted to be together. No one but their family, Erin, Win, and Marvin Earnest knew the true circumstances around their marriage.

Marvin, who had been feared and reviled for years, was changing for the better, and he was learning how to be friends with people. Molly had come to Echo with dreams of being a reporter like Nelly Bly. Originally, she'd wanted to build up a successful newspaper, get her name out there, go on undercover assignments, and write stories about injustice and crime.

She'd been in awe of Thad, who was famous all over the Midwest for his ability to capture the most cunning and dangerous criminals. However, after meeting Keith, falling in love with him, and suffering such a tragedy, she was content with building a successful newspaper. She and Marvin had gone into business and had also developed an unlikely, close friendship. Originally, Thad had been against the partnership since he and Marvin had hated each other.

However, after Marvin and he had come to an understanding, Thad had relented and allowed Molly to go into business with Marvin. The *Echo Express* had grown from a weekly newspaper to a biweekly publication and the partners couldn't be happier about their success.

Keith smiled. "Me, either, but we're very happy."

Roxie asked, "What's it like living with Thad?"

Grinning, Keith said, "Fun. He's the most sarcastic person I've ever met, but he doesn't mean most of what he says. He teases everyone. No one is safe."

Wild Wind said, "You're right about that. I'm glad you're all right, Leah."

"I'm fine. Please don't worry," she signed.

"Well, we'll let you get back to it," Wild Wind said.

They said goodbye to Leah and Keith and went back out into the bitter wind that blew down the street.

Chapter Six

"Honey, I need to run something by you," Win said, coming into the office he shared with Erin.

They had added on to the medical clinic, using the other side for Win's veterinarian practice.

Erin held "Mighty" Mia, as she was known, on her lap, playing with the baby. Mia had a very healthy set of lungs and her cries were much louder than other babies'. Although she had some of her handsome father's Chinese features, she also resembled Erin. She was adorable and even tempered most of the time.

She saw Win and reached for him. He smiled at her and took her from Erin, kissing her soft cheek.

"Hi, Mighty Mia. Are you being a good girl?"

She smiled, her almost black eyes crinkling at the corners a little. Watching father and daughter together always gave Erin a warm feeling in her heart.

"What did you want to run by me?" Erin prompted. Win was easily distracted by his daughter.

"Oh, yeah. You know how everyone always wants me to cut their hair?"

"That's because you're so good at it."

"Thanks. I think I should get paid for it. What do you think of me putting a barber's chair in my side and cutting hair when I'm not busy on vet business?"

Erin smiled as she thought about it. "Why didn't we think of that before? It's a great idea. It would give us more income and it's something Echo needs. You're right; you might as well get paid for it."

Win nodded. "I'll have to order a chair and some other things so I can do a proper job. I might as well put my skills to use."

"That's one of the reasons I love you. You're so smart," Erin said.

Win handed Mia back to Erin and kissed her. "Thanks. You're smart yourself. And beautiful."

They kissed again and Erin grew warm. Her handsome husband always had that effect on her and she suddenly wished that they were at home. When Win pulled back, the same passion was in his eyes. "I'll see you later. I have to go check on that cow for Mr. Terranova."

"Ok. You and Sugar have fun," she said, smiling.

Win groaned. "Don't remind me. I'm sure she's waiting out there for me."

Erin chuckled as Win left and went back to playing with Mia until her next patient arrived.

Wild Wind enjoyed having coffee with Roxie. She was witty, intelligent, and he could see that she was no pushover. Why hadn't he noticed how pretty she was before? Her hazel eyes were sometimes more brown than green and vice versa, and he liked watching them change color. She wore her honey-hued hair pulled back into an intricate bun in the back and he wondered what she looked like with it down.

"Do you like working with Ross?" he asked her.

She shrugged a little. "It's a living. Our pa gave him the business when he took ill and moved to Philadelphia for treatment. I didn't want to go to Philadelphia, so I stayed here and ran it with him."

"Why didn't you want to move? I hear that they have a lot of things there that make life easier. Electricity, running water, and telephones, for example."

"Easier isn't always better. I've been there; I don't like how crowded it is, and certain parts smell terrible," she said. "I went with my parents to help get them settled, but came back. Pa was really strict, too, so it was nice to be out from under his thumb. Ross took responsibility for me, but outside of protecting me, he's never been strict. These days, Callie is the one who helps him in the shop. She loves it and I don't, so it suits me just fine."

"You seem to get along with her," Wild Wind said.

Roxie said, "Callie's the kind of person who gets along with everyone. I couldn't ask for a better sister-in-law and I can't wait to be an aunt. Ross is so excited about becoming a father. He talks to the baby all the time. It's very dear to see such a big man talking to his wife's belly."

Wild Wind grinned. "I know what you mean. Win did that with Erin and Lucky does it with Leah."

"Why didn't you ever marry?" Roxie asked.

"Well, in Cheyenne culture, a man isn't eligible for marriage unless he has counted enough coup to prove himself worthy of a wife and children. He has to be a good warrior, hunter, and provider for his family. I had just earned enough coup when we were captured by the military." His jaw clenched as he fought the old bitterness that still lurked in his soul. "Once I saw what it was like on the reservation—the starvation, the poverty, and suffering—I decided not to marry and bring more children into that sort of life. It wouldn't have been fair to them."

Roxie had heard about the abominable treatment of the Indians, but actually talking to a Cheyenne man who'd lived through it was different— more powerful than anything she could have read in a newspaper. Although he was trying to hide it, she could see the anger and resentment in his eyes and in the set of his jaw.

"I'm so sorry," she said. "You shouldn't have been forced to leave your old life. Would you go back to it if you could?"

His gaze never wavered as he said, "In a heartbeat. You have no idea how much I long for the open plain, to be able to hunt buffalo, and to celebrate our special rituals and dances." He put his hand over his heart. "I keep all of those memories alive in my heart, but I know that there will be no going back. So I'm moving ahead, making a new life for myself, and keeping alive what traditions I can. At least I'm free to hunt and roam wherever I like, within reason. There are many of us who can't say that."

It brought tears to Roxie's eyes to think about a proud warrior like Wild Wind having to give up almost everything about his culture just to be free. She was intelligent enough to know that in some ways, he still wasn't free. He was confined by white man's standards of living, of which many went against what he believed in. It was the sort of thing that would gall anyone.

Wild Wind noticed the sheen of moisture in her eyes. "I'm sorry if I upset you, Roxie."

She blinked her eyes rapidly to clear the tears away. "No need to be sorry. Don't worry about my silliness. Well, I guess I should be on my way and not keep you any longer. Thank you. I had a really nice time."

Under the table, he put his foot on hers, trapping her without anyone noticing. "Did you?" he signed to her. "What did I do to offend you?"

Even if his foot hadn't been pressing down on hers, she would have been pinned by the dark fire in his eyes. "You didn't do anything," she signed. "It's just that what was done to you was terrible and it makes me sad."

His jaw tightened. "I don't want your pity. I don't need it."

Her eyes widened. "It's not pity. I would never pity you, but I am allowed to feel ashamed of something my people did to yours. Don't you have any regrets about something your people did?"

Nodding, he signed, "All people have something their race has done that they are ashamed of."

"Exactly. That's all I meant," she said.

He smiled contritely and lifted his foot from hers. "I'm sorry. I guess I'm a little sensitive sometimes."

Wanting to put it behind them, she resumed their conversation out loud. "You're forgiven, but I do have to be going."

"Ok," he said, standing when she did.

She put money on the table and they walked out together. Roxie said, "I really did enjoy myself and I hope we can do it again sometime."

Wild Wind said, "So did I. I'd like that."

Roxie nodded. "Have a good day."

"You do the same," he said.

She walked away, but turned and gave him a little wave and a smile, which he returned before going in the other direction.

When Arliss didn't find Andi in the church, he almost left town again. He didn't feel right about going to the parsonage, but he'd promised her that he'd come to see her. Leaving the church, he cut around back, heading to the kitchen entrance of the parsonage. He knocked on the door and Bea answered it.

"Oh, hello, Arliss," she said.

"Mornin', ma'am. Is Pastor Thatcher in by chance? She wasn't over at the church."

"Yes. Come on in and have a seat here. Would you like some coffee?" Bea asked.

Arliss said, "I don't want you to go to any trouble on my account." Stepping inside, he closed the door and stayed by it.

"It's no trouble at all. Come sit down," Bea said.

Arliss sat where she'd indicated he should. She poured him some coffee and set it in front of him. "Thank you, ma'am."

"There's cream there, Arliss. I'll go get Andi for you," Bea said.

"I appreciate it," he said.

Bea left the kitchen and went down the hall to the study where Andi was rummaging around on a bookshelf for a different Bible.

"Andi, Arliss is here," she said.

"Oh! Good. I've been worried about him."

Bea smiled at the way Andi touched a hand to her hair, which she had pulled back with some pretty combs, and straightened her blouse that was tucked into riding jodhpurs. Andi caught Bea's amused expression.

"What? I want to look presentable," she said. "I am the pastor, you know."

"Oh, yes, of course you should look presentable. I don't suppose it would have anything to do with the fact that an attractive murderer is sitting at the kitchen table?"

Andi said, "He was protecting the Quinns, and as far as him being good-looking, well, yes, I've noticed that. And he likes the way I look in pants. No one's ever told me that before."

Bea laughed. "Well, you do have a nice figure."

"Thank you. Anyway, I'd better go see him before he decides to leave," she said.

"Yes, don't let him get away," Bea said, grinning.

Andi smiled. "Hush, Bea."

She entered the kitchen and Arliss stood like any good gentleman would do when a woman walked into a room. It showed that he had some breeding.

"Morning, Pastor," he said.

"Good morning, Arliss. Please go ahead and sit," she said.

"Ok. I was enjoying Bea's coffee," he said.

"Bea makes great coffee. Did you eat breakfast?" Andi asked.

Arliss frowned. "No, ma'am. That's not why I came here, though. I just wanted to check in with you like I promised. Thanks for your help last night."

"You're welcome. Are you going to go home today?" she asked.

He shook his head. "I don't know how I'm gonna look them in the eye again after what happened. I don't think so. I'll stay in Echo like I promised you, but I don't want anyone knowin' where I am. It's safer for everyone that way. I just have to get a few things from the store and I'll be fine."

"Arliss, please let me make you something to eat. It'll make me feel better knowing you have something in your stomach."

Arliss chuckled. "How do you do that?"

"Do what?"

"Make me do things that I wouldn't for other people."

"It's magic," Andi teased.

"I can believe it. All right. I'll eat something."

Andi rose to make him some eggs. She knew they still had some bacon from that morning. Cracking eggs into a frying pan, she asked, "Did you stay warm last night?"

"Yeah. I was fine. I hope you weren't worrying all night."

"I couldn't help it. How are you otherwise?"

He shrugged as his gaze traveled over her. "All right, I guess. It's the first time I remember killin' anyone. I feel guilty, but I also don't regret it in a way. Do you know what I mean?"

She poured him more coffee and met his eyes. "You're glad you protected your friends but sorry you took a life."

"Yeah. I wish I hadn't killed him, not only because I shouldn't have, but also because I killed him before I could ask him more about myself. I shoulda just shot him in the leg or something," Arliss said. "Then I coulda questioned him."

Andi moved away from him, thinking he seemed different this morning than he had last night. Of course, he'd had time to process and think about things. Putting his food on a plate, she took it back to the table and sat down with him.

"Arliss, how much do you remember about last night?" she asked.

"I remember that guy coming to the door and him saying he knew me. I remember him pointin' a pistol at us. Otto threw his knife and it's a little fuzzy, but I got ahold of his gun somehow and pulled the trigger. It's like I was a long ways off or something. Then ... then ..." Arliss tried to hold onto it, but it was slipping away. "I remember going into the church and then you were there."

"Do you remember our conversation?" she asked.

He swallowed a bite of toast. "Yeah. You said that you'd drowned as a kid and you have a gift that lets you see and feel things."

"That's right. What did you do yesterday before all of this happened?" she asked.

"I don't know. Got up, helped Lucky or Win. I came to town, I think. I wanted to ask Spike about playing for tips," he said.

"Is Spike going to let you play for tips?" she asked.

"I guess so," Arliss said. He couldn't remember what Spike had told him. "I don't know. Wait. What day did I chop wood for you?"

"A few days ago. Monday, I believe."

Arliss asked, "What's today?"

"Friday."

"Already? Boy, time sure does fly." Arliss was scared. Why couldn't he remember the last few days? Had he played at Spike's? "Andi, did I go home last night?"

Her eyebrows rose. "No. You just told me that you didn't go there this morning, either."

"No, no, no! Not again!" Arliss slammed his hand on the table making Andi jump. "I had this happen to me one other time. It was on the way up here. I lost about a week, I guess. I write in a journal every day because I need to remember what I did the day before sometimes. Once I'm reminded, I'm ok, but—Andi, I don't remember where I went last night after I left the church."

During her work with the Salvation Army, Andi had seen men who'd suffered head trauma act like this. She'd once been told by a neurologist that amnesia was a tricky thing. Some people couldn't remember who they were or certain things after they'd suffered brain injuries. For other people, they couldn't retain memories very long. They couldn't carry short-term memories over to long-term memory. And for other people, they had a combination of the two types. It seemed like Arliss fit that category, but Andi felt that Erin should be consulted.

Andi sensed and saw Arliss' fear and reached for his hand. "Arliss, I want you to come to see Erin with me. I've seen your sort of illness before, but I'm not a doctor. I'd like Erin to check you over. Please?"

"There you go again, talkin' me into things," he said, smiling. "Ok, I'll go with you, but only because you're so pretty and look good in those pants."

Andi laughed. "There's that scoundrel again. You really shouldn't say things like that about me, especially since I'm the pastor."

"Ok. I'll just think them," he said, giving her a wink.

Blushing, she replied, "Do you remember saying those sort of things to me the other day?"

"Yeah. It's strange; I remember every time I've ever talked to you, but other things are hazy sometimes," he said. "I remember how I got to Echo for the most part, and I remember most of what's happened since I've been here, but lately, it's gotten worse, as you can see."

"Maybe Erin can help us figure it out," she said.

Arliss said, "I don't know what I'm gonna do if I never found out who I am—who I was. I hoped so hard that Lucky would be able to help me."

"Just give it some time. I'll help you as much as I can."

"Thanks," he said before finishing his food.

Chapter Seven

"Well, Doc?" Arliss prompted after Erin had finished her examination.

Erin sat down on one of the chairs in the office and looked him in the eye. "I'm afraid there's not much I can do for you. No doctor can. Amnesia is a very hard thing to treat because we can't get into your brain to fix it. You have a combination of retrograde and anterograde amnesia, which is worse than just having one or the other."

"What does that mean?"

"Retrograde amnesia is when you can't remember your past, or even just an event, prior to severe mental or physical trauma. You have that. You don't remember anything before you woke up in the hospital. Anterograde amnesia is when you can't transfer recent memories into long-term memory. You don't remember parts of this past week, which means that some of your recent memories aren't getting into your long-term memory bank, so to speak," she explained.

"And there's no medicine that can help?" he asked.

"No, there's not. There are some things you can do to help strengthen the abilities you do have. You said you keep a journal, so that's a great tool.

It wouldn't hurt to keep a list of tasks that have to be done every day and check them off as you go so that you know they've been done. Amnesia can also resolve itself, so don't give up on that, either."

"Erin, I woke up in September of last year. It's almost March. Tell me I have that much straight."

"Yes, it's February."

"It'll soon be six months. Do you really think it'll improve any? Don't sugarcoat it for me."

She pursed her lips for a moment. "The truth is that the longer the condition persists, the bigger the chance the injury will be permanent."

Arliss put his head down and remained quiet for several minutes. He raised his head as tears filled his eyes. "So I might have to live the rest of my life like this? What would you call it? Mentally impaired? Not knowing who I am or where I come from? Not remembering things from day to day or even moment by moment?"

This was the part of Erin's job she hated the most: telling people disappointing news. There were certain situations in which she was powerless and it tore at her. Now was one such situation.

"I'm afraid so. Any neurologist is going to tell you the same thing," she said.

Arliss said, "Thanks for being honest with me. I'll see you."

He left the office, walking right past Andi and out the door. He didn't want her to feel the brunt of his anger, so it was better not to talk to her. Burning fury consumed him as he strode along the street, not seeing people or his surroundings as he did so. *How am I supposed to live like this? How can I live when I can't remember conversations I've had or what I did yesterday? How can I hold down a job or learn anything new? I'd just forget it again.*

He stopped and retraced his steps to where he needed to cross the street so he could get to the sheriff's office. He walked inside and Evan looked up from his desk.

"Hi, Arliss. How are you?"

"I've come to turn myself in," he said.

Evan got up. "I'm not arresting you. You were defending your friends."

"I shot a man point blank in the head."

"I know, but he represented a direct threat. I'm not arresting you. But there is something I want you to do. I want to see if you can identify the stuff we found on Daniels."

Arliss looked at him sharply. "William Daniels?"

"Yeah," Evan said. "Do you remember him?"

"No. It was the name Andi got from me when she did her psychic thing last night. It doesn't mean anything to me, but I guess he was important to me in the past somehow," he said. "Where's this stuff?"

Evan led him over to the table and pushed a box over to him. "Take your time."

Arliss picked up the money clip and ran his fingertips over it. It seemed familiar somehow, but it wouldn't come to him. When he looked at the matchbook with the letters written inside it, he knew what they meant.

"This is part of the C major scale, but I don't know why he would write it on this matchbook."

Evan took the deposit box key out of his pocket and handed it to Arliss. "How about this?"

Arliss turned the key over in his fingers as an image rose in his mind. Closing his eyes, he concentrated hard on the faint memory. He saw a bank deposit box sitting before him on a table. An attaché case sat next to the deposit box. He took out a thin sheaf of folded papers and unfolded them. They were stocks, but he couldn't read what they were exactly. He refolded them, put them in the box, shut it, and locked it.

A man's voice close to him said, "Are you finished, Mr. Dumont?"

Arliss heard himself say, "Yes. Thank you, Mr. Rollins. I appreciate your assistance."

It was his voice, but he'd spoken with a British accent. The memory faded into nothingness. Arliss opened his eyes and met Evan's gaze.

"I put some sort of stock or bonds in that deposit box and there was a man there named Rollins and he called me Mr. Dumont. I don't know that name, though." He told Evan everything he'd recalled. "I had a British accent, too. Who am I? Dumont or Jackson? Am I really from Alabama or England? I don't understand any of this," Arliss said.

Evan sought to ease Arliss' agitation. "Well, it's more than we had to go on before. Those stocks must be valuable or you wouldn't have put them in the bank. But why did this guy have the key? I'm waiting on word back from some law enforcement people in Alabama. From the sounds of it, this bank seems more upscale. I also have something else in the works. We'll get to the bottom of this. Just have some patience."

Arliss asked, "Do you have some paper I can have? I need to write all of this down so I don't forget it later on."

"Sure," Evan said, going over to his desk. He handed Arliss a large tablet. "Here you go. What do you mean you'll forget it?"

As Arliss sat down, he told Evan about his particular form of amnesia. "It's gonna make it a heck of a lot harder to figure this out. I have to keep a journal every day just so I know what I did the day before. I lost three days this week. I don't remember what I did or where I went. I don't even know where I went last night."

Andi came in the door. "There you are. You left the clinic so fast. I didn't know where you went."

Arliss' jaw clenched. "I just couldn't talk right then. I was too mad. Did Erin fill you in?"

She nodded and sat down at the table with him. "Arliss, you can't be alone right now. What if you don't remember that you belong in Echo or forget to eat or where you're going?"

Arliss bristled. "I don't need a babysitter. I'm a grown man."

Andi's expression softened. "I know you're a grown man, but right now, it's not safe for you to wander around by yourself."

With a frustrated noise, Arliss got up and left the office. Andi went right after him.

"Arliss, please listen to me," she said, catching his arm.

He stopped and turned to her, his eyes shining with anger.

Steeling herself against the ripples of emotions coming off him, Andi released his arm. "I won't pretend to know what you're going through. It must be awful. I'm not suggesting that you're not a grown man, but you're sick right now and need some help, that's all."

He moved closer to her in a predatory fashion, but she held her ground.

"What are you going to do, Andi?" His voice lowered, taking on a rougher timber. "Are you gonna watch me round the clock?" Moving closer yet, he asked, "Are you gonna tuck me in at night? Keep me warm?"

Her eyes widened. She knew exactly what he meant. "If you're trying to scare me or offend me, you're not. I know that this is your anger and frustration talking and you just need someone to take it out on. If that's what you need, then so be it. Go ahead."

Arliss looked skyward for a moment and then back into her eyes. Backing up, he said, "I'm sorry, Andi. I'm not worthy of your time. You've been only kind to me and that's how I treat you? You deserve better."

She smiled to show there were no hard feelings. "It's all right. Then just do better."

He laughed, his anger beginning to dissipate. "You're something else. What do you suggest I do, Andi?"

A smile stole over her face. "I have an idea. Come with me."

Wild Wind watched his nephew push his food around on his plate and almost sighed. Otto had been withdrawn most of that day and evening. He answered when spoken to, but didn't add to the supper conversation going on around him. Wild Wind knew that Otto was confused about what had happened the previous evening. He'd only done what he'd been taught to, but he felt like he was in trouble.

Switching his attention from Otto to Lucky so the boy didn't feel self-conscious, he said, "You know Ross better than I do, Lucky."

Lucky nodded. "Aye."

"And he likes Billy."

"Aye. He likes him very much. That's why he was best man at Ross' wedding," Lucky said, wondering what his friend was getting at.

Leah knew that Roxie had been interested in Wild Wind for a while, and since the brave had been with Roxie that morning, she had an inkling what Wild Wind was working up to asking.

"Ross doesn't seem to have any problem with me or Billy since we're Indians."

Lucky's brows drew together. "He doesn't. Why should he? Did he say somethin'?"

Leah grinned and both men looked at her. "He wants to know if Ross would have any objection to him calling on Roxie."

Lucky turned his eyes on Wild Wind, surprise evident on his handsome face. "Is that right? Yer interested in Roxie?"

"Yes. She brought me a pie earlier this week and made it clear that she was interested in me. We had coffee this morning and had a nice time. I was thinking about inviting her to dinner, but I didn't know how Ross would feel about it."

"Ya never said anything about her before," Lucky said.

"I never thought about her that way until she said something," Wild Wind said. "We've already established that my race and religion doesn't bother her at all. What do you think Ross would say? You told me about the trouble Billy had regarding no parents wanting him to marry their daughters since he's an Indian. I don't want to cause any bad feelings with Ross since we're friends and business partners."

This subject irritated Lucky because even though he was white, he'd faced discrimination just because he was Irish. A lot of people had looked unfavorably upon him and thought he was of lower intelligence and worth. So he understood how Billy and Wild Wind felt to some extent, but he knew it was even worse for them.

Knowing that Ross was a good, fair man with a good head on his shoulders and a kind heart, Lucky didn't think that the butcher would stand in Roxie and Wild Wind's way.

Leah always enjoyed watching Lucky when he was thinking. His expression would change depending on what he was working out in his mind and she could usually tell whether the outcome of what he was thinking about was negative or positive even before he spoke. When Lucky's brow smoothed out, she knew that his conclusion was good.

"I think ya should ask her and let her and Ross talk about it first if he has any objections. Roxie's a strong-willed woman and she won't let anyone push her around, even Ross. That's my advice to ya."

Wild Wind nodded. "Thank you. I appreciate it," he said in Cheyenne.

A strange look crossed Otto's face. "May I be excused?"

Leah said, "You haven't eaten much."

"I'm full, Ma," he said.

"Aren't you feeling well?" she asked.

"I'm just not very hungry. May I be excused?" he asked, giving her a direct look.

"I suppose so."

Sliding off his chair, Otto put on his coat. "I'm going to play with Sugar." He stood still for a moment before pulling out his knife and laying it on the table. "I don't need that anymore." Then he hurried from the house.

Lucky's jaw clenched as he picked up the knife and looked at it. "This is a hard thing to explain to him. I know he did what he thought was right, but he can't go around doing that."

"He did do what was right. If I had had the chance I would have done the same thing and so would you have," Wild Wind said. "It's what he's been trained to do and what I was trained to do—eliminate threats to his family or tribe."

Knowing that Leah was skittish enough about what had happened the night before, Lucky tried to head the argument off that he knew would happen. Wild Wind and he clashed on such issues sometimes. He smiled a little. "I know. We'll figure it out so that he understands."

Wild Wind wasn't willing to drop it, coming to his nephew's defense the way that most Indian men did with children. "What he understands is that it's suddenly wrong for him to act on his training even though his training has continued ever since you brought him here. He saw an opportunity and he acted on it, just as he's trained to do. You're making him feel as though what he did was wrong."

Leah said, "I'm very proud of him for protecting us, but this isn't like it is in your culture. Anything could have happened when he threw that knife. That man could have shot him or any of us. He doesn't have an adult's reasoning about these things."

Wild Wind said, "No, but Arliss did and he also did what I would have. Otto just gave him the opportunity to do it. Another battle move. Otto understands more about strategy at five winters old than many white boys three times his age."

Lucky glared at Wild Wind. "Brother, I think it's time to stop talkin' about this. Like I said, we'll get it figured out."

Since he was a guest in their house, Wild Wind smiled tightly and said, "You're right. I didn't mean to be unpleasant." He finished his meal and said, "Thank you for supper. It was delicious as always, Leah. Have a good night."

Leah said, "You didn't have dessert." She didn't want Wild Wind to be angry at them.

"Next time," he said, putting on his heavy wool-lined buckskin coat. "Goodnight."

Lucky leaned back in his chair and sighed as the brave went out the door.

"He'll always have a warrior's heart and thinks that it's all right for Otto to do the same," he said. "I've tried to explain that it doesn't work that way in this culture. I'm not sure that he'll ever fully understand."

Leah replied, "It'll be all right. I wonder where Arliss is. He hasn't even come back for his things."

"Evan said he's still in Echo, but he wouldn't say where he was stayin'. I think he's too ashamed to come back, but he doesn't need to be. I'll track him down," Lucky said.

"What happened isn't his fault. I just hope he's safe."

Lucky took her hand. "Don't worry, lass. He's resourceful. I'm sure he's fine."

She squeezed his hand. "I'm sure you're right. I'm going to get the dishes done."

"I'll help."

Lucky enjoyed doing domestic chores with Leah. He was a happy man. He had a nice home, a beautiful, intelligent, fun woman by his side, a son he was proud of, and a baby on the way. Both of their businesses were successful and their future looked very bright. Lucky thanked the Lord every day for all of the blessings in his life and in the life of their family. As they did dishes, he prayed for guidance on how to make Otto understand about the situation in a way that wouldn't make him feel worse than he did.

Chapter Eight

As she swept the kitchen floor the next morning, Roxie's mind turned to Wild Wind and their conversation the previous morning. She could understand why he wouldn't want pity and she hadn't meant to give him the impression that she pitied him. He'd accepted her explanation, but Roxie felt that it had been a little lacking. It was hard to have in-depth conversations in public, and conversing in sign language for a long period of time would only draw more attention to themselves. She decided that as soon as she was done with her morning chores, she would ride out to his farm and talk to him about it.

However, as luck would have it, she wouldn't need to. When a knock came at the kitchen door, she opened it to see Wild Wind smiling at her.

"Good morning," he said.

She returned his smile. "Good morning."

"Do you have a few minutes to talk?"

"Certainly. Come in," she said.

As he walked past her, her gaze skimmed over his powerful, lean frame. He'd plaited his beautiful hair into a single braid, which emphasized his chiseled features even more. She shut the door.

"Would you like some coffee or something?" she asked.

"No, thanks. I can't stay, but I wondered if you'd like to have dinner this evening?"

He liked the way her remarkable hazel eyes turned greener as she smiled. "Yes. I'd like that very much."

"Will it be ok to pick you up at six-thirty?"

"That'll be perfect," she said. "I'd like to talk to you about yesterday morning."

He gave her a self-deprecating half smile. "You mean when I lost my temper? It was my fault, Roxie, not yours."

"I need to make you fully understand what I meant," she said. "Please, sit."

Wild Wind gave in to her request and lowered himself into a chair at the kitchen table. Roxie sat in the chair closest to him. "You're right; you don't need my pity and I don't pity you in the least. Quite the opposite. You survived being captured and forced onto a reservation. You faced starvation, cold, and deplorable conditions, but you survived. You stayed true to your friend and got word to Lucky about Avasa and the move west.

"You left the reservation even though you could have been arrested at any time. And then when you got here, you began learning a whole new culture and how to fit in. It's beyond unfair that you had to do all that, and yet you did. You're making a life for yourself and now you're part of a successful business. You're the bravest, strongest person I've ever met. I couldn't have done all that you have, endured everything you've been through. So, no, I don't pity you; I admire you," she said, meeting his gaze.

Wild Wind heard the sincerity in her words and saw it in her eyes. It moved him that she thought about him in such a positive light. "Thank you. No one outside of Lucky and Erin has ever said something like that to me."

"I felt like that the first time I heard your story. I just couldn't tell you," Roxie said.

"Why?"

"Because I was afraid that you would think I was a silly white woman who pitied you and was offering you sympathy instead of admiration. I didn't know you well enough yet."

Wild Wind now saw Roxie as a wise, discerning woman whom he hadn't given careful enough consideration. It wasn't very many women who would look at him in such a way. He felt stupid that he hadn't noticed Roxie's interest in him, but she'd also hidden it well.

"And now?" he prompted.

She gave him a slightly suggestive look. "And now I thought it was time to put my hat in the ring since I know you're looking for a wife."

Her directness pleased him. "There is much more to you than I realized, Roxie. You say that I'm brave, but you are, too, in your own way. Maybe more so."

"How so?"

"It takes just as much courage to reveal feelings and thoughts sometimes as it does surviving ordeals," he said, rising. "I do have to go, but I'm looking forward to this evening."

She followed him to the door. "Me, too."

He smiled and left. Roxie closed the door and got her trembling hands under control before she ran next door to the butcher's shop. She heard Ross chopping meat in the back and bypassed that area to find Callie. Her sister-in-law was arranging some fresh goat cheese on a shelf as she hummed.

"Callie! You'll never guessed what just happened!" she said, hurrying to where Callie was working.

"Does it involve a certain Cheyenne man?" Callie's blue eyes gleamed mischievously.

"Yes! He just asked me to dinner tonight! Isn't that wonderful? Finally!" She twirled around and giggled.

"Did I hear right?" Ross asked from the doorway of the back of the shop. "Wild Wind called on you?"

"Yes, you did, brother dear," Roxie said, lifting her chin defiantly.

Ross' eyebrows drew down. "How come he didn't ask me first? He's supposed to ask me first."

Callie jumped in to help Roxie. "Well, my handsome husband, you know as well as anyone that sometimes we worry about what someone will think about us. Maybe he was worried that he'd ask you for nothing and make a fool of himself if Roxie wasn't receptive to him at all. You remember what that was like."

Ross smiled. "Yeah, I do. I couldn't really ask your pa for permission since he wasn't here, but I was really glad that when I did write him he didn't object any."

Callie smiled. "It wouldn't have mattered to me if he had objected. I fell in love with you and no one would have kept me from marrying you. I knew my own mind and heart, and so does Roxie."

Ross looked at his sister in surprise. "Are you in love with Wild Wind?"

Roxie went to stand before her tall brother. "I don't know yet, but I'd like to see if we're a good match. What if I *was* in love with him and he cared for me? Would you object to him?"

Ross' lips pursed and he shook his head. "It ain't a question of *me* approving or not, Roxie. It's this town, our culture. He's an Indian. Everyone was talking about it when it looked like him and Pastor Andi had taken up together. Most people like him now and they don't mind him being here, but marrying a white woman? I don't know if they're ready for that."

Ross saw anger flare in his sister's eyes and knew he was in for a tongue lashing. "I didn't ask about everyone else. They can go jump for all I care. I asked if *you* would object."

Wild Wind was Ross' friend and he knew the brave was a good man, but he was afraid of what Roxie might endure if she were to marry an Indian. She might be shunned or someone might try to kill Wild Wind for his involvement with a white woman. It wasn't as simple as if only his opinion counted.

"The only reason I'd object is because it's not gonna be accepted, Roxie. Not here or most anywhere in the country, either. Personally I don't have a problem with it, but I'm not the only one living in Echo," Ross said.

"You can't go to dinner with him, Roxie, and that's final."

"Since when do you tell me what to do, Ross?" Roxie said, her temper heating another notch. "I thought the man who did that moved to Philadelphia. Or are you just like him?"

Ross said, "That ain't fair and you know it. No, I don't tell you what to do because most of the time, you don't need me to, but this is different and I'm doing it for your own good. And Wild Wind's. He's lucky someone hasn't turned him into the military by now."

"Is that a threat?" Roxie said, moving even closer to Ross.

His eyebrows rose. "What? No! I'm just saying that he oughta count his blessings and not go making trouble for himself or you. I love you, Roxie, and I'm only looking out for you. You haven't been around when people are talking about him, like the fellas in the saloon. There are some that would lynch him if it weren't for him being friends with Evan and Lucky. If they saw you parading around town with him, even his friendships with them wouldn't keep either of you safe. They tried to kill Billy and Nina, and Billy's lived here all of his life."

Roxie didn't back down. "That may be, but they got out and Evan and Shadow caught the men who did it. There's been no trouble since then and now there's another deputy in town whom no one will want to go up against and Wild Wind is his friend, too. I think we'd be much safer than you imagine we'd be."

Ross did smile a little at the thought of anyone ticking Thad off by going after one of his friends. Deputy or not, Thad wouldn't hesitate to take the law into his own hands to mete out his own brand of justice. His bounty hunter instincts wouldn't let him do any less than that.

"You've got a point, but no one can keep you safe all the time. There's more to consider than just you and Wild Wind. They might come after me, Callie, or anyone else who's associated with Wild Wind. You know it's been done before and for a lot less than courting," Ross said. "There's gotta be another man you're interested in. Someone who's interested in you, right?"

"Why didn't you get married before Callie came along? Wasn't there anyone you were interested in?"

"You know there wasn't, but it's not the same thing," Ross said.

"Why? Because Callie's white?"

Ross' brown eyes showed his anger. "That's not—"

"Not what? Fair? What's unfair is that you get to pick the woman you want, but I'm supposed to settle for some man whom I don't. I never pegged you for a racist, Ross. I guess I misjudged you," Roxie said, storming from the store.

When it looked like Ross was going to follow his sister, Callie said, "I wouldn't do that if I were you, husband. It won't do you any good while she's like that."

"Am I so out of line here, Callie? What would happen in Mississippi if a white woman took up with a black man or an Indian?"

Callie couldn't refute what he was saying, especially because sentiments were even worse about that sort of thing in her home state. "No, you're not wrong about what would happen, but this isn't Mississippi, Ross. We have a black mayor now and look how many people voted for him."

"I voted for Jerry, too," Ross said, "And I always will, but Sonya is black, too. If she was white that wouldn't go over at all and you know it. *I'm* not the problem. If it were up to me, I wouldn't care what color married what color."

"*I* married a white woman. Is that a problem for you or anyone else, Ross?"

Since they'd been so caught up in their conversation, they hadn't heard Win come into the shop. He came around the counter to stand in front of Ross, who towered over him. Win's black eyes never left Ross'.

"And we had a baby, too. No one's ever said anything to my face about it and I don't give a crap what they say about me behind my back. They better not ever harass Erin or me or I'll make them sorry in ways they can only imagine," he said.

"Exactly. You're deadly," Ross said.

Win smiled. "And you think Wild Wind isn't? You've never sparred with him. I have. Plus, he's a lot better with a bow and arrow than I am. If

Roxie isn't scared, why should you be? You're a big strong guy. No one's going to come after you, either. So are you sure the problem isn't your own beliefs?"

Ross shook his head. "No, they're not my beliefs. You oughta know that. I never had any problem with you marrying Erin and I love Mia. I don't care that you're Chinese."

"Is it somehow different because Roxie's your family then?" Win asked.

"No," Ross said. "I didn't want to discuss this in front of Callie because of her condition."

Callie put a hand on Ross' arm. "I'm fine. Now what's going on?"

Ross' jaw clenched. "I've been meaning to talk to Evan about this, but I just haven't gotten around to it. There are some guys who aren't happy with Wild Wind being here. They're not keen on you or Billy, either, but Wild Wind's the one they really don't like. I haven't heard that they're planning anything, but I'm afraid they might."

Knowing that Ross didn't scare easily, Win took what he was saying seriously. "Now I understand why you're saying all this."

"I've never been prejudiced, Win. You know that. Otherwise, I'd have never had you treat our animals all these years, been good friends with Billy, or voted for Jerry," Ross said.

Win's temper cooled. "I believe you. Don't tell me who these jerks are because if I know, I won't be able to keep my mouth shut and it's best if I do. Tell Evan, though, but not Lucky. With his temper, he won't be able to keep quiet and it won't be good for anyone if he goes after them."

"I know. That's why I haven't said anything to anyone yet. Evan was the only one I was going to tell, but I couldn't have you thinking the worst of me," Ross said. "I didn't even say anything to Callie."

She hugged Ross. "Sugar, you can't shut me out like that. I'm pregnant, but I won't break. This is a lot to keep to yourself."

Sighing, he kissed her forehead. "Now what do I tell Roxie? I'm worried that if I tell her the real reason, she'll say something to Wild Wind."

Win thought about it a moment. "It might not be a bad idea for him to know so that he can be on the alert, not that he's not normally anyway, but it won't hurt to be extra cautious. Let Evan tell him."

"That's what I thought, too," Ross said.

"He'll know what to do," Win said. "That's his wheelhouse. In the meantime, I've got more sheep for you to sell."

"Are you sure things are all right between us?" Ross asked.

Win smiled. "I'm sure. Let's get this unloaded. Callie, don't say anything to Roxie, either."

"I won't," she said.

"Good woman. Let's get at it, Ross," Win said.

Chapter Nine

As soon as he and Win were done unloading the sheep Win had brought, Ross went to find his sister. She was in their parlor, working on some mending. She didn't need to look up from her work to see who it was; she knew Ross' step.

"Roxie, I'm sorry about earlier. I need to talk to you about it," he said sitting down on the end of the sofa closest to her chair.

Roxie stayed silent.

"I'm not prejudiced and you know it. Billy was my best man, for cryin' out loud. You know that Wild Wind is my friend." When she still didn't respond, Ross put his hand over hers so she couldn't keep working. "Something's going on that I can't tell you about right now. I know how that sounds, but it's the truth. I've never lied to you, Roxie, and I won't start now. I won't stand in the way of you seeing Wild Wind, but all I ask is that you do it discreetly."

Roxie looked into Ross' eyes and saw that he was sincere. "What's happening?"

"It's best I don't tell you about it. I love you and I like Wild Wind a lot. I don't want to see either of you hurt," Ross said.

"Has someone threatened him?" she asked.

"No and I hope they never do, but, just for now, please do what I'm asking you. Please, Roxie. And you and I never had this conversation. Understand?"

While she was happy that Ross approved of her seeing Wild Wind, she was worried about why Ross wanted her to keep things between them hush-hush. "What am I supposed to tell him when he comes for me this evening? He's taking me to dinner, which I'm assuming means the diner since that's the only restaurant in town."

"I know. Just go this one time, but try to do other things than dinner for a while," Ross said. "Heck, I don't know. I'm no good at this stuff."

"I'll figure it out," Roxie said. "Leave that to me."

"Ok. I'm really sorry about earlier. Friends?" he asked.

She squeezed his hand. "Friends. Thank you for looking out for me."

Smiling, he said, "That's what big brothers are for. All right. I have to go chop up a bunch of sheep now."

"I won't keep you from it, then," Roxie said.

Ross patted her hand and left.

Wild Wind looked at his reflection in the mirror. "Not bad for an Indian," he muttered in Cheyenne as he made sure his tie was straight.

He'd plaited his hair into a single braid. When he'd first come to Echo, he'd considered cutting his hair short to fit in a little more. Then he'd decided against it; he'd already conformed enough as it was by dressing in mainly non-Indian clothing. However, when he knew he wouldn't be going into town that day he wore his native garb.

Smiling as he thought about Roxie, he put on the detested dress shoes. However, he was willing to wear them if it meant that he could spend some time with her. He jerked at the sound of something smashing through a window out in his parlor. Running into it, he saw that his rug was on fire, ignited by a Molotov cocktail.

Pulling a quilt off the sofa, he threw it over the fire and stomped it out.

Another one came through the other window and he knew that whomever was throwing them was prepared to keep on with the attack. They wanted to smoke him out and they were going to succeed.

What they didn't know was that Wild Wind was prepared for just such an occurrence. As an Indian brave, he understood war strategy and how to fortify a camp or residence. One of the ways in which he'd done this was to partially close in the front porch with thick boards that would help protect him from gunfire.

He grabbed his bow, full quiver of arrows, rifle, and ammo. Instead of going out the back, which was what they most likely expected, he went right out the front door. They'd made the mistake of coming before it was completely dark and Wild Wind's keen vision picked them out. When they saw the front door open, a few rifle shots went off.

Keeping low, Wild Wind notched an arrow, aimed, and sent it sailing through the air. It hit his target square in the chest with a muted *thwack*. The man went down. There were four more that he could see, and he was betting that there were more waiting out back. At the sight of their fallen comrade, the others began firing in earnest.

Moving rapidly back and forth on the front porch, Wild Wind was able to take out three more and wound another. However, reinforcements were arriving and while the brave was an excellent marksman and fighter, he knew that he couldn't fend them off much longer by himself. His best chance was to get to the Earnests' ranch, which was closer than Lucky's sheep farm.

Taking a gamble that the men from around back had come around front, Wild Wind ran back through the front door, speeding through the growing flames inside. Cautiously opening the back door, he slipped through it. He already had a bow notched with his last arrow, so when he saw a man raising his rifle, he swiftly fired it into his midsection, making the attacker's shot go wide.

Since he was out of arrows, Wild Wind discarded his bow and empty quiver, picked up his rifle again, and ran for the tree line, knowing that he could lose them in the woods. Streaking across the expanse of meadow, he was suddenly followed by two men who shot at him. He felt a bullet graze his thigh. Although he stumbled, he was able to stay upright.

Pointing his gun behind him, he fired off a shot. He knew he probably wouldn't hit any of them, but it would buy him a few precious seconds so he could reach cover. Running pell-mell into the forest, he heard bullets hitting tree trunks all around him and shouts to find their victim to finish the job.

Wild Wind took off again, but was brought to a halt by a man who was waiting in the woods. He pointed a revolver at the brave.

"Well, looks like I caught myself an Injun," the man said. "Your scalp is gonna look real nice hanging from my porch railing."

Hearing men approaching from his rear, Wild Wind knew that he had to get past this man.

"Drop that rifle."

"I've never done anything to you," Wild Wind said, complying with the order.

"It doesn't matter. A savage is a savage and we need to be rid of all of you. I'm doing my part to make that happen," the man said.

Wild Wind grinned. "Lucky! I'm glad to see you!"

The man turned to look at the place Wild Wind was smiling at and that was all the opening the brave needed. He jumped the man as he drew his knife. His assailant turned back in time to get his revolver up and fired at the same time Wild Wind's knife plunged into his chest, piercing his heart.

The man sagged to the ground and Wild Wind fell on top of him, blood running from his stomach where the bullet was now lodged. Knowing that he had to get away from there, Wild Wind found the strength to get up and make his way through the trees and bushes.

He had to get the bleeding stopped so that he didn't leave a blood trail that would be easy to follow. His strength was rapidly leaving him and he knew that he couldn't keep running. Looking around, he saw a group of thorny bushes that would provide thick cover for him. Keeping his hand pressed to his wound, he hurried to it, dropped to his knees, and pushed his way inside it. His suit jacket and pants protected him somewhat from the sharp thorns, but he still sustained some bad scratches.

Once he lay curled up inside the bushes, he worked on slowing his heart rate to slow down the bleeding and quieting his breathing to avoid detection. Slowly, so as to make as little noise as possible, he unbuttoned his shirt. Then he carefully moved leaves aside so he could dig up whatever loose earth was underneath of them.

Scraping up a handful, Wild Wind worked up what saliva he could and spat it onto the dirt, making it as moist as possible. He pressed the mixture hard against the wound, gritting his teeth against the increased pain. The whole time he was doing this, he heard voices all around him and prayed to the Great Spirit that his cover was good enough to keep them from finding him.

Although the mudpack helped slow the bleeding, it didn't stop it completely. Wild Wind had to fight hard to stay conscious. He had to wait out his enemies until he was sure they were gone and then make his way to the Earnest ranch for help.

Time ceased to have any meaning as he lay on the cold ground. He had no idea how long it was until the voices faded away completely. Still, he didn't move for quite some time for fear that someone waited in the woods for him. He began shivering from the cold and shock and he knew that he had to take a chance on moving on.

His side and thigh had stiffened and moving was excruciating. Wild Wind crawled slowly out of the bush, being as quiet as he could. Once he was free, he stood up as much as he could and started walking through the forest, praying that he reached the Earnests' before he passed out.

"It's time for bed, sweet Eva," Ronni said, picking up her daughter.

Eva shook her head. "No. No bed."

"Yes. I know you don't think you're tired, but as soon as your pretty head hits the pillow, you'll go to sleep," Ronni insisted.

Eva let out a noise of dissent.

Carrying Eva upstairs, Ronni took her into her new bedroom and set her on her feet. As she started changing Eva into her nightgown, she heard something outside. Going to the window, she tried to see what it was. The sound came again and she recognized it as a voice.

Opening the window so she could hear it more clearly, Ronni leaned out a little.

"Help! Help!"

The voice was hoarse and as Ronni's gaze roamed over the yard below, she was barely able to see a figure moving across the grass. It looked like they were crawling.

"Marvin! Shadow! Help!"

Ronni shouted, "Help is coming! I hear you! Help is on the way!" She closed the window. "Eva, you stay right here," she said sternly to the little girl. "I mean it."

"Ok, Mommy," Eva said, nodding her head.

Ronni rushed downstairs to the parlor where her housemates were.

"There's someone shouting outside who needs help," she said. "I don't know who it is, but they're crawling across the yard."

Shadow got up and retrieved his revolver from the mantle. He always made sure to have a firearm handy no matter where he was. He moved past Ronni, exiting out the front door with Marvin following closely.

"Help! Please help me!"

Shadow recognized the voice at the same time he saw the person. "Wild Wind? Is that you?"

"Yes! I've been shot!"

The twins hurried to the injured brave and got him up off his knees, but his legs buckled when he tried to stand. Marvin and Shadow carried Wild Wind up the front veranda stairs and through the open front door.

Ronni stood just inside and she shut it after them. They took Wild Wind into the parlor and laid him on one of the sofas. The amount of blood that soaked Wild Wind's clothing was alarming.

"Oh my God," Ronni said. "What happened?"

Wild Wind struggled to get the words out. "Bunch of men attacked me at home. Too many to fight off. Hid and came here. Burned down cabin."

All of them were sorely angered by this news.

"I'll go inform Erin that we need her help and then go get Evan and Thad to go out to Wild Wind's farm with me," Shadow said.

His wife, Bree, kissed him. "Be careful."

He smiled. "Count on it." He threw on his coat and ran to the barn to saddle a horse. In a matter of minutes, he was racing along the path the led to Lucky's farm.

Inside the Earnest house, Marvin directed Ronni to bring him their medical supplies. Ever since Shadow had been severely injured a couple of years ago, Marvin made sure to keep bandages, carbolic acid, and gauze on hand, just in case something like this arose.

"He's still bleeding," Marvin said. "Bree, help me get his clothes off. Ronni, get water boiling and wet some cloths in the meantime so I can start cleaning his wounds."

Wild Wind grunted in pain as Marvin palpated his abdomen. His vision began turning gray and even though he fought valiantly, he lost consciousness.

"That's probably for the best," Marvin said.

Bree watched Marvin work. "How could someone do this? He's never hurt anyone since he came here."

"Prejudice, plain and simple," Marvin said in a cold, angry tone. "I've heard people make comments about him. I've heard them make the same sort of remarks about the Belkers—Win and Billy, too. Even Nina, despite the fact that she's white."

Shaking her head in dismay, Bree began helping Marvin tend to Wild Wind.

Chapter Ten

Evan, both his deputies, Lucky, and Win approached Wild Wind's place cautiously. Since Shadow had literally grown up in darkness, his night vision was extremely powerful. He didn't need the starlight overhead to help him see that there was no movement on the place.

"They've killed the sheep," Shadow said, looking at all the carnage, both men and animals. "Wild Wind was quite successful in his counterattack. I count five bodies lying near the cabin, but there may be more out back."

"What?" Lucky shouted. "Those sons of bitches! It's not bad enough that Wild Wind might die, they went after the sheep, too!"

He began whistling, heard a whine in response, and headed in that direction. Suddenly Rafe sprang at Lucky and the Irishman fell back.

"Rafe, it's just me. It's ok, lad. Easy," he said.

The coyote mix whined and then limped over to where Bubba lay panting in the grass. Lucky knelt beside him and began searching for the dog's injuries. Under Bubba's right front shoulder blade he found a gunshot wound, but he couldn't tell the extent of the injury.

While Win saw to the dog, the others moved slowly through the sea of slaughtered sheep. The closer they came to the smoldering, burned-out shell of a cabin, the angrier Evan grew. They examined each of the human bodies. As Evan was checking the last of the fallen men in front of the cabin, the man moved and opened his eyes.

"Help," he whispered, fingering the arrow that stuck out of his chest.

"Rusty?" Evan asked, recognizing the man.

Rusty nodded.

"You want help?"

"Yeah."

Fury took hold of Evan. "Ok. I'll help you. I'm gonna put you out of your misery." He put a bullet in Rusty's head.

Thad came up beside him and Evan looked at him. Nudging Rusty with his boot, Thad said, "Nice work, Sheriff. Couldn't have done better myself. He was gonna die anyway."

"Never let it be said that I don't have compassion for my fellow man," Evan said. Normally the sheriff wasn't callous about human life, but, in this case, he felt justified.

They went around the back of the cabin and found two more dead men. They were shocked to see that one of them was Hank Winston, the school teacher.

Thad said, "Hank was in on this? It don't make sense. I didn't know he was an Indian hater."

Lucky said, "Some people hide that sort of thing really well. I'll bet he didn't vote for Jerry, either. He probably agreed to sit on the council just to make it look good."

Evan said, "I hope Adam is ready to take over for Hank. I know he was planning on going to college, but we need him to finish out the school year if he's willing."

Adam Harris was in the process of finishing up his senior year himself, but he was actually smart enough that he could have gone to college the year before. He'd been working and saving money towards his tuition. He always helped Hank with the other students who were having trouble learning, so he had some experience and could at least get them through the last few months. The council could start looking for a new teacher once summer came.

Thad had come to know Adam very well since he was courting his oldest stepdaughter, Allie. "He's sharp as a tack. He can do it."

Shadow said, "It seems as if our Cheyenne friend put up quite a fight."

Lucky said, "Aye. Ye've never seen him in battle, but I have. Wild Wind doesn't believe in takin' captives. He doesn't give anyone a second chance to get up and fight again. He puts 'em down and makes sure they stay down." Searching the ground, Lucky found Wild Wind's trail. Others wouldn't have seen it, but Lucky was an excellent tracker, trained by Wild Wind and other Cheyenne braves when he'd lived with their tribe. "We don't need to go in there right now, but I'm bettin' there's at least one more fella dead," he said, pointing towards the woods.

Evan sighed. "I'm glad we already brought a wagon. Looks like the undertaker and Andi are gonna be busy the next few days."

Lucky said, "I'm gonna go see how Win's making out with Bubba."

A gunshot rang out, giving the Irishman his answer. Lucky let out a scream of fury and anguish and shot the body closest to him until he was out of bullets. Then he stood panting, his gray eyes glowing silver in the moonlight that now shone down on the farm.

"I'm gonna kill every last one of them, I swear I will," he said. "I'll find out who else is involved and I'll hunt them down like the curs they are."

Evan put a hand on his shoulder. "No, you won't, Lucky. You let us take care of this. You need to concentrate on your wife and family. You've got a baby on the way and your Cheyenne brother to help take care of. Not to mention dealing with the farm here."

Lucky groaned. "We've lost a fortune. I'll have to start butcherin' right away and try to sell what meat I can. Good thing it's cold out. The meat will keep longer. At least we can sell the wool, too."

Footsteps sounded behind them and Win joined them. "I'm sorry about that, Lucky. He wasn't going to make it. He'd lost too much blood. I'm gonna miss him, too. He was a good dog and still young."

"Aye," Lucky said in a thick voice. "That he was. I'm gonna go see if Ross can help me with these sheep. Adam, too."

Win said, "I'll help, too. I'll get started while you go get them."

Thad said, "Get Big Keith, too. His muscle will come in handy. Too bad Billy's no help since he can't stand blood."

Lucky said, "He can help shear them, he just can't field dress them. I'll check to see if Erin and Marvin have Wild Wind back at the clinic while I'm in town. It's gonna be a long night."

Erin was glad to have Andi helping her with Wild Wind's surgery since Win couldn't assist her. Andi had been a nurse in the Salvation Army and she was skilled with everything from field surgery to treating common ailments. As they worked, Erin could tell that if Andi wanted to further her training, she would make a fine doctor. However, Andi was happiest healing and saving people's souls.

As Andi blotted away blood from where Erin was suturing, she said, "I have a message for Lucky from Arliss."

Erin briefly glanced at her. "You know where Arliss is? No one has seen him since that night."

"I know. He feels terrible and he's too ashamed to come back. He's also afraid that he'll bring more trouble on you all," Andi said.

Looking at Wild Wind's face, Erin said, "Looks like more trouble came without Arliss' involvement."

"I'll let him know what happened," she said. "I'll convince him to come see you all."

Erin asked, "How's his memory?"

"Um, better some days than others. He seemed a little clearer today. I'm worried about him. Sometimes he doesn't remember eating or a conversation we've already had. Then there's his temper, too. He becomes so frustrated with himself."

"Do you feel threatened by him?"

Andi smiled. "No. Never. He gets mad and yells and then he apologizes and he's sweet again."

"So you see him every day?"

"Yes."

Erin had already removed the bullet and she now finished repairing the damage done by the deadly missile. She closed the incision and Andi cleaned Wild Wind off again before they bandaged his midsection. The bullet graze to his thigh had already been taken care of by Marvin, and Erin was happy with the job he'd done, so she and Andi left it alone.

Andi's considerable strength came in handy in moving Wild Wind from the small surgical area to the two-bed ward and getting him into a bed.

"I'll stay with him tonight, Erin," Andi said. "You have a baby to go home to."

"Are you sure?" Erin asked.

"Absolutely. If I need anything, I'll have someone come get you."

"All right," Erin said just as Lucky came into the ward.

He didn't go near Wild Wind since he was dirty, but his eyes never wavered from the man he considered a brother. "Will he be all right?"

"I think so," Erin said. "He's a strong man to have survived that kind of injury while traveling all that way on foot to get help."

"Aye. He's a warrior through and through. He killed seven that we know of and I'm not a bit sorry that he did. They had no business comin' after him. They'll think twice about doin' it again, too. I don't know how many more of the cowards went after him, but the ones he didn't take down killed all the sheep on the farm. They shot Bubba and hurt Rafe. Win had to put Bubba down. There was nothin' he could do for him."

"Oh, Lucky," Erin said, hugging him despite his dirty state. She wasn't going close to Wild Wind again and she could change her clothes. Right then, offering her friend support was uppermost in her mind. "I'm so sorry."

Lucky accepted her embrace. "Thanks, lass. I don't have hate in me heart for too many people, but I hate all of those buggars. I pray that they rot in Hell for what they've done. I'll have to answer to the Lord for that, but I'll try to forgive them someday. Just not tonight."

Andi stayed silent, knowing that this wasn't the time to offer spiritual counseling. Emotions were too raw and close to the surface for that.

"It's times like these I wish we had a medicine man here," Lucky said. He switched to Cheyenne. "Rest, my brother. Know that the guilty will be dealt with. You have earned much coup and can be proud of the brave way you fought. You are a warrior to be reckoned with. You must get better so we can go hunting and pick on Billy together. Sleep well and I will come see you tomorrow." Looking at Erin, he said, "Are ya goin' home then?"

She nodded. "Yeah. I'll need to feed Mia soon."

Andi said, "I'm staying with him tonight."

"God bless ya, Andi. Yer a good woman and we're lucky to have ya," Lucky said.

"Thank you. Arliss said to tell you hello and that he's very sorry about everything that happened. He's been afraid to come see you because he doesn't want anyone else to follow him," she said.

Lucky offered her a slight smile. "Tell Arliss that no one blames him and that there's no reason he can't come see us. Truth be told, I could use his help right now."

"I'll let him know," Andi said.

Lucky nodded. "Come, Erin. I'll escort ya home."

"All right. Good night, Andi. I'll be back first thing to check on him and take over," Erin said.

Andi bid them both goodnight, checked Wild Wind, and settled in for the night.

Almost daily, Arliss discovered new things about himself. That night, he found out that he knew how to pick locks. When Erin had left the clinic, she'd locked the door. Arliss had it open in a matter of seconds. His memory loss frustrated him no end, but for some reason everything Andi told him stuck like glue. Earlier in the evening, she'd told him that she was going to the clinic to help Erin with Wild Wind.

He hadn't been able to sleep, so he thought he'd go see how Wild Wind was doing. He walked through the darkened waiting room, past the office, and into the ward. Andi lay on a cot by the bed where Wild Wind still slept. Arliss quietly walked over to the brave and hated the slightly pale pallor beneath his normal skin tone.

"So much for me stayin' away to keep everyone safe," he whispered.

"Arliss?"

He saw that she was awake now. "Aw, I'm sorry, darlin'. I didn't mean to wake you up. How's he doin'?"

Andi sat up. "Erin was able to get the bullet out and she repaired what she could. The rest is up to him now."

"He's strong. He'll make it. You gotta stay all night?"

She nodded. "Erin will be back in the morning, of course. Lucky said that no one wants you to stay away and that they don't blame you for what happened. He also said that they could use an extra pair of hands."

"He said that, huh?"

"Yes."

"All right. Remind me to go over there in the morning."

Andi said, "It's such a sad situation. They burned down Wild Wind's cabin and killed the sheep and one of the dogs."

"Damn. Sorry. How many of them did he pick off? You don't mess with this ole boy. I've seen him shoot and throw a knife."

"Seven."

Arliss nodded. "I knew it had to be a lot."

Getting up, Andi checked Wild Wind for fever and was relieved to find that his temperature was normal. There had been no seepage of blood through the bandages around his stomach, which was also a good sign.

Arliss watched her work. She was competent and efficient. Andi pulled the covers over Wild Wind, tucking them around his shoulders. Noticing the intense way Arliss watched her, she felt a spark of desire when she saw the warmth in his eyes.

"You're such a pretty woman, Andi. I don't think you know it, though," he said, not apologizing for staring.

A blush stained her cheeks as she smiled. "No, I guess I don't. Men want their women to be petite and fragile, not six feet tall and muscular."

He surprised her by moving close enough that he could slip an arm around her waist. "That's just because you ain't met the right man—until now, that is."

Andi didn't have to look up very much to meet Arliss' eyes. "What are you saying?"

He smiled. "Don't tell me you don't know that I'm sweet on you. You know it without your special powers."

She did know. Andi often caught him watching her with desire in his eyes and he always treated her in a way that went beyond simple gentlemanly courtesy. He wasn't shy about taking her hand for a few moments or briefly touching her arm or shoulder. This was the first time he'd gone beyond that.

The attraction wasn't one-sided. With his deep blue eyes, sandy brown hair, and strong jaw, he was very desirable. Since coming to Echo, he'd had food on a regular basis and combined with all the work he did with Lucky and others around town, he'd gained a lot of muscle; he now had a fine physique.

Arliss was considerate and made her laugh all the time when they were together. He was smarter than he first appeared to people, showing them that he was more than just a "dumb Alabama boy," as he called himself. He was a gifted fiddle player and had many talents that were hidden, even to him. The only problem was he didn't know who he was.

What if he was married? If he really was from England, he might have a wife and children over there. Was he a spy of some sort? He was obviously a trained killer, but who had trained him and why? There were so many questions surrounding Arliss that she was afraid to get involved with him for fear that both of them would be hurt in the future.

"Yes, I can tell," she said.

She shouldn't let him hold her like this, but his hands just rested lightly on her waist and it felt good.

"Andi, I know I don't have anything to offer you and you'd be takin' a big gamble on me, but I'll promise you this much: I'll always do everything in my power to make sure you don't get hurt in any way," he said. "I know it's not enough, but it's the best I can do at the moment."

Andi didn't know why, but she was drawn to this mystery man with his mostly easygoing personality and winsome smile. She had to admit that she loved his accent, too. There was a naughty part of her that hoped he really wasn't British because if and when he regained his memory, his voice might change. She couldn't imagine him with a British accent.

"Is it enough for now, Andi?" he asked with a serious expression.

Was it? All she knew was that she enjoyed being around him, was attracted to him, and was deeply concerned about him. Like many other times in her life, Andi decided to take a leap of faith. "Yes, it's enough."

The grin that lit his face made her smile in return.

"I can't tell you how happy that makes me," he said. "I don't know how this works with pastors. Are you allowed to kiss a man or not?"

She chuckled. "Yes, I can kiss a man."

"I sure am glad to hear that," he said. "I'd like to right now, but this isn't the time or place." He nodded in Wild Wind's direction and stepped away from her a little. "Soon though. I'm gonna go make some coffee for you and then I'll head out to Wild Wind's place. That's a shame about all those sheep."

"Yes, it is," she said.

"I'll get that coffee going."

She watched him leave the ward, feeling disappointed that he hadn't kissed her, even though she knew he was right about it being the wrong time. Shaking it off, she turned her attention back to her patient.

Chapter Eleven

Roxie hurried along the street very early the next morning. Ross had told her what had happened to Wild Wind the previous night. She'd wanted to rush to the clinic, but she knew that Erin needed time to work on him and that she would only be in the way. However, she hadn't been able to sleep and therefore had gotten dressed and ready to go.

She hadn't said anything to Ross, but she was angry at him for not telling Evan sooner about what he'd overheard men saying about Wild Wind. If he had, Wild Wind wouldn't be fighting for his life.

There were a couple of people in the waiting room, including Molly Watson. The young brunette woman smiled at her.

"Hi, Roxie," she said. "Are you feeling poorly?"

"No. I'm here to see Wild Wind," she said.

"Me, too, but I haven't seen Erin to ask if it's all right to yet. She's in with someone right now," Molly said.

Roxie said, "I'm going to sneak back to see him. I need to see him."

Molly was a newspaper woman to the hilt, even at her young age. "Can I come with you in case he wakes up and says something about what happened? I want to see how he is, too, of course."

Smiling, Roxie shook her head. "Fine. Let's go."

Quickly the two women went back through the hallway, past the office and exam rooms, and into the ward. They found Wild Wind in the second bed. Both of them were shocked by how weak and pale he looked. Given what he'd been through, it was no wonder, but Roxie was so used to seeing him as a strong, active man that it was hard to see him this way.

Going over to his bedside, Roxie tentatively reached out to stroke his hair.

"What a strong man he is to be able to withstand such terrible injuries and reach help the way he did," she said.

Molly agreed. "He's tough, all right. He's a hero as far as I'm concerned. Those cowards he killed deserved it for going after an innocent man that way." Her blue eyes shone with righteous anger. "That's just how I'm going to write it, too. He singlehandedly staved off an ambush and lived to tell the tale. Now's not the time, though." Molly might be a reporter, but she wasn't insensitive. She took Wild Wind's slack hand in hers. "You fight, Wild Wind. You gotta get better. Don't let them beat you. I'll be back to see you."

She took her leave then and Roxie was alone with him. She ran a hand over his brow and caressed his cheek. "Molly's right. You have to show them that you're stronger than they are. So don't you even think about leaving us. There are so many people who love you and need you. Please fight, my brave warrior."

The pain in his abdomen brought Wild Wind to consciousness, but he didn't know where he was. The last thing he remembered was crawling through the woods trying to get to the Earnest ranch. He felt cool fingers touching his face and a hand holding his and surmised that he'd been successful in reaching help.

He closed his hand around that of whoever held his and could tell that it was a woman.

A pleased feminine chuckle met his ears. "Wild Wind? That's it. Wake up."

Roxie? Why are you here? Where is here? Only one way to find out.

Lifting his eyelids was a surprising struggle, but he managed it. Roxie's beautiful blue eyes met his gaze.

"Hello," she said. "I guess you had a good excuse to stand me up last night."

If he'd had the strength, he would have grinned at her humorous statement, but he was only able to give her a slight smile. "Sorry," he whispered.

"You're not the one who should be sorry," she said. Angry fire suddenly lit her eyes. "I'm so proud of you for defending yourself the way you did. Let me get you some water."

His eyes followed her as she filled a glass from a pitcher and brought it to him. Carefully, she helped him drink some and then readjusted his pillow for him.

"Thanks," he said. "Did I get to Earnests'?"

Roxie nodded as someone else came into the ward.

"I do believe I heard my name," Marvin said, smiling as he walked over to the other side of Wild Wind's bed. "I see my patient is awake. That's encouraging."

Wild Wind's forehead creased. "Patient?"

"Oh, yes. Ronni was upstairs and heard your distress call. She alerted the rest of us and Shadow and I took you into the house where I put some of my meager medical knowledge to use," Marvin said. "I guess it helped, for which I'm glad."

"I don't remember that. Thank you." Wild Wind tried to hold up his right hand for Marvin to shake, but he was tired again.

Marvin clasped his hand, resting both of theirs back down on the bed. "Think nothing of it. We were happy to help. I won't stay. I just wanted to see how you were doing. You did a heck of a job on those Cretans who attacked you. I don't know how many of them there were, but I'd say you killing seven of them put a nice dent in their numbers. Well done."

"Seven? That is much coup," Wild Wind said.

"I would say so. I'm sorry about the sheep, though. And Bubba. He was such a good dog and very friendly."

Wild Wind's eyes widened. "What do you mean?"

Marvin passed a hand over his eyes as he realized his faux pas. "Forgive me. I didn't know that you weren't informed yet. Well, there's no getting around it now. I'm afraid they killed all of the sheep and Bubba, too. Rafe is all right, although he has a broken paw, according to Win. I'm so sorry."

Roxie put a hand on his arm. "Wild Wind, I know how furious you must be, but you can't let that concern you right now. Getting upset will only make you weaker and prevent you from getting better."

Marvin's smile was malicious. "Rest assured, Wild Wind, I'll help ferret out who all was there or knew about it. Evan is doing the same thing. They better pray that he finds them before I do because I don't have his sense of honor about these things. Mine is rather more Biblical in nature. An eye for an eye and all that. Get your rest as Roxie is advising you. I'll come see you again tomorrow." He nodded at Roxie. "Good day, Roxie. He's in capable hands."

Wild Wind tried to contain his rage and only succeeded by picturing himself putting to death whatever men remained from the group that had attacked him. That image, along with Roxie's touch, calmed him.

"How about another drink and then you should sleep," Roxie said.

He nodded and let her help him drink again.

She put a hand to his forehead. "Sleep. I'll be here."

Closing his eyes, he let slumber overtake him.

When she'd treated Wild Wind and installed him in the ward, Erin hadn't realized that the clinic would be essentially commandeered by Lucky. He was a force of nature and between his charm, reasoning, and stubbornness, he was not to be denied, either. He'd shown up the evening after the attack with a bunch of stuff that Erin recognized from Wild Wind's tipi, which Arliss had been living in until the night Arliss' "friend" had shown up.

"What are you doing with those?" she asked, following him down the hall to the ward.

"Well, ye've never treated a Cheyenne man before and there are things that he needs besides just the medicine you have. Ya hafta treat his spirit and mind as well as his body," Lucky said.

He was quiet as they entered the ward in case Wild Wind was asleep. He carefully sat down the crate he carried and looked at his friend. Roxie sat beside the bed reading a book. She was staying with Wild Wind overnight. She saw the angry look that passed over Lucky's face as he watched Wild Wind sleep. As kind and considerate as the Irishman could be, he was also quick to anger and not afraid to mete out physical punishment when his loved ones had been wronged.

"How is he?" he asked Erin.

"Holding his own. He's still with us, so I'd say that's a good sign," Erin replied.

"Aye."

The women watched as Lucky crouched down and pulled out what they knew was sweet grass.

"You can't burn that in here," Erin said. "You shouldn't even have that stuff in here. It's not sanitary, and if I have to have another patient stay, they shouldn't breathe it in."

Lucky smiled at her. "C'mon, lass. I'll only let it burn a few minutes. The scent will be comforting to him and purifying, too. Just a little bit? Please?"

"Dang it! How do you always get your way? Just a few minutes," Erin said.

He chuckled, pulled out a blackened bowl in which Wild Wind often burned the grass, set it on the table near Wild Wind's bed, and lit a little of the grass. Then he got a sack out of the crate and handed it to Erin.

"Wasna. He might eat that before he will anything else and it's good for him. I made some venison stew, too."

"Lucky, we have food here," Erin said.

"I know and there's nothin' wrong with it, it's just that this is what he prefers and since he's not feelin' well, the more we can coax him into eatin', the better. I'll put the stew over here on the stove to keep warm."

Roxie felt Wild Wind squeeze her hand and saw a smile play around the brave's mouth. When she would have spoken, he gave a tiny shake of his head and squeezed her hand again.

"Ok. Thank you. I'm sure he'll enjoy it," Erin said.

Lucky wasn't done. He pulled out a deerskin blanket.

Erin pointed at him. "You put that on his bed and you'll need your own bed here, and I'll be the one to put you in it."

"I washed it," Lucky said, clearly offended.

"I've seen the way you wash clothing. No. It's not going on his bed."

Scowling, Lucky put it down, but picked up a small dream catcher. "Otto made this for him." He grinned when he saw Erin nod.

One by one, Lucky took things out of the crate for Erin's approval. The brand-new moccasins Nina had made for him were allowed to stay, as were the dream catcher, a small ceremonial bone rattle, the wasna, and a few other items. Roxie had a difficult time not laughing over the barter-and-trade-like way Erin and Lucky negotiated. At the end of it, Lucky got sneaky. He'd rolled up the deerskin blanket. Quickly, he took it over to Wild Wind's bed and spread it out so that most of it was underneath the bed, with some sticking out as though it were a rug.

At Erin's look of disbelief, Lucky said, "What? Ya said he couldn't have it *on* the bed, but ya didn't say it couldn't be *underneath* it."

Erin couldn't stay angry with Lucky and she laughed. Roxie couldn't hold back any longer and Wild Wind laughed weakly while he held a hand over his side.

"Aw, I'm sorry, lad," Lucky said. "I didn't mean to wake you."

Grinning, Wild Wind said, "I've been awake for all of it, so don't worry. It's your big mouth. Even when you think you're being quiet, you're not."

"I know. Hard as I try, I'm still noisy, which is why ya taught me Indian sign," Lucky said.

"That's right. Thank you for all of the presents," Wild Wind said.

"Yer welcome."

Erin put on her coat. "Roxie, if you need anything, Andi said she'll be home tonight after eight. The council meets tonight. If something serious happens, send someone to get me."

"I will," Roxie said. "I used to help take care of Pa, so I'm used to this sort of thing."

She pinched Lucky's arm and said, "No making him laugh hard. If you make him break his stitches, I'm gonna scalp you."

He rubbed his arm, but laughed. "All right. I'll try to behave. Go home to yer family."

"Goodnight, everyone," Erin said and left the ward.

Normally, there wouldn't have been a council meeting that night, but after what had happened to Wild Wind, Jerry had called one.

"Where are we with the investigation, Sheriff?" he asked as soon as it began.

Evan said, "I'm making headway, but I'm not releasing any names yet. I don't need a vigilante group loose on the streets. It'll only start an all-out bloodbath and I don't want any more innocent people hurt. What I want is for everyone to go about their daily business and not live in constant fear. Acting afraid will show these guys that they hold power and that we don't want."

Spike said, "You know I'll do whatever I can to help, Evan. If I even get a whiff of anyone being involved, I'll let you know."

Evan nodded. "That's what I will ask for: information. Don't act on it, just pass it along to me or my deputies. No one else. We'll deal with them."

"All right. I know you'll catch these guys," Jerry said.

"I wouldn't look for them to try anything again for a little while or maybe they never will, but either way, we'll get them," Evan said.

"Ok. Now, we have the matter of replacing Hank to deal with. I'd hate to end the school year early, especially with a couple of our students graduating this year," Jerry said. "I move that if he'll accept the position, Adam Harris take over the job until the end of the year."

"I second that," Edna Taft, head of town council said. "He could have graduated last year, so as far as I'm concerned, he's smart enough for the position."

Adam's mouth hung open a little. "Me?"

Evan smiled. "Unless you know another Adam Harris. Yes, you."

Marvin asked, "Will you do it, Adam?"

For as long as he could remember, Adam had wanted to be a schoolteacher, but having it suddenly thrust at him before attending a teacher's college was a little daunting. Then he thought, why should he go all the way to Massachusetts for a degree? It was the closest teaching college that gave a degree so that he could teach anywhere, not just in that state. There was one in Colorado, but it was only for residents of the state and the teacher had to teach within Colorado once they'd graduated.

He practically had Hank's lesson plans memorized anyway. He could certainly get the rest of the kids through until the end of May. Then he'd have the summer to figure things out for the next year. He just had to convince everyone that they wouldn't need to look for a replacement.

"I'll do it," he solemnly said.

Jerry said, "All those in favor of Adam Harris temporarily taking over as Echo's teacher, say 'aye.'"

All of them except Adam did since he couldn't vote for himself.

"Next order of business: Adam, you know that Hank was our town clerk. Do you wanna do that, too?" Jerry asked.

"I don't know; I mean, do I have the authority to do that sort of thing?" Adam asked.

Spike said, "You do if we say you do. Do you know how to file documents and stuff like that?"

Adam nodded. "Sure. It's simple, really. And I know how to record minutes."

Jerry said, "Do I hear a motion to appoint Adam the new town clerk since our old one is dead?"

"I'll make the motion," Marvin said.

"I'll second it," Spike said.

"All those in favor?" Jerry asked.

Everyone said "aye." And that's how Adam ended up with two important positions in Echo.

Chapter Twelve

On the third night after the attack, Wild Wind awoke during the night. Roxie slept on the cot near his bed. She'd turned down the lamp so the lighting was dim. Her blonde hair looked coppery in the flickering flames and they made shadows dance over the blanket she lay beneath.

She'd been there every night to take care of him when she didn't have to be, which told him several things. First, she was a very kind woman since she wouldn't accept any money from Erin for doing it. She also cared for him a great deal and she was skilled at this sort of work. There was no task that she'd balked at doing and she often did things for him without being asked.

Looking around the room, he smiled as his eyes rested on the dream catcher Otto had made for him. His mind returned to the woman on the cot. How long had she had feelings for him? Why hadn't she said anything to him sooner? Fear, most likely. Not fear of what other people would think, he knew. She'd probably been afraid that he would reject her.

He could understand that. It was one of the things that he'd feared with Andi and he'd been right in a way. What had happened between them couldn't really be called rejection, but a mutual agreement that they'd never be able to see eye-to-eye on the differences in their religions. They'd tried, but after a little while it had become very apparent, and they'd both known there was no use in trying to force things when neither could go against their beliefs. Although he'd regretted the situation, Wild Wind knew that he and Andi had done the right thing in breaking things off.

Perhaps the Great Spirit had made him and Andi try briefly so that it would spur Roxie to come forward once he and Andi had stopped seeing each other. It was entirely possible. After all, the Great Spirit saw and knew all. Was Roxie the real reason that he'd felt in his soul that he was meant to leave the reservation with Lucky? If she was the woman that he was meant to be with, why a white woman? Why not another Indian woman, even if it was from another tribe?

As if she knew he was thinking about her, Roxie stirred and opened her eyes to see him looking at her. She raised her head.

"Are you all right? Do you need something?"

"I'm fine. Just couldn't sleep. I'm not used to sleeping so much," he said.

"You needed it after being injured so badly. How is your pain? Do you want more laudanum?" she asked.

"No. I don't like the way it makes me feel."

"Willow bark tea? It feels chilly. I better put more wood in the stove anyway. I don't mind brewing some for you," she said, rising.

He didn't refuse. The tea would taste good and alleviate his pain a little, although it wasn't bad at the moment. "Thanks."

"You're welcome."

She built up the fire in the stove and put tea on to steep. Coming to his bed, she put her hand on his forehead. Although it was warm, it wasn't overly so. "Good. No fever." She pulled the covers back and checked his bandage while trying to ignore the rest of his muscular torso. "No bleeding. That's good, too. Are you sure you don't want a shirt? Aren't you cold?"

"I don't bother with a shirt at night. Most of the time I just wear a breechcloth." He liked the blush that came to her cheeks and couldn't help being amused. "I don't sleep in a bed the way you do, either. I never bought a bed." His amusement turned to dismay and anger. "It's a good thing I still have my tipi since Lucky said that only a few things from the cabin were salvageable."

"I'm so sorry about all of your belongings and home being ruined, but I'm so glad that you're still with us," she said. "Especially because you still owe me dinner. You're not getting out of that."

He chuckled. "I haven't forgotten, and I'll make good on that."

She fixed their tea and put a few cookies on a plate for them to share. "We'll have a little snack," she said, putting them down on the table tray she placed over him. Then she pulled her chair close and sat down.

Although he wasn't hungry, Wild Wind picked up one of the oatmeal cookies and took a bite to humor her. It tasted good and he was surprised that it actually activated his appetite.

"Did you make these?" he asked.

"Yes. Yesterday."

"They're very good," he said.

"Thank you. Other people like cakes or pies best for dessert, but cookies are my favorite sweet," Roxie told him. "I like almost any kind of cookie."

"Otto loves those coconut ones you make."

She smiled. "Every time he sees me, he asks me to bake him some. He's so sweet and funny. He's good at mimicking people. I like it when he copies Lucky."

"He has Lucky's personality, although he can be serious, too."

"How is he doing after what happened with that man who showed up at Leah and Lucky's?" Roxie asked.

"He's confused because he's been trained as a warrior and only did what he'd been taught to do. So he doesn't understand Lucky and Leah's disapproval of his actions. I don't, either. It was really no different than me defending my home or myself. I'm proud of him," Wild Wind responded.

"I think it's different because we don't see children in the same light as you do. We don't think that children should handle weapons at such an early age, so it's rather shocking that Otto would do such a thing."

"I see what you mean. I'm still learning some of the differences in our two cultures. May I ask you a question?"

Roxie nodded. "Of course."

"Why are you interested in me? I'm an Indian and you're white."

While his blunt question surprised her at first, she saw that it was a good opening for the subject.

"I'm very aware that you're an Indian," she said. "You're different from any other man I've ever met. You're very handsome and I'm sure you're considered so by your own people, too. I suppose exotic is a good way to describe you, but it's much more than that. You're a very intelligent man, you're kind, you're skilled at many things, and I like how good you are with children. I've already told you that I think you're brave, which you are. In short, you're the sort of man every woman dreams of, Indian or not."

He was flattered by her positive response and impressed that she hadn't avoided his question in some way. She'd been forthright and specific, which pleased him.

"And you truly would have no problem with our different religions and not expect me to convert to Christianity?" he asked.

Her eyes widened. "I would never ask you to convert! Why should I impose my beliefs on you? Say that we were to marry and have children: Would you stand in the way of them being baptized?"

"No. They should be able to decide their own beliefs when they're old enough to understand. Everyone should have the right to believe as they like. Erin and Win have a similar agreement since he doesn't believe in any god or religion," Wild Wind said.

"Well, then, there would be no problem. What about celebrating Christmas and Easter?"

He shrugged. "I do so now; not because I believe in Jesus, but because I like exchanging gifts and getting together with everyone. Does that bother you?"

"Not at all." Their conversation was enlightening and exciting to Roxie because they were able to agree on such things. It meant that there would be no issue with them later on.

He nodded. "This is good. I'm glad that we think alike on the subject."

She smiled and it brought attention to how pretty her lips were. Even in his weakened condition, he would have liked to kiss her. He knew that he needed to talk to Ross.

"When you go home today, will you tell Ross that I'd like to see him? I have some sheep business to talk to him about." It wasn't a lie; he did, but it wasn't the main reason he wanted to see Ross.

"Certainly," Roxie asked. "Can I get you anything else?"

"No, thanks." He took her hand brought it to his lips, placing a kiss to the back of it. "Thank you for all of your help."

Roxie almost gasped at the little tingle that streaked up her arm at the contact from his warm, supple lips. Her imagination immediately went to what it would be like to kiss him. Their gazes met and held for several moments before Roxie regained her wits.

"You're welcome. I'll clean this up and get it out of the way so you can rest again," she said.

Wild Wind's gaze followed her as she cleared away their dishes and put the bed tray off to the side. Suddenly his eyes were completely opened to what a vibrant, beautiful woman Roxie was and he was hungry for something besides food. As she went over to her chair, his arm shot out and he grasped her upper arm, pulling her towards him. Looking into his dark eyes, Roxie saw that he'd been thinking the same thing as her. Since he was propped up against pillows, she didn't have to lean over much to kiss him.

As their lips met, Wild Wind kept the contact light, but he was still strongly affected by the feel of Roxie's soft mouth against his. However, she made it apparent that she wasn't done with him. Her warm hand moved over his chest, over his shoulder, and under his long hair as she deepened the kiss.

Roxie's heartbeat sped up as he responded to her, kissing her back fiercely. His skin was smooth and the strong muscles underneath it fascinated her as he moved. Remembering his injuries, she reluctantly pulled away from him. Her breathing was rapid as she looked in his eyes and ran a hand down over his powerful arm.

"I think I got a little carried away," she said.

"No more than me," Wild Wind responded. "I take it you've done that before."

Roxie gave him a sassy smile. "Yes, I have. Are you shocked?"

He laughed. "No. Not at all. I'd be shocked if a beautiful woman like you hadn't been kissed."

Roxie straightened and moved away from him. "I'm glad it doesn't bother you."

"No, it doesn't." He was beginning to feel sleepy again, and even though he'd have liked to either kiss her more or talk to her more, he began nodding off.

Roxie saw and smiled as she lay back down on her cot and covered up. She yawned and curled up, letting her mind drift along until she fell asleep.

Chapter Thirteen

Arliss wiped sweat from his brow and then went back to throwing charred boards from Wild Wind's ruined cabin into Lucky's wagon. It was such a shame that the brand-new home had been destroyed. He'd liked the way Wild Wind had decorated it. As he picked up another board, he thought about all of the beautiful things his friend had lost to the fire. There had been very few things untouched by the flames.

"Arliss?"

He put the board in his hands in the wagon before turning to the source of the voice. Marvin stood a short distance away, surveying the damage.

"Yeah? What can I do for you, Mr. Earnest?"

"No need to be so formal. I need some information from you."

Arliss put a hand on the wagon and leaned on it a little. "About what?"

"Well, I've been asked to go on a mission to help find out who you are and what you may have been involved in and I was wondering if you'd remembered anything else about your former life?" Marvin asked.

Arliss let out a short laugh. "Well, I can give you my journal. It'd be better to read that since my memory seems to be getting worse."

Marvin arched a brow. "Worse? How so?"

"Well, it's possible that by this time tomorrow, I won't remember this conversation or that I helped with the cleanup here. That's why I've been keeping a journal every day. That way, I can read it and it sort of jogs my memory about things," he said. "Erin says it might clear up or it might be permanent. She said that keeping a journal like that is a good way to deal with the problem, and it's working pretty good so far."

"I'm sorry to hear that, Arliss. Perhaps reading your diary would be good."

"Where are you going?" Arliss asked.

"To Alabama to see what's in that deposit box. It would give us a better—"

In mere seconds, Arliss had Marvin by his shirt collar. "Whose harebrained scheme was this? It won't work. They'll be waiting to see who shows up there and once they get their hands on those documents, they'll kill whoever has them with no remorse."

It wasn't only Arliss' physical assault of him that shocked him. Arliss now spoke in a clipped British accent, but the man didn't seem to be aware of it. Marvin didn't try to resist Arliss as their eyes met.

"Who would come after us, Dumont? What sort of plot are you involved in?" Marvin asked, playing on a hunch.

Arliss' smile held no mirth. "Who are you? Are you working for Stanton? Are you one of his men?" he asked in the same British voice.

Marvin played along, letting out a derisive snort. "What kind of fool do you take me for? I wouldn't work with him if he were the last operative on the planet. What do you suspect him of?"

"I don't suspect; I know. I've only to get those documents to the proper—"

"Here now, Arliss!" Lucky shouted, riding up to the wagon. "Let Marvin go!"

Marvin watched in stunned fascination as Arliss' whole demeanor changed from that of a sophisticated British spy of some sort to a down-to-earth Alabama boy. Arliss' saw that he had a grip on Marvin's shirt and was confused about why he was roughing up the man. The last thing he remembered was saying something to Marvin about his journal.

"Mr. Dumont?" Marvin queried.

"What?" Arliss asked. He turned Marvin loose and smoothed down his shirt as best he could. "I'm sorry. What happened?"

"That's all right," Marvin said. "You weren't yourself for a little bit. Mr. Dumont paid us a little visit."

Lucky had dismounted and come to stand with them. "What's this now?"

"I was informing Arliss that I was going to Alabama to retrieve the contents of a bank deposit box there and suddenly I wasn't talking to Arliss anymore, but Dumont."

Arliss' brow furrowed. "What do you mean?"

"Well, you thought I was an operative and accused me of working with someone called Stanton. Then you said that you had documents that needed to go to someone, but we were interrupted by Lucky, so I don't know who they're supposed to go to," Marvin explained. "Does any of that sound familiar?"

"Dumont again? Documents?" Arliss dragged a hand through his hair and closed his eyes as he concentrated on the name. Nothing came to him. "Gosh!" He grabbed a piece of board from the wagon and angrily hurled it through the air. "What is wrong with me? How can I be two different people? I don't understand. Who am I? Which one is the real me?"

Lucky heard the severe strain in his voice and knew a panic attack was imminent. "Arliss, we'll get this figured out. Ya were Arliss when we first met and I never saw or heard about anyone named Dumont. It's my belief that Arliss is the real you, not this other fella. I don't know what ya might have been mixed up in, but you're the man I spent so much time with, not Dumont."

Marvin said, "Listen to Mr. Quinn. There's an answer, we only have to keep digging in order to find it. I'd like to talk to Erin again, but it's my belief that this Mr. Dumont didn't appear until after your … misfortune. Sometimes trauma can do strange things to a person psychologically. I should know. Anyway, could I stop by to get your journal from you this evening?"

"No. I'll bring it to your place," Arliss said. Andi was still the only one who knew where he stayed.

Lucky's jaw clenched. "This is ridiculous, Arliss. If someone wanted ya, they could just watch for ya around town or something. What if I need ya for something? I gotta hunt Andi down first and if it's an emergency, I won't have the time to do that. Like this with Wild Wind. I had no idea how to find you to tell ya. Why don't you come back to the farm?"

"No!" Arliss said. "I'm not taking the chance that any of you might get hurt."

Lucky asked, "Has it ever occurred to ya that they might come lookin' for ya and when we don't know where ya are, try something anyway?"

Arliss let out a rough groan of frustration. "I'm damned if I do and damned if I don't! I feel like I'm losing my mind! Do you know what it's like to have gaps in your memory or to not remember conversations or what you did the day before? It's damn scary! Now I'm starting to act like some other man and I don't remember it? I'll tell you where I'm stayin', but you can't come there. There's a small carriage house out in back of the parsonage that was converted to a little apartment several years ago, I guess. That's where I am."

Lucky grinned. "No wonder Andi can find ya. Yer not far from her."

Arliss smiled. "Nope. Not far at all."

"It looks as if Mr. Jackson is a little smitten with our pastor," Marvin said.

"Are ya, now?" Lucky asked.

There was no sense denying it. "Yeah, I'm pretty sweet on her. Can y'all blame me? I don't know what women I've seen before I woke up in the hospital, but she's the best-lookin' woman I remember ever seeing."

Clapping his shoulder, Lucky said, "That's great. Does she know?"

"Yeah, she knows. Seems like she sorta feels the same way even though I'm crazier than a bed bug. She helps keep me straight. I don't remember a lot of things, but if she tells them to me, I do. It's strange."

Marvin replied, "It may have something to do with her unusual abilities."

"She had feelings about things and she knew about Daniels before Evan knew the identity of the fella I shot. It came to her when she tried to do a reading for me. She said there's been a lot of death around me, but she doesn't know if I did the killing or I just saw a lot of killing," Arliss said.

"She did? Do you think she'd be willing to try another reading?" Marvin asked.

"I hate to ask, but after what just happened here, it might be a big help," he said. "I'll see if she'll do one tonight. Marvin, I don't think it's a good idea for you to go to Alabama."

Marvin said, "You need to find out who you are and there is no one else to go at the present."

Arliss sighed. "You shouldn't go alone. I should go with you. Maybe it'll jog my memory."

Marvin smiled. "I won't be going alone. I've convinced Dr. Wu to go with me as my valet. I think I'll be quite fine between his fighting skills and mine."

"Maybe, but I'm going with you. Don't tell me no or I'll just go back by myself," Arliss said.

"Lad, that's not a good idea," Lucky said.

"How am I supposed to move on with my life if I don't know about my past, Lucky? How can I offer Andi anything when I'm like this? What if it were you? What would you do?"

Determination was etched on Arliss' face and Lucky remembered that look; there would be no deterring Arliss.

"I see yer point. Marvin and Win will keep ya safe. I can't believe ya convinced Win to go with ya. Yer not his favorite person," Lucky said.

Marvin's mouth curved upwards. "I know, but I have my ways. Perhaps a shared adventure will help that situation. It did for you and me."

Lucky smiled. "Aye. That it did."

Marvin, Ronni, and their daughter, Eva, had gone to California with Lucky a year ago to meet Leah's parents and escort her and Lucky back to

Echo. Marvin had been hated in Echo for years and there were many who still hated him. However, over the past year and half, he'd been working to repair his image. More accustomed to making enemies and intimidating others, making friends was hard for Marvin, but he was testing the waters. Lucky and Leah were his biggest supporters outside of his family. The Quinns believed that people could change if they wanted to, and they were happy to see the way Marvin was growing.

They knew that Ronni and their children were the main reasons that Marvin had begun to reform. Despite the dark part of Marvin's personality, Ronni loved him and saw the good in him, too. Shadow's wife, Bree, felt the same way about her husband. Both women had cared enough to find the men beneath all of the hard darkness and see the better aspects of their husbands.

"When do we leave?" Arliss asked.

"The day after tomorrow. I'll change our travel arrangements to accommodate three instead of two," Marvin said. "I'm still not sure about this, but I understand why you need to go."

"Thanks," Arliss said.

Marvin nodded. "How big of a dent does this put in your business, Lucky?"

"A big one, but we'll survive. We were able to sell a lot of the meat and all of the wool was bought, so that'll offset some of the damage. Once Wild Wind is back on his feet, we'll rebuild his cabin and start up another herd here. We've started out with less." Lucky speared Marvin with a hard look. "It's a good thing Travis decided to leave our operation and stay with you."

"Well, we may be friends, Lucky, but business is business and Travis is vital to mine. Sorry. I hope there are no hard feelings about it," Marvin said.

"There aren't. Truth be told, it was better for him with being a single father and all. I'm glad for him and glad that ya wised up and started treating him the way he deserves to be treated," Lucky replied.

"As am I. Well, I'd better go take care of those changes, and I have some business to take care of before we leave since we don't know how long we'll be gone," Marvin said. "Good day, gentlemen."

"'Bye, Marvin," Arliss said.

———✦———

"I'll understand if you don't want to," Arliss said to Andi as they sat in his carriage house. "I'm just trying anything to find some answers."

"Of course I want to help you," Andi said. "I hate the thought of you going back there, however."

"I won't lie and tell you I'm not nervous about it," he said. "But with Marvin and Win along, I'm sure it'll be safe."

Andi nodded. "Give me your hands and just let your mind drift."

It was no hardship holding hands with her. No sooner had they joined hands than Andi said, "Stop that sort of thinking. I didn't mean let it drift there."

Arliss actually felt his face flush. "Sorry. It's your fault for bein' so pretty."

Now she blushed. "Stop it! I can't concentrate."

"I'm sorry. Ok. I'll be good," he said.

Arliss took a couple of deep breaths and began concentrating on the name Dumont. He also thought about what Marvin had told him about his episode at Wild Wind's farm. He was glad that he'd been able to hang onto that memory so that he had been able to tell Andi about it. He'd also written it down in his journal before taking it to Marvin's.

The direction of Arliss' thoughts helped Andi navigate to the wall in his mind. The sea of blood didn't last as long this time and since he wasn't fighting against the memories, she was able to get over the wall easier.

As she dropped to the ground, she stood facing Arliss, but it wasn't Arliss. This man wore a very dapper English suit and top hat and his brown hair was much shorter. He had a completely different air about him, as well. Even his smile was different, although the sparkle in his blue eyes was the same.

"Well, what a pleasure it is to meet the fair Pastor Thatcher," he said in an elegant British voice.

Andi didn't know what to do. She'd had many visions, dreams, and feelings over the years, but she'd never actually spoken to someone in one of them before. She was always an outsider, an observer, never an active participant. However, there was no mistaking that this man was speaking directly to her and expecting a response.

"Hello, Mr. Dumont," she said. "I'm hoping that you can help me—and Arliss, too."

"Ah, yes, Arliss. He's a delightful chap. Always good for a laugh and a snappy fiddle song," Dumont said. "So he told you about me, did he?"

"Yes, but no one knows much about you, not even him," she said. "Who are you?"

"Come for a stroll with me and I shall impart some answers," he said, offering her his arm.

Hesitantly, she put her hand through it, letting him lead her through a splendid spring garden.

"I certainly see why Arliss fancies you. You're quite an attractive woman," Dumont said.

"Thank you, but please stay on track. I'm not sure how long I can keep this up."

"Oh, I see."

"Is Arliss, or you, a spy or government operative of some sort? And what are these documents in a bank deposit box in Alabama?" she asked. "Did you put them there?"

Dumont's pleasant exterior faded and was replaced by a sober expression. "Yes, I put them there. It's imperative that they get into the proper hands."

"Whose hands?"

Dumont said, "Arliss knows."

Andi pulled on his arm, stopping him. "No, he doesn't. That's why I'm here: to find out. He can't reach you, wherever you are. He's tried. Just tell me what they are and who they need to go to."

"My dear, it's too dangerous for you to know. It's best left with Arliss. He'll remember at the appropriate time."

The stony expression on his face told her that he wasn't going to budge on this. Since she felt her strength beginning to fade, she moved on. "Fine. Who are you? Are you the operative or is Arliss? Which is the actual person?"

"I'm afraid I don't follow," he said.

"Are you Arliss' cover or is he yours?" she asked.

"Oh, I see. Well, we're each other's, I guess you'd say."

She put a hand to her temple. "I don't understand."

"It's very simple. Sometimes I need to be in charge and sometimes he does. It depends on the situation, I suppose you'd say."

"In charge of what?"

"Ourself."

"That's not even a word. It makes no sense."

He chuckled patronizingly. "It does if you think about it. You see, Arliss and I have a partnership. We inhabit the same body, but we are two separate conscious beings. Dr. Elders can tell you all about it. We're very good friends of his. Have Arliss get in touch with him."

Dumont began fading.

"No. Don't go. Do you know if Arliss is married or has family anywhere?" she asked.

"That I can answer. No. Arliss has no one, the poor man. But perhaps we do now?" he asked.

"What?"

"Never mind."

"What about his sister?"

Dumont sighed. "Dead, I'm afraid."

A sucking motion began pulling Andi away from Dumont and she clutched his arm tightly. However, it was stronger than her and she gave up, letting it pull her back over the wall into the sea of blood and then back to herself.

"Andi? Andi."

She felt someone patting her cheek. Opening her eyes, she found that Arliss sat on the small love seat with her, holding her in his arms.

"There you are," he said, his eyes filled with worry. "Are you all right? You've been gone a long time."

She smiled, glad to hear his Alabama accent. "I'm ok. I just need to rest for a few moments." She laid her head against his solid shoulder.

Arliss held her closer and stayed quiet to let her have the time she needed even though he was very curious about what she may have experienced. As she regained her strength, Andi tried to decide where to start with Arliss. She sat up a little straighter and he smiled at her.

"Feeling better?"

"Yes. Arliss, who is Dr. Elders?"

The name seemed to echo inside Arliss' mind. It was very familiar to him. "Dr. Elders. Dr. Elders! He was one of my doctors while I was in the hospital. He's a brain doctor of some sort. I forget what Erin called that kind of doctor. He kept giving me tests and stuff like that to see how I was coming along."

"So he does exist then? That's good. You'll be able to get some answers from him," Andi said. "Especially with this next part. I spoke with Dumont, who looks like you except for his shorter hair. He wore an expensive suit and spoke with a British accent. He said some very strange things."

"Ok. Go ahead and tell me."

"He said that you're one and same person, that you have a partnership. Does that make any sense to you?"

"No. If we're the same person, how can we have a partnership?"

"I don't know. He said that sometimes you're in charge and sometimes he is. He said that he put the documents in the deposit box and that you'd remember who to give them to when you were supposed to remember," Andi replied.

"Why is this Dumont talkin' in riddles? Why can't he just answer a damn question? Who the heck is he? He can't be me and me him, right?"

Andi put a hand to his cheek. "You said Dr. Elders is a neurologist at the hospital in Mobile. Maybe you should postpone this trip just long enough to get some answers from him. He may be able to shed a lot of light on some things."

He sighed and closed his eyes, fighting against his impatience. What she said made sense. It would be better to go armed with as much information as possible, and Dr. Elders could provide some. Opening his eyes, he nodded. "Ok. I'll tell Marvin and Win tomorrow and send a telegram to Dr. Elders. I'll have to go to Dickensville. I'll see if one of them can go with me. Did Dumont say anything else?"

"I'm sorry to have to tell you this, but he said your sister is deceased."

He smiled sadly. "I was wondering if she wasn't, but I don't know why I thought she might be."

Andi bit her lip and then asked, "Arliss, does the word 'ourself' mean anything to you?"

"Ourselves?"

"No. 'Ourself'," she said and spelled it for him.

"I didn't know that was a word."

"It's not. When Dumont said that you take turns being in charge, I asked him what you were in charge of. He said, 'Ourself.' I have no idea what that means, though," she said.

Arliss noticed that she looked tired. "Darlin', don't worry about it anymore tonight. You need to get yourself some rest. I'll go to Dickensville tomorrow to get that telegram out."

"I *am* tired."

"I'll walk you over home. I better get you back before Bea comes looking for you," he said.

Andi smiled. "She knows that I can take care of myself. There's no need to walk me to the door."

"Humor me, ok?" he asked. "You know, we never did get around to that kiss. What sort of kiss am I allowed to give you since you're a pastor?"

The idea of kissing him created a warmth inside her chest. "A chaste kiss."

"Chaste. What's a chaste kiss? Why don't you kiss me and quit when it's appropriate. Then I'll know for the next time," he suggested.

"The next time?"

MAIL ORDER BRIDE: *Montana Hearts*

"Yeah. That's if we both like it. Ain't no sense kissing again if we don't like it."

She smiled at his logic. "I can't kiss you."

"Why?"

A blush blossomed in her cheeks. "I just can't."

"I got an idea. Just tell me when to stop then," he said.

He covered her mouth with his before she could answer and held her closely. At first she hesitated, a little shocked by his forwardness, but she soon relinquished control to him. He gentled the kiss, coaxing rather than demanding, and Andi grew a little bolder, wrapping her free arm around his neck.

Images played through her mind, some not so chaste, but she blocked them out, knowing it was rude to invade people's thoughts. She felt Arliss' hand rub her knee and jerked away from him.

"That's enough," she said.

She'd startled him. "I'm sorry. I was letting you lead," he said, loosening his hold on her.

"It's not your fault. I let myself enjoy it a little too long, that's all," she said. "I really should go." She stood up and moved towards the door. "I don't need you to walk me over. I'll be fine."

He stood as well, but, seeing how spooked she was, he didn't move towards her. He hadn't meant to scare her. "Ok. I'm sorry, Andi. Thanks for helping me, darlin'."

"You're welcome. Goodnight." Andi went out the door before she gave into temptation and went right back into his arms. It wasn't Arliss she was scared of, it was herself. She would have to explain that to him sometime when she was ready. Just not yet.

Chapter Fourteen

Hunkered down in his black woolen coat, Evan patiently waited outside the back door of the medical clinic. It was cold out, but the coat Lucky had had made for him kept him cozy. Ever since the night of Wild Wind's attack, he and Shadow had been keeping watch at night in case someone came to finish off the job on the brave. Evan always acted on his hunches and this was one he wasn't going to ignore.

Shadow was around the corner of the front of the clinic. They'd elected not to inform anyone about their surveillance so that Wild Wind wasn't alarmed, although both lawmen knew that the thought couldn't be far from his mind. So far no one had shown up, which was a good thing, but Evan wasn't ready to call it quits yet.

A noise to his right made him stiffen. He knew it wasn't Shadow because his deputy could move as silently as the thing for which he was named. Barely moving his head, he searched for the source of the noise. A figure moved stealthily towards the back door, testing the doorknob.

Evan drew his gun. "If I were you, I'd stop right where you are or else I'll shoot your head off."

As Evan drew closer, the figure put his hands up. "Ok. Don't shoot."

"Saul?"

"Yeah."

"I don't believe it. Turn around and keep your hands on the building," Evan said in a disgusted tone.

Saul moved to turn, but then rushed Evan. The sheriff sidestepped a little and slammed his gun butt into the side of Saul's head. The man went down on his face and Evan stepped on his back. Saul let out a holler of pain.

"Serves you right, you coward," Evan said. "Believe me that was a lot of fun for me. Keep fighting, Saul. I'd enjoy doing some more damage."

"No. I'm done."

Evan knelt and put handcuffs on Saul. Just as he finished, gunfire sounded from inside the clinic.

"You move from here, Saul, and I'll hunt you down and do you in. You hear me?" he growled.

"Yeah! Ok! I'll stay right here."

Evan had a key to many of the businesses in town in case he needed to get into them in a hurry, but he didn't have sufficient light to find the right one for the back door. He ran around front and found the door open. Cautiously, he entered the waiting room and moved towards the exam rooms.

Just then, he heard the sound of a fist connecting with a body and a grunt of pain.

"Shadow?"

"In here, boss."

Even in the tense situation, Evan smiled because it always sounded funny when Shadow called him that in his cultured manner of speaking. He followed Shadow's voice to the second exam room. Shadow struck a match and lit the lantern there, moving away from the bright light that hurt his eyes.

A man lay on the floor; Evan recognized him as Artie Hirsch. Blood showed on his shirt, but when Evan saw it dripping down onto the man, he realized that it was coming from Shadow.

Hurrying to his deputy, Evan asked, "Where are you hurt?"

"It'll keep. There's another one in the office. He's dead."

"I'll just check on Wild Wind and whoever's with him, but I'll be right back," Evan said.

"All right."

Evan moved back the hallway to the door of the ward. "It's just Evan. I'm coming in," he called out before he went through the door.

He was surprised to see that Wild Wind was alone and that he had a revolver pointed at the door. The light of battle shone in his dark eyes.

"Are you all right?" Evan asked.

Wild Wind nodded. "Are there more?"

"No. Are you alone?"

"No. Roxie, come out now. It's safe," he said.

Roxie poked her head out from under the bed and then started to crawl out. Evan holstered his gun and helped her to her feet. She trembled a little, but seemed unhurt.

"Are they gone?" she asked.

"No, but they're contained," Evan said.

Wild Wind asked, "How many?"

"Three."

He nodded. Roxie sat down on the chair by the bed and Wild Wind took her hand. "You're safe, Roxie. I wouldn't let anyone hurt you," he said.

"I know," she said.

"Keep that gun, just in case. I don't expect any problems though," Evan said. "I have to get back to Shadow. He's hurt, but I don't know how badly." Taking out his gun, he asked, "Roxie, you know how to shoot a gun, right?"

"Yes."

"Ok. I need you to go get Billy. He's closest. Bring him back here. If anyone bothers you, shoot them," Evan said. "As of right now, you're a deputy. Go on."

Roxie took his revolver hesitantly, but then left the clinic, taking off down the street at a run.

Going back to Shadow, Evan saw him sitting bare-chested on a chair, a bandage wrapped around his left elbow. He hadn't done too bad of a job considering he only had one hand to work with, but blood was seeping through the bandage at an alarming rate.

"What happened?" Evan asked.

"I knocked the gun out of this guy's hand, but he's quite tricky with a knife. Of course, he had an opening because his cohort grabbed me from behind. I was knocked off balance and he got in a quick slice before I kicked him in the chest. I still had my gun, and I simply reached behind me and shot into the other one's stomach. He fell back and I shot him again. He fell into the office and I came back after this one and knocked him out. You'll want to cuff him," Shadow said.

As he'd spoken, Evan had gathered more bandages and suturing supplies.

"Ok. Let's see what we have here. I'm no surgeon, but I can do some field knots that'll help stop the bleeding until we get you out to Erin's. It'll be quicker for us to just ride out there instead of waiting for her to get here," Evan said.

He unwrapped the bandage and saw that it was bleeding too much for him to stitch it. "Damn it. Stay here." Evan ran into the office, found a can of coffee, and ran back. "Hold your arm out."

Shadow did, watching Evan with curiosity. "How is coffee going to help?"

Smiling, Evan said, "This is an old trick that Uncle Reb taught me. Field medics during the war used to use it as a temporary way to stop bleeding." He packed the deep cut with the coffee, pressing it hard into the wound before wrapping it back up very tightly. Then he took a strip of bandage and wound it around the top of Shadow's bicep and tied it as tightly as he could. "There. That'll have to do for now."

Roxie returned with Billy, who took one look at all the blood and blanched. "Holy crap. What do you want me to do, Evan?"

"Get Shadow out to Erin on the double. He's got a real deep cut that needs to be fixed. It's bleeding badly," Evan replied.

Billy quelled his queasiness. "Ok."

Shadow stood up and swayed a little. Billy grabbed him. "Easy, Shadow. We're gonna ride double so you don't fall off."

"Good idea," Shadow said, feeling dizzy.

Evan watched the two men leave the room and then looked down at the man on the floor. He handcuffed him and then remembered that Saul was still out back. He hoped. This man didn't show any signs of waking up anytime soon, so Evan went through the ward, into the back hallway, and out the back door. Saul had taken Evan at his word and was still lying on the ground.

"Ok, Saul. On your feet," Evan said, hauling the man up. "To the jail. Run."

They made it to the sheriff's office in a matter of minutes and Evan put Saul in a cell, locked it, and ran back to the clinic. He was glad to see that the man on the floor still hadn't moved. Going over to him, he bent down and felt for a pulse. There was none. Shadow must have hit him harder than he'd thought.

"More funerals. Poor Andi," Evan said.

The day after the thwarted attempt on his life, Wild Wind began working on regaining his strength. Against Erin's wishes, he got out of bed and started to take short walks. After he'd made three brief trips around the clinic, he informed the doctor that he was well enough to go home.

"Wild Wind, you really should stay in case you run into infection," she protested.

"No. I know the signs. If my wound does become infected, I can fight it just as well there as here. I have willow bark tea and I'll take some laudanum with me just in case I need it. I can't keep lying here. Besides, that way you won't have people breaking in here again," Wild Wind said, packing up his belongings.

"You should let me do that," Erin said. "Or wait until Roxie gets here."

"I'll be fine. I'll stop by her house to see if she'll take me out to the farm in their buggy. I know that I can't walk that far."

Seeing that he wasn't going to change his mind, Erin gave up arguing with him. She gave him a bottle of laudanum and wrote down instructions for him. "I'll see you at home tonight," she said.

Wild Wind gave her a careful hug. "Thank you for saving my life. I'm in your debt."

"No, you're not. I'm just glad you're still here," she said. "I can't imagine my life without you."

He smiled. "Have a good day and stop worrying about me."

"I'll attempt to do both," she said.

He shouldered his buckskin bag. "It's light," he said, catching her worried look. He gave her shoulder a squeeze and left through the back door of the clinic.

Chapter Fifteen

The alarm clock on her nightstand told Roxie that she'd been lying in her bed for three hours, but she hadn't slept in all that time. She was still too keyed up over the events of the previous night. When they'd heard the fight between Shadow and the two intruders break out, Wild Wind had pulled a gun out from under one of his pillows and told her to get under the bed.

He'd been prepared to fight, but Roxie had been worried about his safety because of his condition. He'd told her in a stern tone to do as he told her and the fierce expression on his face had convinced her to follow his order. So under the bed she'd gone. What a relief it had been to hear Evan's voice after all of the ruckus.

Ross had taught her to shoot a gun, but it had been a long time since she'd had one in her hands. Therefore, when Evan had given his to her and sent her for Billy, she'd prayed hard that no one came after her because she hadn't been sure she could actually shoot someone. This was not only because she didn't know if she had it in her to take a human life, but also because she wasn't a proficient shooter.

Once she'd gotten Billy, she'd given him Evan's gun, glad to be relieved of it. Better that than her accidentally discharging it. When she'd told Ross what had happened, he'd been shocked and worried over both her and Wild Wind's welfare. He'd hugged her, relieved that his little sister was safe and sound. Ross hadn't said it, but Roxie could tell that he didn't want her staying at the clinic with Wild Wind anymore. She wasn't going to abandon him, however.

The doorbell rang. Roxie got up and threw on her robe since she was in her nightgown. Rushing down the stairs, she opened the door, surprised to see Wild Wind on the porch.

"What are you doing here? Why did you leave the clinic? Get in here and out of the cold!"

He smiled at her scolding tone and stepped into the small foyer. The male in him took in her slightly tussled, long, wavy blonde hair and how pretty she looked in her lavender silk robe. He'd wondered how she'd look with her hair down and now he knew—incredibly beautiful.

"I'm here to impose on you for a ride to the farm. I can't stay at the clinic anymore. It's time I went home. I need to get up and move now to regain my strength. I'm also bored there and I need fresh air," he said.

Roxie said, "I'm certainly willing to take you to the farm, but are you sure you're really ready to go home?"

"I'm sure. I need to stop by Billy's to borrow some clothes from him," he said. "All mine are gone. I have a few things in my tipi, but they're not what I want to wear. I'll give them away."

Roxie frowned. "What do you mean?"

His jaw squared and anger filled his eyes. "Ever since I came here, I've been trying to fit in, to be more like the people in your culture. I've dressed like you, learned to talk like you, and learned skills that the people of your culture have. I've learned how to live in a house, eat your kinds of food, sit at a table, and eat with utensils.

And for what? I know now that I will never be fully accepted here and that I was foolish to think that I would be. So I'm done trying to be something I'm not. I'm Cheyenne and I'll always be Cheyenne. It's time that I be true to myself and live the way I've always lived. I need one of

Billy's Cheyenne outfits. Then I need to hunt and get some hides to give to Nina so she can make me some clothes. I will never put on another dress shirt, tie, or shoes after today. I am a Cheyenne brave and I don't care if people like it or not."

For some inexplicable reason, tears filled Roxie's eyes. Her chin rose. "I can't tell you how happy I am to hear you say that. I've thought for a long time that you shouldn't be tamed, that you must be so uncomfortable with our ways and trying to live a life so foreign from yours.

"I've been proud of you for the things you've accomplished, but I've also wanted to see you return to your original way of dressing and doing things. It's not right for you to have to conform. I've sometimes seen the wistfulness in your eyes as you were doing something unfamiliar. You're right; if people don't like it, who cares? Now they know what a formidable foe you are and will leave you alone."

Wild Wind could hardly believe he was hearing all of this from a white woman or that she was so attuned to him. He'd no idea that she'd been paying such close attention to him so as to be able to discern his thoughts.

"I hope you're right, but anyone who does come after me will die. I am through playing by the rules of your culture," he said, testing her. If he were to seriously consider her as a mate, she needed to understand who he truly was and accept him as such.

She surprised him by giving him a pleased smile. "As far as I'm concerned, you'd be well within your rights."

"I will no longer live in a house."

"I don't think you should."

He smiled. "You would live in a tipi?"

"Happily."

"And what of all your fine clothing and jewelry?"

Roxie laughed. "What need would I have for them in a tipi? Besides, I don't wear very fine clothing and I actually find it very constricting. I only wear it because it's required of me. I wouldn't mind wearing much simpler clothing."

"You would have to learn Cheyenne cooking."

"Nina and Lucky can show me."

Wild Wind was growing more excited with her every answer. "Do not tell me any of this if you are really not sure. I can't seriously consider you for a wife if you don't mean it."

He was happy to see the indignant look she gave him. "Why would I do that? Do you think this is just a game for me? If it were, why would I agree to see you in the first place? Why would I have let you know my feelings for you in the first place? Why would I have stayed with you while you were hurt? I've loved you for a long time and you don't play games with those you love, Wild Wind."

His eyebrows rose and he couldn't think of anything to say.

"I'm well aware of how different our cultures are, but I don't care. I fell in love with you, and your culture is who you are," she said.

Wild Wind found his voice. "But what about *your* culture?"

"We may need to make a few compromises, but you've tried mine and it's just too stifling for someone like you. I hated to see it. I want you to live the way you're happiest," Roxie said.

"You're truly in love with me? Why?"

She was amused by his confusion. "For all of the reasons I've already told you about why I'm attracted to you. Does it have to be anything more specific than that?"

"I don't know. I can't believe we're talking about this right now. It wasn't my intention to," he said. "Roxie, I don't know what to say when you tell me you love me. I—"

"You don't need to say anything. Until a couple of weeks ago, you didn't even really notice me, and that's partly my fault because I didn't say anything. I don't expect you to be in love with me. I hope that'll come in time, but I'm not in any rush for it. I'll settle for your liking me and being attracted to me," she said.

It seemed as though he was to be constantly surprised by Roxie. She was incredibly generous and levelheaded about the situation. Those were good traits in a mate. Along with her kindness, sense of humor, fierce nature, and beauty, she would be a wife of whom any man could be proud.

Stepping closer, he said, "Make no mistake, I do like you very much and you are a beautiful, desirable woman." He reached out, caressing her cheek before sliding his fingers into her hair, pulling her to him. "You must understand that if we did marry, I would never let you go. Although divorce is a fairly easy thing in Cheyenne culture, I would never divorce. Do you understand?"

"Yes. I would never want to divorce," she said.

Wild Wind smiled. "That's good to hear."

Roxie rested her hands on his chest, enjoying the feel of the cool buckskin. "I would do my best to make any man a good wife."

Jealously unexpectedly spiked inside Wild Wind as he thought about Roxie with some other man. With a growl, he captured her lips in a demanding kiss, claiming her without words. Her soft mouth under his thrilled him as did her immediate response from her. She wound her arms around his neck, giving herself over to the strong desire he stirred in her. The times she'd dreamt of kissing him like this were innumerable and she felt not one bit of shame in indulging herself.

The kitchen door opened and she pulled away from Wild Wind quickly.

"Roxie! Are you up?" Ross called.

Roxie turned and scurried quietly up the steps while Wild Wind slipped out the door and stood on the porch, calming his racing heart while trying to look like he hadn't just been passionately kissing one of the women of the house.

Inside, Roxie made it seem as though she'd just gotten up, coming out into the hallway in her robe to stand at the top of the stairs.

"What are you shouting about, Ross?"

Standing at the bottom of the stairs, Ross said, "Oh, good. You're up. Callie and I are really busy in the shop, but I was wondering if you could go to the store for us. We need more twine and a couple of other things."

"Certainly. I have to take Wild Wind out to the farm, but I'll pick them up on the way back home," she said. "Erin released him today. He's waiting out on the front porch."

Ross looked out the small window in the door to see the brave standing by the steps leading to the walkway. "Oh. I'm glad he's feeling better. Ok. That'll be fine. I'll go say hello while you dress."

"All right," Roxie said, relieved that they hadn't gotten caught. "I'll be down very shortly."

Ross nodded and stepped out the front door, giving Wild Wind a smile. "I'm glad to see you up and around," he said, closing the door behind him. "How's the pain?"

"It could be worse," Wild Wind said. "I'll live."

"I'm glad for that. Look, I want to apologize to you for something," Ross said.

Wild Wind just gave him a confused look.

Ross shuffled his feet a little. "I heard some guys talking about you a couple of times, but they never said they had any specific plans or anything. I was gonna tell Evan, but I sort of forgot about it and then I got busy and never got around to it. I should have gone to him right away. Maybe it would have made a difference. I don't know, but I'm sorry about that."

"There's nothing to apologize for. Hearing someone talk doesn't mean they'll take action. Unless Evan was going to put a guard on my farm, there would have been nothing he could have done to prevent it. He can't arrest someone until they do something," Wild Wind said. "Maybe it's good that things happened the way they did. At least this way there are less men who want to kill me. Whoever else was in on it now knows that I'm not an easy target. Let your conscious be clear."

"Thanks. They sure did find out that you're not to be messed with," Ross said. "It's nothing I, or most any man, wouldn't have done."

Wild Wind nodded then fixed Ross with a speculative stare. "There is one thing you could do to perhaps make it up to me."

"Sure," Ross said eagerly. "Name it."

"Give me permission to court Roxie."

Ross' eyes widened a moment in surprise, but he held Wild Wind's gaze. "Do you promise to be good to her and respect her?"

"Yes."

Before agreeing, Ross gave it careful consideration as he thought of all of Wild Wind's positive attributes. He was a good provider, a skilled protector, intelligent, and considerate. The fact that Wild Wind was an Indian didn't influence Ross' decision one way or another. He only looked at Wild Wind as a man, not an Indian man.

"I give you permission, but just know that if you break her heart, nothing will keep you safe," Ross said.

"I understand."

Smiling, Ross held out his hand to Wild Wind. "Ok, then. You have my permission."

They shook hands as Roxie came out onto the porch. "I'm ready," she said. "I'll hitch up the horse."

Ross said, "I'll do it for you. I don't think it would be a good idea for Wild Wind to do it yet."

Wild Wind smiled wryly. "No, not yet." His pain was increasing and he knew that he needed to get home so he could rest.

Roxie said, "Come sit with me while Ross gets the buggy ready. You should be resting."

Wild Wind nodded and followed the brother and sister into the house.

Chapter Sixteen

L ying in his tipi felt strange to Wild Wind after staying in the clinic and before that living in a cabin. He felt relaxed to be in his natural element again. This was where he was meant to live, not in a box. Looking across the firelight at Leah, he smiled at her.

"You don't have to stay with me," he said.

She smiled at him and signed, "I know, but I can't help being worried about you. What if you need something? There's no one to help you."

Wild Wind said, "Have Otto stay with me. If I need help, he'll come get you."

She shook her head. "I should have thought of that. I swear this baby is robbing me of my wits."

"I've heard women say that's often the case when they're pregnant."

She rubbed her slightly rounded stomach with a loving look on her face. "I love this baby so much already. July seems so far away."

Wild Wind said, "It will be here and you'll wonder where the time went. Do you like staying in a tipi?"

Leah smiled. "Yes. Very much."

"Would you ever live in one?"

"I'm not sure that I would live in one forever, but I wouldn't mind living in one temporarily," Leah said.

"What would you miss the most about living in a house?"

"That's easy to answer: the kitchen. I've tried, but I just can't learn to cook the way Lucky and Nina do," she signed. "And I'm used to sleeping in a bed. Why?"

"I wanted a white woman's perspective on it."

"Why?"

"Do you promise to keep a secret?" he asked.

Leah couldn't resist a secret. "Of course. I swear not to tell anyone. Even Lucky."

"Ross gave me permission to court Roxie. I haven't officially asked her, but we have talked about it somewhat. She said that she wouldn't mind living in a tipi, but I'm worried that she would regret it later on. I will never live in a house again, just as I won't wear clothing from your culture anymore. Perhaps maybe for a formal occasion, but that's it."

Grinning, Leah crawled over to him and patted his shoulder. "I'm so happy for you. Roxie is a good woman. She's had feelings for you for a while now."

With a chagrined expression, he said, "So she told me. I would like your opinion on something else."

"Go ahead. Ask away," Leah said.

"I've been thinking of a way to combine the dwellings of each of our culture. Did you like the lodge that you and Lucky were married in? Did you like staying there for your honeymoon?"

Leah thought back to the wonderful week she and Lucky had spent in the large lodge. Her mind went over all of the fun they'd had and how much passion they'd shared. Thinking about that made Leah smile. "I loved our time there. It was very comfortable and beautiful inside."

He grunted. "If you had a kitchen and a bed in a large lodge like that, would you live there?"

Leah envisioned that and was surprised by how appealing that idea was. "I think I might. I'd have to see it, though. How would you safely have a stove in one? You'd need a stove pipe."

"I've been thinking about that. I've seen a couple of railroad camps where they had houses that were really just tents. They had stoves with pipes coming out of the wall. Maybe Lucky knows how to do that. Someone around here must know how."

"What is it about a house that you don't like?" Leah asked.

"You already know that circles are sacred to us. Houses are square and harder to heat than a tipi. I'd rather walk on soft furs or woven mats than hard, cold wooden floors. I like the sound of the rain on a tipi. It's a softer sound than when it pounds down on a roof and much more soothing. When it thunders, the tipi doesn't shake the way a house does and there are no windows for lighting to flash in. Most of our children aren't as scared of storms as children in your culture. There are more things, but those are just a few differences that make me prefer tipis." Sudden inspiration hit him and he sat up much too quickly in his excitement. Fire ripped through his stomach and he flopped back down with a groan of pain.

"Wild Wind!" Leah said aloud. "Are you all right?"

He nodded as the pain receded. After a few more moments of lying still, he could speak again. "I forgot about my wound. Will you hand me that drawing paper of Otto's over there, please?"

"Sure." Leah retrieved the paper and a pencil for him.

"Thanks." He sat up much more carefully this time.

Wild Wind wasn't an artist, but he only wanted to draw a basic idea of what he was thinking while it was fresh in his mind. "Will you get Lucky for me?" he asked as he finished the first drawing.

"Of course," Leah said, hurrying from the tipi. She was curious to see what Wild Wind was thinking.

In a few minutes, she was back with her husband and son.

"Leah says yer hatchin' some sort of idea," Lucky said.

"Yeah. Look at this and tell me if it can be done. You know about building both houses and tipis, so I figure you're the best one to ask," Wild Wind said, handing Lucky his first drawing.

Leah and Otto crowded close to Lucky so they could see, too. Wild Wind finished the second drawing and gave that to the three of them.

Lucky grinned. "Yer a genius. Leah said ya mentioned the railroad tents. They did the same sort of thing—combined a tent and house. A lot of them have frames and doors, but they're covered with canvas. So what you want to do would work. You just want to attach a small kitchen to a large lodge. It wouldn't be hard to do at all and it wouldn't take very long. Now the question is, why are ya thinkin' about it to begin with?"

"I might as well tell you. Ross gave me permission to court Roxie."

"That's fantastic!" Lucky said.

"I think so, too," Wild Wind said. "I don't want to live in a house, but I know there are some things that women in your culture are used to having. Leah said the thing she would miss most about a house is a kitchen. Building a small kitchen onto a tipi would solve that problem. I would also be willing to make it big enough so that we could have a bed in it."

Lucky said, "The railroad bigwigs had beds in theirs, so there's no reason you couldn't. Some of them were big enough that they could section off rooms, too. That might be something to keep in mind for when little ones come along. It would allow for privacy, but it would still have the feel of a tipi. And if ya used the sort of heavy canvases the railroads do, they allow in more light during the daytime, so that would sort of compensate for not havin' windows. Roxie would appreciate that, I think."

"Good idea," Wild Wind said, writing that down on the list he was making on another piece of paper. "What else?"

They spent the rest of the evening planning the building of an unusual structure, and when bedtime came they had it pretty well fleshed out. As he laid there after Lucky and Leah had gone over home, Wild Wind thought about the money he now had in the bank and planned to start figuring out how much it was going to cost to do what he wanted to do. His heart filled with determination and hope that he and Roxie would have a bright future. As he watched Otto sleep and listened to the crackling flames, Wild Wind resolved to make it happen no matter what he had to do.

Chapter Seventeen

No sooner had Win hung out a barber's pole than customers started coming through the door for haircuts. The afternoon after Wild Wind had gone home Arliss entered the shop. Sugar shoved her way in the door with him, almost knocking Arliss over.

"Sugar!" Win protested. "Knock it off! Sorry about that, Arliss. I've tried everything, but I can't break her of it." He pointed at a large, thick sleeping mat over in the corner. "You go lay down," he told Sugar.

The burro put her ears back but did as she'd been told. She turned a circle and settled down on the mat.

"Think nothing of it, my good man," Arliss said.

Win stared at him a moment. "Why are you talking like that?"

"Like what?"

"Like you're British," Win said.

Arliss smiled. "Because I am."

The hair rose on Win's neck as he looked at Arliss. There was a vast difference in his demeanor, smile, and the way he moved and walked. He'd hung up his hat with very precise movements and straightened his denim coat as he'd put it on a peg. All that combined with the accent convinced

Win that he wasn't talking to Arliss.

Still, he asked, "Arliss?"

"No. Arliss is resting at the present. I've come for a haircut. I'm not sure the poor boy knows what one is."

"Dumont then?" Win asked.

"Right you are. You can call me R.J. I prefer my friends to call me that instead of Reginald," R.J. said, sitting down in the chair.

Win put the sheet over him. "I'll be right back, R.J."

"Take your time. I'm in no hurry."

Win opened the door into the medical clinic's ward and went through it to the office he and Erin shared. She wasn't in it, so he knocked on one of the exam room doors.

"Come in," she said.

Opening the door, Win was relieved to see that she was alone. She'd been straightening up the room after her patient had left.

"Did you read that stuff you got from Dr. Elders yet?" Win asked.

"No. Why?"

"You need to because I've got Arliss over in my chair, but he's not Arliss right now. He's Dumont, who prefers to be called R.J.," Win said. "This would be a good time to observe him."

Erin was concerned and yet fascinated from a clinician's point of view. "Ok. I'll come right now. I'll get the file and be right there."

Win nodded and went back to his shop.

"R.J." was still in the chair.

"R.J., are you sure Arliss wants his hair cut? I know he likes it a little longer," Win said.

R.J. smiled. "It's been long for a while now and it's time to clean up a bit and look presentable. I am taking Pastor Thatcher to dinner tonight and I'd prefer to be presentable."

"You are? Not Arliss?" Win asked.

Erin joined them just then.

"Ah, there's the good doctor now," R.J. said. "We haven't been formally introduced yet." Holding out a hand, he said, "I'm Reginald Joshua Dumont, but you may call me R.J."

Erin couldn't believe that this was the man she'd come to know as Arliss. There was no trace of a Southern accent and none of Arliss' mannerisms showed at all.

Slowly, she gave R.J. her hand. "It's nice to meet you. Very strange, but nice."

R.J. chuckled. "Yes, I understand that it's a rather unusual situation."

"So you know who I am?" she asked.

"Of course. You see, Arliss and I share information so that we both know what's occurring," R.J. said.

Erin consulted the file notes that Dr. Elders had sent. "I hope you don't mind, but Arliss contacted Dr. Elders and had him send Arliss' file to me."

"Not at all. Dr. Elders is a good man and very intelligent, I might add. He understands us very well and has been helpful in helping us understand each other," R.J. said.

Win asked, "How is it that you know all about Arliss, but he doesn't remember anything about you?"

R.J. sighed. "I think it's because of the attack on us. We fought valiantly, but there were too many of them to fend off. It's a miracle that we're alive."

"So you remember the attack? Why doesn't Arliss?" Erin asked, sitting down. She was absolutely riveted by this situation.

R.J. thought how best to explain that. "Because he wasn't in control at the time. I was."

Win said, "That makes no sense. Arliss, quit playing games."

Erin said, "He's not playing games, Win. He has Multiple Personality Disorder. Dr. Elders is a very prominent psychiatrist and neurologist in Alabama and he's published a lot of papers on all sorts of mental disorders. R.J., Dr. Elders says that there's a third personality named Blake Morgan. Do you know Blake?"

R.J. laughed. "Oh yes. You don't want to meet Blake. He's not a very nice person, I'm afraid. Fortunately, he doesn't appear very much. When he does, I can usually control him."

"Is he the one who shot the man who came looking for Arliss?" Erin asked.

"No. That was Arliss—with a little help from me." He looked at Win. "Are you going to cut my hair or not?"

"I guess so," Win said, picking up his scissors.

"R.J., are you always conscious, aware of what Arliss is doing?" Erin asked.

"Yes. Arliss used to be conscious of me, too, until the attack. I'm having trouble getting through to him, though," R.J. said, genuine regret tinging his voice.

"You and Arliss are friends then?" Erin asked, taking notes.

"Yes. Very good friends. More like brothers since we share the same body. As I told Pastor Thatcher, we have a partnership and it works very well."

"Andi knows about you?" Win asked as he worked on the back of R.J.'s hair.

R.J. smiled. "In a manner of speaking. She was able to reach me with her psychic abilities. She's quite the woman. Beautiful, kind, intelligent, and she's very patient with Arliss. We're quite enamored of her, you know."

Win and Erin laughed at the idea of two men who inhabited the same body being attracted to Andi.

"Which of you is taking Andi to dinner?" Win asked.

"I am," R.J. said. "I thought it was time that she and I become acquainted."

Erin said, "I don't think that's a good idea. You should let Arliss take her. After all, he asked her."

R.J. said, "No, he didn't. She doesn't know we're going yet. I plan to ask her as soon as I leave here."

"I can't let you walk around by yourself like this," Erin said. "You don't know where you're going or anything."

"My dear, I know precisely where I'm going and what I'm doing. I knew how to get here, didn't I? You must remember that I know everything Arliss does. I hope to be able to get through to him soon," R.J. said.

"How do we get Arliss back? Does he control you?"

"No, it's a partnership."

Erin said, "I want to talk with Arliss. Can you get him for me?"

"No. I told you I can't get through to him."

"We have to get him back," Erin said. "He doesn't know any of this. He thinks he's insane."

Win finished up the haircut and stood back to inspect his work. Although the man before them looked very different with the nicely styled hair, he was still very handsome.

"Do you want a shave?" Win asked.

Erin gave him a disbelieving stare.

Win smiled. "Sorry. Force of habit."

"Thank you, but no, Win. I'll take care of that later. I must go buy a suit," R.J. said.

Erin said, "Are you going to pretend to be Arliss? No one knows you and I'm afraid that if you act strangely, something bad will happen."

He gave her a patronizing smile as he stood up. "Why do you think he has memory gaps? Normally he wouldn't, but, as I said, the attack changed that. Do you have a piece of paper so I can write Arliss a note?"

"Write Arliss a note?" Win asked.

"Are you deaf, daft, or both?" R.J. gave him an irritated look.

Erin hid her smile while Win gave him a small notepad and a pencil. R.J. wrote something down, ripped off the page, and put it in his jeans pocket. "Thank you, Win. Erin, it's been lovely chatting with you. I'll keep trying to reach Arliss."

Win asked, "What about Stanton? Who is he?"

R.J.'s jaw clenched so hard that he was sure his teeth would crack. Win and Erin were startled by the furious expression on his face. "Stanton is the vilest man who has ever lived. He betrayed us, blew our cover. That's how we ended up in the hospital. But I didn't let them defeat us."

"What's in that bank deposit box? We need to know," Win said. "We're going to Alabama to get it. Who do we give it to?"

"Arliss will know what to do with it. Leave it to him—or me, I should say," R.J. said. He took a breath to calm himself.

Erin still didn't want to let R.J. leave, but there wasn't much she could do to stop him. The man was in full control of his faculties. He knew where he was, who she and Win were, and all about Arliss' life. Everything in Dr. Elders' file indicated that all three personalities were fully capable of leading a full life.

"Can I ask you one last question before you leave?" Erin said.

"Certainly."

"Why did Arliss' mind create you and Blake?"

"That, my good woman, is a long story. One I don't have time to tell right now. Have a pleasant evening," R.J. said. He put on his coat and hat and walked out the door.

Win and Erin looked at each other.

Win said, "Does it make me a bad person because I find this somewhat funny?"

Erin said, "If it does, then I am, too. I've never encountered anything like this. I don't know whether or not to tell Andi so she's prepared. What do you think?"

"It might be a good idea," Win said. "I'd like to know what's on that note he wrote."

"Me, too. All right. I have a couple more patients to see," she said.

"I can go tell Andi if you want," Win said.

"All right," Erin said. "I'll see you at home then."

Win gave her a lingering kiss. "You sure will. We have a love scene to read."

Erin grinned. "My favorite."

"Mine, too." He winked at her before she went back over to the other side.

After Win's visit, Andi sat in her office, unable to concentrate on her work. She didn't know what to expect from Arliss, a.k.a. R.J. He'd seemed nice enough when she'd met him, but it wasn't like with Arliss. Win had said that R.J. had thought it was time for her to meet him. What if she liked him, too? Did that make her a cheater? She didn't even know what she and Arliss were. They were certainly more than friends, but not quite a couple.

Did she want to be? There were too many questions surrounding the man for her to answer that. She was sympathetic to Arliss having a mental condition, especially one for which there was no cure. He was bright, funny, and attentive. She loved hearing him play fiddle, too.

There was a knock on her door and her heart began racing as she saw Arliss enter her office, but she could tell that this wasn't her Alabama man. Standing in front of her desk was the man she'd met in the garden the night she'd used her gift to try to find answers about Arliss' past.

"R.J.?" she asked timidly.

He smiled as she took in the nice gray suit he wore and noticed that his hair was now nicely cut. "So we meet again, Andi. You're looking splendid, as always. How did you know to call me R.J.?"

"Win told me."

"I had a hunch he might. He's a good friend to watch out for you like that. May I sit?"

"Yes. Please do."

He did. "You were hoping for Arliss, I think."

Andi smiled. "Yes. I know him. I don't know anything about you."

"Precisely why I would like to spend the evening with you. Will you take pity on me and have dinner with me?" he asked.

Searching his face, Andi tried to find some trace of Arliss, but other than the twinkle in his blue eyes and the same facial structure, she couldn't.

"I don't know if I want to," Andi said. "You make me very uneasy."

R.J. said, "I know. That's why I want to show you that you've nothing to fear from me. I'm a part of Arliss and he's a part of me. We're partners and great friends." He pulled out a piece of paper from his pocket. "I'm going to give you this note to Arliss. If you really want to see him, read what it says aloud. If you're willing to get to know me a little, keep it to yourself for now. It's the key to bring out either of us."

She took the paper and saw the hopeful look in his eyes. *Come out, come out, wherever you are* was written on the paper. It struck her as funny that the key to changing his personalities was a phrase from a childhood game and she chuckled.

"Is this a joke?"

R.J. grinned. "No. Try it once if you like, but I hope you'll switch back to me. It works in seconds."

Deciding to call his bluff, she said, "Come out, come out, wherever you are."

The lines of his face softened a little and a confused look settled on his face. He looked at her and then around at her office. "Andi, how did I get here?"

The Southern accent was back and Arliss' more relaxed body posture, too.

"R.J. paid me a visit," she said.

This didn't make sense to Arliss. "Who's R.J.?"

"Your other you—Dumont. R.J. is what he goes by," Andi said, watching his reaction closely.

Arliss' brows drew down as he tried in vain to make the name make sense to him. He stood up, pacing across the floor. "That's his name?"

"So he says."

"I don't know any R.J. Dumont," Arliss said. "Who is R.J. Dumont?" He was startled when a wave of dizziness hit him. He grabbed the chair and went to his knees. "R.J. Dumont," he said weakly before falling unconscious to the floor.

Arliss came to in stages, birdsong greeting his ears and the smell of roses wafting in the air. He felt cool grass against his cheek and palms. Slowly raising his head, he saw that he lay in a beautiful garden filled with vibrantly colored flowers. Pushing up onto his knees, he tried to figure out where he was.

A hand slipping under his arm scared him and he pulled away.

"Arliss, it's just me. R.J. Let me help you up, lad."

He allowed the other man to assist him in getting to his feet and was stunned to be looking at his own face.

"Who are you?" he asked. "Why do you look like me?"

A sad look settled on R.J.'s face. "You really don't remember me, do you?"

"No. Where are we? I was just in Andi's office and now I'm here. I don't know what's happening," Arliss said.

"Come sit with me, Arliss." R.J. motioned towards an ornately carved stone bench.

Arliss sat down by him.

R.J. sighed. "You and I are the same person, but not the same. We exist inside of you together and we're best friends. It's so good to see you again. I've been trying to get through to you, but ever since the attack, I haven't been able to. It's the brain injury, I suppose."

Arliss frowned. "How can we both be inside of me?"

"Technically, it's your body, but we share it. So does Blake, but we don't let him come out to play very much, so to speak. Only when absolutely needed." R.J. waved towards a third version of Arliss, who stood a little ways off from them. There was a malevolent look about this other version that scared Arliss a little.

R.J. saw this. "Don't worry. He'd never hurt either you or I. He loves us—so much so that he won't hesitate to do anything to protect us, which he's done a few times over the years."

Arliss remembered the man he'd shot in the Quinns' house. "Did he shoot that fella that came after me?"

"No. You did, but I helped you. You didn't know how to recall me, so I stepped to the fore, although it was very difficult. We can only do that in extreme cases."

"There are three of us in one brain?"

"Yes. You see, each of us have certain skills and knowledge that combine to create the perfect man. You are our intelligence gatherer, thief, and all around good guy who is a talented fiddle player. You're a skilled physical laborer and understand many aspects of construction," R.J. said.

Much of this Arliss already knew, but to hear it confirmed was a relief to him in a strange way. "What do you do?"

"I am able to infiltrate the upper echelons of society when it's called for. I am also a superbly trained assassin and accomplished gambler. This has helped keep us afloat many times. Blake is our muscle power and he doesn't care who he offends. There are only certain things we use him for, but that's not important right now. Is any of this sounding familiar?"

Arliss felt a dull pain in his head as he concentrated.

R.J. saw that he was on the verge of something and said, "Stanton. That has to mean something to you. Stanton!"

It came to him the way ocean waves at high tide smash into a sea wall. Arliss reached out and grabbed R.J.'s shoulder to steady himself so he didn't fall off the bench. Memories crashed down on him so rapidly that it was a wonder that he could take it all in, but he did. Eventually they slowed down. R.J. kept a hold on Arliss until the other man looked at him again.

R.J. saw the light of recognition in Arliss' eyes and grinned. Arliss smiled back and R.J. grabbed him in an impulsive hug. "It's so good to have you back. I've missed you so much."

Arliss laughed and returned the embrace. "Same here, R.J. I just didn't know I was missin' you since I didn't remember about you."

R.J. drew back and clapped him on the shoulder. "Well, we're back together again now. You're going to be angry with me."

"Why?"

"I cut our hair and I'm taking our lady to dinner," R.J. told him.

Arliss smiled. "So you like our lady, huh? Ain't she something?"

"Yes, she is. I only hope that she can deal with all of us. To that end, don't you think it's time she got to know me?" R.J. asked.

"I guess so," Arliss said. "She's a pastor, so you be on good behavior. I know how you are with women."

R.J. said, "No worse than you are."

"Yeah, but she's different, R.J. Hey, did you make those memory gaps?"

"Yes, I'm afraid I did," R.J. said. "I know we have a rule about that, but you didn't remember me and there were times when it was necessary. I needed to know what was happening and who was important in our life now. We didn't have Dr. Elders here, so there was no one who understood about us. I'm sorry for overriding you like that, but I had to."

"It's all right. I'm glad you did. You never know when you might have been needed. We gotta go back to Alabama; you know that," Arliss said.

"Yes, I do know that. The sooner the better," R.J. said. "We can't take the chance that someone will go after those documents."

"I know. But for now, you have a dinner date. I'll tell Andi it's ok," Arliss told him.

"Thank you," R.J. said.

Chapter Eighteen

Arliss awoke with a start to find himself lying with his head in Andi's lap while she sat on her knees and fanned him with some papers from her desk.

"Hi, darlin'," he said, smiling.

She smoothed back his hair. "Are you all right?"

"Yeah, I'm fine. I feel sorta stupid for fainting like that, but I'm ok. It's a good thing I did. I talked to R.J. and I remember everything now. Who I am, what happened, and who he is," he replied. "Let's get off the floor."

He sat up, stood, and helped her up. Looking down at himself, he laughed. "Oh, boy. R.J.'s got us all gussied up. Well, that's him, all right. Anything you wanna know about clothes he can tell you."

Andi couldn't stop staring at him. "You know who he is now? Is he someone you knew once?"

"Come on and sit down. No, he's not. I'm not going into detail, but there were some things that happened when I was a teenager and after that I met R.J. I'm not sure how else to describe it to you. I need him and he needs me to survive certain things and to do certain things that the other can't. It's been that way ever since I was fourteen. I just didn't have a name for what it was called until I met Dr. Elders."

"Win said it's called Multiple Personality Disorder and that there's also another personality."

"That's right. Blake is the very darkest part of me and R.J. and I don't let him out much."

"Does he come out with the same phrase?" Andi asked.

"No, and I'll never tell you what it is, either. That's just how dangerous he is," Arliss said. "Andi, I'll understand if you tell me to get lost right now. I know you didn't expect all of this craziness when you met me. If you tell me to, I'll go pack up and leave."

"Do you ever want to get rid of them?" she asked.

"In the beginning, I did, but we became friends, and I love them like brothers now," Arliss said. "You have to understand that I wasn't able to get rid of them and now, I don't want to. They're my family. If you accept me, you have to accept them, too. If you can't, then there's no point in you and I seeing each other because they're a part of me. The three parts make a whole, as R.J. likes to say. He likes you, by the way."

Strange as it was, Andi was flattered. "Does he now?"

"Oh, yeah. He'd really like to take you to dinner, too. That's why he cut our hair and dressed us up," Arliss said.

She noticed the way he talked about himself as a plural. "And his taking me to dinner doesn't make you jealous since he's a different man?"

"He is and he isn't a different man. No, it doesn't. See, we're all aware of what's going on. So while you're having dinner with him, I'll know what's happening, but I'm just an observer. It's the same when I'm in control. We all know what's happening, but we hardly ever override each other. R.J. has been off and on lately because he couldn't get in touch with me. That's why I couldn't remember a lot of stuff," Arliss told her.

"I think I'm crazy. This is so bizarre, so unbelievable, but I'm so curious," Andi said. "And for the record, I'm rather fond of you and I don't want you to leave."

"Being fond of me is one thing, but being able to accept us is another, Andi. Truth is, we're crazy about you, but I don't want to get any deeper into this if all of us are only going to end up heartbroken."

She smiled coyly. "Can I wait until after I have dinner with R.J. to decide? And shouldn't I meet Blake, too?"

"I'm not comfortable with you meeting Blake yet," Arliss said. "How about you have dinner with R.J. and then decide. Don't worry about Blake right now."

"Ok, but I want to meet him soon," Andi said. "How can I accept all of you if I never meet him?"

Arliss saw her point. "All right. Are you ready for R.J.?"

She nodded.

"You know the magic words. Go ahead," Arliss said. "Have a good time. R.J. is a lot of fun, just in a different way than I am."

Andi arched a brow at him. "What if he tries to kiss me?"

"That's up to you if you kiss him, but I did warn him about being good," Arliss said.

"I can't believe that doesn't make you jealous."

"It would if it was some other man outside of the three of us. You know, someone else's body, but not mine. The three make a whole. That's the key," Arliss said.

Shaking her head, Andi said, "I'll see you later on."

"Have a good night."

"Come out, come out, wherever you are," Andi said.

Arliss began changing immediately, taking on a more regal bearing and sitting up straighter.

"Hello again, Andi. I take it we're going to dinner then?" R.J. said, smiling at her.

Andi heard his British accent, started laughing, and couldn't stop for a minute or two. R.J. didn't take offense and laughed with her.

"I feel like I'm in some sort of weird dream," she said, once her laughter had abated. "Arliss said that it was fine with him if we had dinner."

"Yes, I know. I'm glad that you're open minded enough to do so. Perhaps your unique gifts make you so," R.J. said. "Is seven a good time at which to collect you?"

"Yes. That will be fine," she said.

He gave a curt nod. "Wonderful. I shall leave you now, but I'm looking forward to our time together later."

"Me, too," Andi said, surprised to find that she really was.

———

Thad sat outside on the porch that evening, smoking a cigarette when Adam rode up to their house.

"Evenin', Adam. Here to see your girl?" he asked.

"Actually, I'd like to talk to you," Adam said, dismounting.

"Ok. Plant yourself."

Adam tied his horse to the porch railing and took the chair closest to Thad.

"What's on your mind, son?"

It was cold out, but Adam was sweating inside his coat from nerves. He willed his heartbeat to slow down. Knowing that Thad didn't ever beat around the bush about anything, he thought that it was best to do the same with the bounty hunter turned deputy.

"Well, since Allie and I started seeing each other, I've fallen in love with her. I can't imagine my life without her now. She's more than I ever dreamed of in a woman. I'm a hard worker and I always treat her with respect, just like you asked me to that day in the barn last year," Adam said. "And you know what I mean."

"Yep. I do. I'm glad to hear it. I'd still like to kick Keith's ass once in a while, but what's done is done. Him and Molly are happy and that's what matters at this point, I guess. Anyway, go on."

"Thad, I've come to ask for your permission to marry Allie," Adam said.

Thad smiled. "I had a hunch that you'd ask me soon. You haven't asked her already, have you?"

"No, sir. I wanted to talk with you first."

"Good boy. How do you plan to support her and your kids when they come along?"

"I have this teaching position now and I'll still work for Lucky in the summers. I can pick up other odd jobs if I need to, too."

Thad fixed him with a steely gaze. "You being a teacher is only temporary and you only work for Lucky part-time."

"This teaching position is going to be permanent, Thad. I'll make sure of that. I can do the job and these kids know me. By the time summer comes, I'll have shown the council that I'm the best choice for the job and they won't look for anyone else," Adam said without flinching away from Thad's eyes. "I've also talked to Ma and, depending on how Allie feels, we can live with her. With our combined incomes, we'll be fine. Allie and I can also save up money for whenever we have kids and she can't work for a while after they're born."

Thad liked Adam's quiet confidence and the determination he saw in the young man's eyes. He knew Adam was smart, kind, and good-tempered. He could tell that he'd never mistreat Allie in any way. "All right. You can ask her."

Adam's grin made Thad smile.

"Thanks, Thad. You won't regret it," Adam said, holding out his hand.

Thad shook it. "I know I won't. When are you gonna ask her?"

"Soon, but I have to get a ring and I want to plan out how I'm going to ask her. I want it to be really special," Adam said.

"Fair 'nuff. You and Keith. I ain't had those girls even a year and you're already stealing them away from me," Thad said. "You know, you have Jerry to thank for that."

"How do you figure?" Adam asked.

"Well, he's the one who started off all these mail-order brides. If he hadn't, I wouldn't have met Jess and she wouldn't have brought her girls here," Thad said.

"I'll thank him next time I see him."

Thad made a face. "Don't do that. It'll go to his head and he's already got a big enough ego."

Adam laughed. "Ok. He's a really good mayor. Echo is certainly benefiting from his leadership—he put together a good council."

"Yep," Thad agreed. "Everyone has different things they're good at, so they make a good team."

"Do you like being a deputy?"

Thad laughed. "Yeah. I started out as a deputy when I was about twenty, but I got fired because I couldn't follow orders. I did things my way and my boss didn't like that. That's when I became a bounty hunter. I could hunt down scum and do it on my terms. I've filled in for Evan a lot over the years whenever he needed to go out of town or helped him on cases. So it's not anything I'm not familiar with.

"Every once in a while I get an itch to go out on the road, but then I think about my family and I don't want to leave them. The itch goes away."

Adam said, "I'll bet you never thought you'd have such a big family."

"Nope. But I'm a happy fella. It's nice havin' a houseful of people I love around me. It's never dull."

"And now your baby will be here soon."

Thad chuckled. "That sure was a surprise. Jessie's ready for Mini Mac to be born."

The nickname that Jessie and Thad had given their baby cracked Adam up. "I love it when you call the baby that. It's so funny."

"Well, I don't like to call the baby 'it' and it's a pain in the ass to call it 'him or her' all of the time, so that's what we came up with," Thad said.

"Do you want a boy or a girl?" Adam asked.

"Don't matter to me. I'll love Mini Mac either way."

Adam nodded. "Well, I'll go see Allie for a little while before I have to go grade some papers for tomorrow."

"Ok."

"Thanks again, Thad."

"You're welcome."

Adam went inside and Thad sighed and lit up another cigarette. "Looks like I'll be walking another one down the aisle before too long," he mumbled to himself.

Roxie scratched on the flap of Wild Wind's tipi and tried to control the giddiness that she always felt when she was going to see him.

"Come in."

Ducking inside, she saw him sitting on a sleeping pallet. "Hello. How are you feeling tonight?"

He smiled and patted the spot next to him. Roxie took off her shoes and padded over to him. Sitting down, she arranged her skirts so that they covered her feet. She had forgotten to change her dress shoes before she'd left the house. Walking around on the furs and mats that lined the tipi floor could be difficult with such shoes. Boots were fine, but dress shoe heels tended to get caught and sometimes ended up getting pulled off her foot. It was simpler to just go barefoot and she liked doing it.

"I feel fine. You need some moccasins. Have Nina make you some," he said.

Patting his knee, she said, "I'm one step ahead of you. I already asked her and she said she'd have them tomorrow."

"Good. How was your day?"

"Busy. Callie was very tired today so I helped Ross in the shop. People really love that goat cheese and it's no wonder. I don't know how you make it, but it's delicious," she said.

"I'll show you sometime. It's not hard," Wild Wind said. "I'm glad it's selling so well. Are you hungry? I have some roast and potatoes left."

"No, thank you. We had dinner." She looked around at the tipi, taking in the colorful paintings on the sloping, deer and steer hide walls. "Did you paint them?"

"Yes."

"They're very nice. So what do the Cheyenne do at night?"

"The women make clothing, jewelry, or other things. Some men will weave baskets, but mainly they repair or make weapons. When we're not doing those things, we play games and entertain the children and just visit with each other," he said.

"So it's not much different than our culture," she remarked. "It sounds very nice."

"It is. There is also a large central fire where everyone can gather and visit. A lot of times there's gambling and people make trades, too. It's a lot of fun," he said. "I miss that."

"What do you trade for?" Roxie was very curious about his culture and wanted to become familiar with it the way he was with hers.

"All kinds of things. Sometimes it's goods being traded, but it can also be services. Listening to the trading is fun because people haggle back and forth," he said.

"I'd like to see that," she said. "I'm sorry that I'll never get to."

"Me, too."

Roxie grew quiet for a few moments. Wild Wind could tell that something was on her mind and just left her to her thoughts. He wasn't a person who felt the need to fill the silences with words. In his culture, sometimes silences said more than talking did.

"Wild Wind, do you think your family would have liked me?"

He gave her a kind smile. "You mean because you're white?"

She nodded. "Yes. Would they have accepted me?"

"We're very welcoming of white people as a rule as long as they are peaceful. Yes, they would have liked you and welcomed you."

Her smile made his stomach drop pleasantly and desire spread through his body.

"I'm glad you think so. I'd be devastated if they'd hate me. I wish I could meet them," she said.

"I wish the same thing," he said, running a hand up over her arm and shoulder until his hand cupped the back of her neck.

Roxie shivered at the contact of his warm palm against her skin. His eyes seemed to have darkened even more and she read the passion in them. Her pulse jumped as he held her in place while he leaned closer so he could kiss her. His lips were warm and supple and she wanted more. Kissing him harder, she looped her arms around his neck and pulled him closer.

His powerful arms encircled her waist and he pressed his body against hers, reveling in her feminine softness in contrast with his hard muscles. When she buried her hands in his hair, he shuddered as her fingers slid over his scalp, groaning his excitement against her sweet lips.

One of her hands slid down the back of his buckskin shirt, heightening his passion even further. He couldn't think as her fingers skimmed over his skin. Suddenly she pulled away from him, leaving his senses reeling. They stared into each other's eyes for several moments.

"Oh, my," Roxie said. "I'm so sorry."

"Why?"

She moved away from him a little. "I didn't mean to be so forward."

Wild Wind said, "You weren't the only one. There's nothing to be sorry about. At least we know that we're attracted to each other. That's a good thing."

"Yes, it is."

To distract the both of them from the current of desire that still ran between them, Wild Wind asked, "Would you like to learn how to play knuckles?"

She pounced on the idea. "Yes. I've heard you and Lucky talk about it, but I'd like to know how to play. Maybe I'll win." A mischievous gleam entered her lovely blue eyes.

Wild Wind gave her a cocky smile. "We'll see about that."

They laughed and teased each other for the next hour over the game and Roxie loved hearing his deep-timbered laugh and his mesmerizing smile. His hands were strong and nimble and she couldn't help but think about how good they had felt on her. When the current round ended, Roxie decided that she should get home before Ross started worrying about her.

"Thank you for a lovely evening," she said. "I had so much fun."

"So did I. Thanks for coming to see me."

She said, "Truthfully, I couldn't stay away. Is there anything you need before I go?"

He liked that she felt so strongly about him. He was quickly coming to feel the same way. "No. I'll be fine. Otto's been sleeping with me in case I need help, but I'm feeling much better."

"All right."

She rose and he carefully did the same. Fast movement was still painful, so he made sure to move slowly. "I'd ride home with you, but I can't quite yet. I'm sorry."

Roxie smiled, putting a hand on his cheek. "It's ok. I'll be fine. I'll come see you tomorrow night after the town hall meeting."

"Ok. I won't be there; it'll only cause more trouble if I go," he said.

The whole situation made Roxie burn with anger. "It's not right. I know that Jerry and the rest of the council and our sheriff won't put up with anymore of that behavior. Things will be fine."

He nodded. "Yes. Why didn't I see how beautiful you were before?"

His question rendered her motionless.

He traced her bottom lip with his thumb. "How pretty your lips are and how soft your skin is? Your hair is the color of golden wheat and your eyes remind me of some of the beautiful lakes I've seen—such a bright, sparkling blue. I'll never get tired of looking into them."

Roxie's breath came a little faster and her mouth was slightly parted. No man had ever said such things to her and it had a powerful effect on her. She made no objection when he ran his hands down her sides and rested them on her waist.

"You feel so good in my arms. So soft and womanly." He gathered her to him, just holding her while resting his cheek on the top of her head.

Roxie smiled against his chest. "You feel good, too. So strong and virile."

They stayed that way for a few minutes before Wild Wind slowly pulled back from her. "You should go so you get home before it gets much later."

"Yes. You're right," she said.

Once she'd put on her cloak and shoes, he gave her a brief yet passionate kiss before walking her out to her buggy.

"See you tomorrow night," Roxie said.

"See you then."

The buggy moved away across the meadow to the road at the lower end that led into town. Wild Wind watched her until he couldn't see her any longer and then went back into his tipi.

Chapter Nineteen

THE ECHO EXPRESS

Violent Attack Sparks Outrage
By Molly Watson

March 20ᵗʰ, 1894—Last night's Echo council meeting was rife with anger and unrest as the council members all voiced their disgust over the attack of Wild Wind, a Cheyenne brave who has lived in Echo for almost two years. The attack took place a week ago, resulting in the death of seven townsmen at the hand of the victim.

The number of attackers is unknown. They surrounded Wild Wind's cabin, armed with rifles and other guns. The skirmish began when they threw Molotov cocktails through the windows, setting the dwelling on fire in an attempt to drive Wild Wind from his home.

However, they weren't expecting Wild Wind to be such a fierce, competent fighter, and he was able to take out five of them before being forced to run. Running out the back of the cabin, he encountered another assailant, whom he quickly dispatched into the next life and kept going.

Upon reaching the woods, where he hoped to lose his enemies, he ran into yet another attacker. They fought and even though Wild Wind succeeded in killing him, he sustained a serious gunshot wound that almost killed him. He was able to make it to the Earnest ranch, where

Marvin Earnest gave him rudimentary medical care until Wild Wind could be transported to Dr. Erin Avery's medical practice.

Mr. Earnest said, "I was shocked to hear of this heinous attack, which Wild Wind imparted to me while myself and my sister-in-law, Bree, administered medical care to him. In my opinion, those that were foolhardy enough to have gone after such a dangerous adversary got their just desserts. I'm very happy that Wild Wind came through it all and is now recovering well."

Mr. Earnest wasn't the only one to condemn the brutal attack and to commend the victim for standing up so well for himself.

Sheriff Evan Taft said, "Listen up! This kind of thing isn't going to be tolerated in Echo, and me and my deputies will do whatever it takes to make sure something like this never happens again. So if you're thinking about pulling another trick like that against anyone, you better think again, because I have no problem putting scum like you in the ground. Going after someone like that is cowardly and despicable and whoever else was in on it should be ashamed of themselves. This is the only warning I'm going to give about this. From now on there won't be any talking on the matter, only action, and you won't like the action I take. Remember what I've said here tonight."

In addition to the assault on Wild Wind, the culprits also killed thirty-four sheep and one of the victim's sheepdogs.

When interviewed about the attack and subsequent attempt to take his life a few days later as he lay wounded in the medical clinic, Wild Wind had this to say: "I've never done anything but treat everyone I've met with decency and respect. I mind my own business and I've never caused any trouble for anyone. Prejudice is an evil thing and drives people to do stupid, horrible things and I feel sorry for them. I guess they know now that I won't back down from a fight and I'm very capable of inflicting damage. I show no mercy in a battle and now the rest of Echo knows it.

"I'd like to thank the Earnests, Dr. Avery, Pastor Thatcher, and Miss Roxie Ryder for all of their help in saving my life and caring for me. I'm also grateful for the protection Sheriff Taft and Deputy Earnest gave me and Miss Ryder the night the cowards tried to kill me at the clinic."

The investigation into who else may have been included in the conspiracy to murder Wild Wind is ongoing and this reporter personally knows that Echo's lawmen are dogged in their determination to bring criminals to justice. It's only a matter of time before their identities are uncovered and they are punished.

More updates will follow as they become available.

Roxie finished reading Molly's article and put the paper down on the kitchen table. "That should fix their wagons," she said.

Ross smiled. "Yeah. I don't think anyone will bother Wild Wind again."

"That's right," Roxie said proudly. "He's not to be trifled with."

Callie grinned as she put jam on a piece of toast. "And you'd say that even if you weren't so taken with him, right?"

"Yes, I would. Anyone who can do what he did deserves to be praised." Deciding to change the subject, she asked, "Are you feeling up to helping Ross today or do you want me to?"

"I am raring to go after resting and sleeping so much the past couple of days," Callie said. "I actually feel hyper, so I think it'll be good for me to help my handsome husband."

Smiling, Ross said, "I'd be glad to have my beautiful wife help me."

"And what are you going to do today?" Callie asked Roxie.

"I'm going to do a few chores around here and make some cookies," Roxie said. "Otto asked me to make those coconut cookies he loves so much."

"That kid's gonna start looking like a coconut cookie," Ross said. "He's so cute that it's hard to tell him no."

Roxie said, "Why do you think I'm making them? I couldn't refuse him when he looked at me with those big brown eyes of his."

They finished their breakfast and went their separate ways to begin their various tasks.

The Ryders weren't the only ones who were busy that day. Wild Wind and Lucky finished up their morning work and then set about making out an order for all of the supplies they'd need to build Wild Wind's unusual new home. Wild Wind couldn't hunt yet, but he planned to go in a few days when he could walk longer and drag deer home.

Although they had ordered canvas, they would still need deer hides. Billy, Adam, and Keith had also offered to hunt and bring in deer. They would all share the meat, however, so there was no danger of it going to waste. Once their order was sent off, they went over to Wild Wind's farm and plotted out where they were going to situate the house/tipi.

Using stakes, they marked it off so that it was ready for when their supplies arrived. Over the next couple of days, they were able to build the kitchen part, complete with a good-sized pantry, shelves, and a place for the stove. They covered it with tarpaulins to protect it until the other building materials came.

They selected a tall, thinner tree that would serve well as a center pole for the lodge and Lucky and Adam cut it down. They still had some of the support poles and hide walls from Lucky and Leah's wedding lodge, which would come in handy.

All of this was done without Roxie's knowledge. Wild Wind wanted to surprise her with it when it was done. She had no reason to go to his farm since he was living in his old tipi on Lucky's farm, which made it easier to keep secret.

By the end of the week, Wild Wind was able to hunt again, but only for a short period of time. His wound made it hard to stretch and hold his bow the way he need to, so he used a rifle instead since shooting it didn't require that sort of muscle action. He usually brought down a deer every other day, and the other days, he hunted other animals for their coats and feathers.

Nina and Leah would use them to make sitting cushions for his new home. Some of the feathers he would hold back to dye and decorate clothing with. All during this time, he and Roxie saw each other every day and most evenings. They played games with the Quinns and whomever else dropped by, including the Earnests, who had started coming over at Lucky and Leah's repeated requests.

Little Isaac Earnest, Marvin and Ronni's four-month-old son, looked just like Marvin, which delighted Ronni. He was a happy baby and adored by his family, as were Shadow and Bree's fourteen-month-old twins, Rory and Lucas. This was also true for Eva, Ronni and Marvin's toddler. Otto was a good sport and played with the younger children. He'd started teaching them Cheyenne and it was funny to hear Eva going around saying a word or two of it here and there.

Every Tuesday the Quinns entertained, Lucky cooking Cheyenne-style and the Tafts, McIntyres, and Two Moons always came over. With the addition of the Earnests attending, it was evident that the Quinns' lodge wasn't going to be big enough. Therefore, quite a few of them worked together to enlarge it, including Marvin and Shadow who were very curious about the process.

Shadow helping didn't seem unusual, but Marvin assisting was very strange since he didn't seem the type to do manual labor.

Thad remarked upon this. "Seein' you in jeans and an old shirt is about the weirdest thing I've ever seen."

"I'll have you know that I don't always wear suits. When needed, I wear the sort of outfit you see me in now. It's just that I'm normally conducting business. When I help Molly at the paper, this is how I dress. You're just not there when I am."

Billy said, "I'm with Thad: it just looks weird."

"Perhaps to you, but Ronni has informed me that she likes the way my ass looks in jeans," Marvin said.

Billy almost dropped the rope he was using to haul a support pole in place to that Lucky could hammer it in place when he laughed. The sudden slack in the line made Lucky miss the nail he was hammering and he hit his thumb.

"Damn it, Billy! Hold it still!" Lucky said around the injured appendage.

"Sorry," Billy said, still grinning.

Leah didn't help things when she said aloud, "I think Ronni is right. Marvin's rear does look good."

Lucky almost hit his thumb again. "You quit lookin' at his rear!"

Leah laughed and moved back further so she was out of the way.

The large group had the new lodge assembled by the end of the day and they all ate together that night, except for Thad who went home to Jessie, who wasn't up to the outing since she was so far along. He didn't mind going home to her since he was nervous about the impending birth and didn't like being away from her longer than he had to. He kept his black stallion, Killer, at a fast canter and made it home in good time.

Jessie loved sleeping in Thad's arms. It was something that her first husband had rarely done with her. In the beginning of her and Mile's marriage, he'd been sweet and affectionate, but that had begun changing and other than love making, he didn't really touch her in bed much.

Thad was completely different. It was rare that they didn't fall asleep with him holding her and he always knew when she got up in the night for something. As soon as she got back in bed, he pulled her back to him, snuggling up to her again. It was something she never would have suspected of the rough-talking man, but it was a very pleasant surprise.

In her advanced pregnancy it was more comfortable for her to sleep on her side and Thad had taken to spooning her, letting her rest back against him to give her back added support. That had happened by accident one night, but Jessie had mentioned how comfortable it was and Thad hadn't forgotten. They'd slept that way ever since.

Two mornings after the enlargement of the Quinns' lodge, she began having contractions. Thad's arm rested loosely around her and she smiled. Even when he was sleeping, she felt his love for her and was once again awed by it. Being around Thad was so easy and fun, even in the mornings when he was very cranky before he'd had his first cigarette and cup of coffee.

She rubbed his arm as a slight contraction came upon her. It wasn't all that painful and she didn't feel any rush for anyone to go get Erin. It was funny how calm she felt even though she was about to give birth. She'd been a wreck with Allie and worried with Molly, but not with this baby. Maybe it was because she'd been through it a couple of times and knew what to expect.

Thad's arm tightened around her a little and he kissed her shoulder. "Is it time to get up already?"

"Not quite yet," she said.

"How come you're awake then? Go back to sleep. Why are you waking me up?"

She found his cantankerous morning attitude amusing and never took anything he said personally. "Well, I just thought you might want to share in the birth of our baby."

"Of course, I want to."

"Well, you can't do that when you're asleep."

"I don't plan on sleeping whenever it happens."

"Do you want to be with me? I know that's not the normal way it's done, but I won't mind," she said.

Thad had been thinking about that and hadn't made up his mind. Men weren't supposed to be present in the birthing room, but several of his male friends had been present during the births of their children and they'd told him that they were happy they'd gotten the chance to witness it.

He smiled and kissed the side of Jessie's head. "I'd like to help Mini Mac come out into this big world. I have no idea what to do, but you'll just have to tell me."

A stronger contraction made her breathe a little faster. "Well, you're going to get the chance very, very soon."

Thad became completely awake and rose up on his elbow, looking down into her face. "Are you in labor?"

"Yep."

"Why didn't you say so, for Pete's sake! I'll have Porter go get Erin," Thad said.

"No, not yet. There's no hurry," Jessie said. "Just lay here with me a while."

Seeing how calm she was eased Thad's sudden nerves. He relaxed back down on the bed and held her again. "I'm going to be a father again. You know I love all the kids, but I have to admit this is a little different because I helped make this one and I'm gonna watch Mini Mac be born."

Jessie smiled. "Of course it's different. I don't doubt your love for our other kids, but I understand what you mean."

"I never expected to be a father, but I really never expected to be a father at my age. Funny thing is that between you and our brood, I'm the happiest I've ever been. I think I'm about to get even happier though."

They lay talking for almost an hour until Jessie's contractions became more painful and she felt the need to walk. Thad helped her up and went to get Allie. He knocked on her bedroom door and worked on quieting his anxiety. He put his experience of dealing with high stress situations to use and focused on what needed to be done.

Allie opened her door.

"Good morning, sweetheart," he said. "Looks like it's time for the baby to come."

Allie grinned and bounced up and down a little. "Oh my gosh! I can't wait."

"Me, either. Will you stay with Jess while I get Porter up to go get Erin?" He wanted each of the kids to have a part in the event so that they didn't feel slighted and he'd worked out how to do it.

"Sure," Allie said, trotting across the hall to their room.

Thad knocked on Porter's door.

"What?" came the boy's response.

"Look alive in there," Thad said.

Porter groaned, but Thad heard him get up from his bed. Porter opened his door and gave Thad a sleepy glare. "What is it? It's too soon to get up for school."

"Well, you're not goin' to school today. I need you to go get Erin," Thad said.

"How come?"

"Jessie's havin' the baby," Thad said. "So it's your job to go Erin. Got it?"

Porter nodded, his eyes wide open now.

"Get going, son."

"Yes, sir!" Porter shut his door and got dressed in record time. Going out into the hallway, he saw that his parents' door was open and peeked inside. "Mama?"

Jessie was sitting up in bed now and she smiled at Porter. "You can come in, honey."

Porter had never been around a woman who was about to have a baby. He went over to Jessie. "Does it hurt a lot?"

"Some, but not bad right now. It'll get worse later on, but it'll all be worth it in the end," she said.

"Can I touch it?" he asked.

Jessie took his hand and put it on the spot where the baby had last moved. It moved again and Porter grinned. "That's my little brother."

Allie said, "Or sister."

Porter rubbed over the spot a little. "Nah. It's a boy. I better go get Erin before Pa has a fit. He's probably down having a cigarette."

Jessie said, "That's all right."

Porter kissed her cheek and left the room. Soon they heard Molly's footsteps on the stairs. There was no mistaking them because she always ran up and down them.

"Mama!" she said, running in the room. "Pa says were having a baby today! I'm so excited."

Jessie and Allie laughed at her. Molly tended to be excitable and curious about everything and she was looking forward to the birth of her sibling as much as the rest of the household.

Jessie said, "Yep. We're having a baby today."

"How's your pain?" Molly asked.

"Not too bad yet," Jessie said.

"That's good. I'm going to get the girls up so they can milk the cows and feed the chickens while I start breakfast," Molly said. "Keith is filling the cook stove and building the fires back up."

Jessie noticed that everyone seemed to have a job to do. "Did you decide that on your own?"

"No. Pa woke us up and asked us to."

"Oh, ok," Jessie said, smiling inwardly. *You're a slick one, Mr. McIntyre.*

Their huge cat, Sometimes, came meandering into the room, curious as to what the excitement was all about. The bobcat/domestic cat mix leapt onto the bed and nudged Jessie's hand to be petted. She stroked the big feline's silky head and was rewarded with his rumbling purr. His big green eyes stared into hers and it seemed like he was trying to tell Jessie that he was also excited about the impending birth.

Since marrying Thad, the cat had taken to Jessie and followed her almost everywhere whenever he was around. J.J., their youngest daughter, had given the cat that name because sometimes he was around and sometimes he wasn't. Jessie loved Sometimes and spoiled him by giving him his favorite treat of raw eggs and other snacks.

Keith came up the stairs with two armloads of wood. He'd grown another half inch over the winter and he was even more muscular. Molly loved her husband and thought he was the most handsome man on Earth. His brown eyes shone as he smiled at Jessie.

"Baby day, huh?"

Jessie laughed and then groaned. "Mmm hmm."

Allie held her hand.

"Molly, help me put wood in the fireplaces. I'll hold the wood and you unload it," he said.

They started their chore in Jessie's room and continued around the house, waking J.J. and her sister, Liz. Once they heard what was happening, the two little girls ran in to see Jessie before they went down to do their chores. She chuckled as the two blondes trotted off again. They were lively girls, but very different in personality.

J.J. was more outgoing and feminine while Liz was quieter and more tomboyish. They reminded her of Allie and Molly. Allie was more feminine and quiet while Molly was the tomboy who liked to shoot guns, fish, and play baseball.

While all this was going on, Thad sat out on the back porch, not smoking, just getting his mind in the right frame of mind to help Jessie through the birth. She was the one doing all of the hard work. Thad could handle any dangerous situation and he'd been in quite a few tight spots over the years, but he was more terrified at that moment than he'd ever been in the past.

He was almost powerless in this situation; there wasn't much he could do to help Jessie except encourage her and support her in any way he could. Thad was used to being in control, and not being in control of the situation was nerve-wracking for him. He now fully understood what Evan and his other friends had gone through when their wives were giving birth.

"Get it together, McIntyre," he muttered under his breath right before J.J. and Liz came out the door.

"Good morning, Pa," J.J. said. "It's baby day!"

This was what they'd all started calling the day when the baby would be born.

He chuckled while she hugged him. "Yep. You don't seem excited, though," he teased her.

She kissed his cheek. "Oh, yes, I am! We'll have a live baby doll."

Liz said, "It's not a baby doll; it's a baby."

J.J. released Thad and turned her blue eyes on Liz. "I know that, but it'll be sort of like it, only better." She shook her head and went on her way.

Liz gave Thad a calmer hug. "I'm glad baby day is finally here."

"Me, too, honey," Thad said. "Thanks for milking the cows. It's a big help."

"You're welcome," she said with a pleased smile.

"All right. Get to it."

"Yes, sir," Liz said and trotted off the porch while she smiled at him.

He chuckled, stood up, took a huge breath, and went back into the house.

Six and a half hours later, Jessie was in the last stage of labor. The family had all been with her and Thad off and on until the final stage. Then they'd all been gently kicked out so that Erin could work and Jessie and Thad had privacy. Even though he was a wreck inside, Thad kept up his calm exterior.

"You're doin' great, Blue Eyes," he told Jessie as he wiped sweat from her forehead.

Jessie nodded and bore down. "Oh my God. This was so much easier when I was younger," she ground out through gritted teeth."

"You're tough, Jess. You gotta be to put up with me," he quipped.

"Very true," Jessie said.

She grunted and pushed again before relaxing and saying, "Erin, just reach in and pull it out. I don't mind."

Erin smiled. "That's not a good idea."

"What kind of friend are you?" Jessie asked.

"The kind who's going to deliver a healthy baby," Erin said.

Thad kissed Jessie's cheek. "That's right. We have to get our Mini Mac out here."

Erin laughed. Hearing the nickname never failed to amuse her.

Jessie leaned against him. "You do it. You get Mini Mac out here."

"I would if I could, but it doesn't work like that."

"You men get out of all of the hard stuff. You don't have a monthly, you don't have babies, and you don't have to do laundry," Jessie said.

"I do laundry," Thad said. "I've done my own for years and then—" He shut up when Jessie glared at him. "What? You brought it up."

Erin said, "Ok, Jessie. Push hard. You're crowning."

Thad put a supporting arm behind Jessie and helped her sit up farther to make it easier for her to push. "C'mon, Blue Eyes. You can do it."

Jessie thought about how much she wanted to hold their baby and dug down deep for the energy to push. With Thad and Erin urging her on, Jessie grunted and strained and little Mini Mac was born.

"It's a boy," Erin said, grinning. "Congratulations."

The baby began crying and Jessie cried with relief and happiness. A cheer rose out in the hallway as the family heard the baby.

"What is it?" Allie called through the door.

"A boy," Thad responded. They heard more cheering. "They must have been standing out there the whole time," he said with a chuckle.

Jessie nodded and Thad hugged his wife. "You did fantastic, honey," he told her. "I'm so proud of you. Even if I had the right equipment, I don't think I could do that."

Jessie smiled. "I don't think you could, either."

"Thanks for the vote of confidence," he said, watching Erin tend to the baby.

Erin came over and placed the baby in Jessie's waiting arms.

Jessie looked down into his pink little face and felt joy surge through her. Here was the baby that she and the man she loved so much had been waiting on. Finally, she was able to hold their son. "He's gorgeous, just like you, honey," she told Thad. He didn't get a chance to respond because she suddenly hugged the baby to her and gave him a fierce look. "We're naming him Thaddeus Elroy McIntyre, Jr. and that's that. We'll call him T.J. If you want to hold him, you'll agree with me."

Thad's eyebrows rose over her attitude. "Ok. Fine by me," he said. "I like the idea of havin' a junior. After all, he is Mini Mac."

Jessie shook with tired laughter. Then she kissed the baby. "Hello, T.J. I'm your mama and this guy over here is your pa. He's cranky in the morning, but other than that, he's a pretty nice guy."

"Don't point out my flaws to him right off," Thad complained. "Give him a chance to worship me a little."

Jessie held the little bundle over to Thad. "I think he wants to see you."

Thad had been around babies before and was used to holding them, so he took T.J. with no trouble. Holding his son in his hands for the first time was an experience so moving that Thad couldn't contain his tears as hard as he tried. "You are a handsome devil, all right," he said. "Welcome to the world, Mini Mac." He could have watched the baby forever, but he knew that Erin needed to finish up with Jessie.

"What do you say we go meet the rest of the posse, huh? We'll be back," Thad said, kissing Jessie.

Chapter Twenty

By that evening, the McIntyre household was filled with their friends who'd been told about T.J.'s birth. Enough food had been brought that the McIntyres wouldn't have to cook for a couple of days. T.J. was passed around and everyone visited briefly with Jessie in between feeding T.J. and her napping.

Wild Wind and Roxie weren't among them because he was afraid that one of the kids who knew they were building his new home would accidentally spill the beans about it to Roxie. As a rule, he didn't lie, but he was willing to go against his principles in this case. He told Roxie he was in too much pain so he was going to stay home and go the next day.

She'd scolded him about overdoing it lately and said she'd stay with him, as he'd been hoping that she would. Besides, he enjoyed the time they spent alone. Roxie felt the same way and liked how she and Wild Wind could just sit with each other, not saying much sometimes. Their conversations never felt forced and she appreciated not having to make small talk.

When it grew later, Roxie left him, even though she hated to. Wild Wind wistfully watched her ride off into the night and when his heart called out for her, he knew that something wonderful had happened; he'd fallen in love with Roxie. He smiled as he went inside his tipi and lay down. He was filled with impatience to have his home completed and he decided that he was going to work harder to get it done as soon as possible.

The new home was completed by the first week of April and Wild Wind was thrilled with how it had turned out. It was beyond his expectations and it had been a group effort. He would always be grateful to his *he-vo'éstanemo*—his family—for helping him. As he surveyed their handiwork, Wild Wind knew it was time to put the rest of his plan into action.

Roxie was surprised that Friday when Wild Wind showed up at her house early in the afternoon. She opened to door to see his handsome, smiling face.

"*Pave-esheeva,*" she said, using the Cheyenne greeting, which meant "good day" and was about the closest thing in the Cheyenne language to the English word "hello". Wild Wind had begun teaching her Cheyenne and she was catching on to simple words and phrases fairly well. "Did I forget you were coming?" she asked, motioning him inside.

"*Pave-esheeva. Hová'áháne.* No. Is it possible for me to steal you away?" he asked, taking in the way she looked in her simple blue calico dress that brought out her eyes.

She gave him a playful look. "You're in luck, my brave. I just finished with my work and I was actually going to come see you. Where are we going?"

"I have a surprise for you, so I can't tell you," he said.

"You're not going to give me a hint? Just a little one?"

He liked her coaxing smile. "Nope. Not one."

"That's not very nice."

"I know," he said, taking her cloak from the coatrack and draping it over her shoulders.

Seeing that she wasn't going to get any more information out of him, she let him lead her out to his buggy. Fortunately, his attackers had spared his small barn, goats, two horses, and his buggy. He helped her into the buggy and joined her on the seat. Starting out the buggy, he noticed the way the sunlight turned her hair an even more golden shade of blonde. Her deep blue eyes roamed over the town and met his as they talked and her lilac-scented soap reached his nostrils.

From head to toe, Roxie was a beautiful woman, and he saw the way other men looked at her. He was proud that he was the man she loved and he didn't care who saw them together. It was time for everyone to accept him and he wasn't going to hide his relationship with Roxie as though it was something of which to be ashamed.

Roxie noticed that they didn't turn off on the road that led to Lucky's farm. "Where are we going?" she asked.

"To see your surprise," Wild Wind said, smiling.

"Still not going to tell me anything, hmm?"

"That's right."

She sniffed and pretended to be offended, which made him chuckle.

"You won't be angry once you see it," he told her.

"We'll see about that," she said.

As they rode up the road that led to Wild Wind's farm, Roxie saw an odd yet beautiful structure standing on it. It looked like a huge tipi, but not a tipi. There was a small part that looked like a house sticking out from the back of the round, white structure. The "house" part was also white. Two offshoots, one on opposite sides of the main tipi, gave the home an even more exotic look. They were each shaped like half of a tipi, making it appear as though they were emerging from the main section.

"What is that?" she asked.

"My new home," he said.

She looked at him in disbelief. "Your new home? You didn't tell me you were rebuilding."

"That's because it was a surprise," he said, smiling.

On the outside, various animals had been painted and she thought the large, colorful figures were beautiful against the white canvas and the blue sky above it.

"It's wonderful," she said, getting out of the buggy without waiting for him to help her. She'd begun adopting some of the ways a Cheyenne woman acted. He'd told her that men didn't normally help women up and down off horses and she equated the same thing with buggies.

This wasn't because the men were inconsiderate, but rather because it was important for women to be independent when the men were out on hunts or fighting. Plus, a woman couldn't go searching for a man every time she needed to ride a horse.

This wasn't something Wild Wind expected her to do, however. Roxie had taken it upon herself to do it. He'd been disconcerted by it at first because he'd become accustomed to the practice of helping women in and out of conveyances and up and down off horses. The woman he'd come to love had informed him that she could do it herself and he'd abided by her wishes, secretly proud of her.

Wild Wind said, "Go ahead on in."

Roxie grinned and ran to the tipi. It had an unusual entrance for a tipi: a door instead of a flap. It was engraved with various Cheyenne and Irish symbols. Wild Wind was following her and laughed when she closed it right before he arrived at the entrance. He knocked on it and called out, "Can I come in?"

Roxie ran back to the door and opened it, peeking out at him. "And just who would you be?"

"Chief Wild Wind, and I have come to ravage the beautiful white woman with the hair the color of the sun," he said, playing along.

"Oh, well, in that case, come right on in," Roxie said with a seductive smile.

He smiled and followed her inside. Roxie saw that there was a large flap a short ways inside. The space between the door and the flap reminded her of a foyer. There was a beautiful rendering of a dragon on the flap and she traced it with her fingers.

"Did Billy paint this?"

"Yeah. Win gave him the idea. He said that this dragon is for protection and good luck."

"It's gorgeous," she said, going through the second flap.

As she stepped inside the main living area of the tipi, her eyes took in the height of the tipi and the way light was able to come through the canvas walls, giving the inside a warm glow and plenty of light to see by. The floor was largely outlined with furs, woven rugs, and even a few carpets. Standing back the way she was, she could see that they'd been arranged to create a huge mosaic picture of the sun and was astounded by the beauty of the work. The very outside ring of the floor was still grass and she noticed that it was becoming green quicker than the grass outside since it was warmer inside the tipi.

There were rolled-up canvases hung around the perimeter of the tipi that reminded her of window blinds. She went to one and saw how to untie it, but she looked at Wild Wind for permission since it wasn't her home. He nodded so she quickly undid the leather thong. The canvas unfurled and she gasped as she saw the intricate design of mallard ducks in flight.

"Are all of them decorated?" she asked.

"Several of them are, but there are some blank ones, too," he replied. "Go ahead and look at them."

She noticed that two of them were already down and that they were unpainted and placed higher than the other ones. She left them alone for the moment and let the other five hide panels down. Two were blank and three were decorated. One showed an eagle soaring high against the sun, deer leapt across a stream on another, and the last one was covered by a small herd of bison.

Roxie stared in wonder at the beauty surrounding her and fell in love with the home in that instant. "What are the big panels for?"

"Why don't you go look and find out?"

She gave him a quizzical glance and ran to the first one, pulling aside the buckskin panel. She noticed that it was very heavy and wondered why. Walking behind it, she saw that a very large "room" had been set up in one of the offshoots, complete with a large bed, two night stands, a bureau, and a small camping stove. Two large Persian rugs had been cut and fitted together to create one rug that completely covered the half-circle floor.

The last piece of furniture was even more unusual for Wild Wind to have than the other furniture. A beautiful wardrobe sat to the left of the bed. In fact, it was strange that he would have such a room at all, but it was an exquisite space. Perplexed, she left the room and gave him a confused look. He just smiled and motioned for her to go to the other large panel across the tipi.

She went to it and slipped inside the other offshoot. It was devoid of furniture, but its floor was covered by a very pretty woven rug and there was another small camping stove off to one side. Coming out, she saw Wild Wind standing by a doorway at the back of the tipi and surmised that this had to be the entrance into the house part of the "building". He waved her inside it as she drew near. It was a large kitchen done in light pine, including the wooden floor that was flush with the tipi floor.

A window in two of the three walls let in more sunlight and allowed her to closely inspect the kitchen. A door in the third wall provided a second entrance into the home. Pretty red-and-white gingham curtains lined the windows. There was a sink with a water pump, a six-plate cook stove, large eight-place table and chair set, and plenty of counter and cupboard space. Seeing a door in the far wall of the room, she opened it and discovered a big pantry.

Wild Wind enjoyed the expression of wonder that showed on Roxie's face. It told him that she liked everything and that was of the utmost importance to him if they were going to share the home.

She looked at him and he said, "Come with me, Roxie."

She took the hand he held out to her and walked with him to the center of the lodge where she saw a central fire pit. In her awe, she hadn't noticed it earlier. It was large and a big, black, cast iron pot hung over it. The area around it was lined with colorful stones that had been cemented together to catch any food that might fall instead of getting the floor covering dirty. It would be easy to wipe it off if necessary.

Wild Wind had Roxie sit down with him and took her hands in his. "Roxie, the past few weeks have meant so much to me. I'm glad that you had the courage to open my eyes to how you feel about me and I'm sorry that I didn't see it before then. Men can sometimes be dense about things like that, but I usually pick up on them. I don't know why I didn't.

"I can't thank you enough for taking care of me and keeping me from being bored. I've enjoyed all the time we've spent together and I now know what a wonderful woman you are. You make me smile and laugh and I'm always happy when you're with me. Your kindness and generosity touches me and you're a very intelligent woman. Everything about you is beautiful, from your sunshine hair to your pretty little toes."

Roxie laughed a little over that.

Wild Wind continued. "I've seen how skilled you are at running a household and how good you are at helping Ross with your shop. I can't imagine my life without you now and I have come to love you so much that sometimes I can hardly bear to be parted from you."

Roxie was startled by his statement. "You love me? You really do?"

He took her face in his hands. "Yes. I will never lie to you, Roxie. It's not in my nature to lie and I'll always be honest with you. *Né-méhotàtse.* I love you."

Tears of happiness welled in her eyes. "I love you, too. You make me so happy."

"I'm very glad to hear that. I have a couple of questions for you," he said, releasing her. "What do you think of my new home?"

A smile of such beauty settled on her face that it seemed as though it lit up the whole tipi. "It's the most magnificent, beautiful home I've ever seen. It's so light and spacious and very romantic. I feel as though I'm in a castle or some sort of exotic place. I've never seen anything like it."

Moving close so he could embrace her, he said, "I'm so happy that you like it so much because I want you to share it with me, as my wife. Will you marry me, Roxie?"

If it was possible, her smile became even brighter as tears spilled from her eyes. She surprised him by kissing him firmly. She broke the kiss and smiled into his eyes. "Yes, I'll marry you and share this wonderful home with you, my handsome brave."

He kissed her soundly, conveying his happiness to her silently. When they parted, he said, "I would be very proud if you would wear this ring."

Roxie gasped as she saw the lovely ring that was really a work of art. Instead of a diamond, a tiny, highly detailed depiction of hummingbird in flight was centered on a ring. An even tinier diamond had been used for the bird's eye.

"Oh, Wild Wind, it's stunning," she said as he slid it onto her finger. "I wasn't expecting a ring since I know that the Cheyenne don't give them for engagements."

"I know, but I wanted to honor your culture, too. Besides, now everyone will know that you belong to me."

"I love the sound of that. Why a hummingbird?"

Running his thumb over it lightly as he held her hand, he replied, "To us a hummingbird represents love, peace, and happiness, and those are all things I want us to have in our marriage."

She shook her head. "I can't believe any of this. I can't believe that you would build such a … splendid home for us to live in or give me such a beautiful ring. It's all so overwhelming. I feel like I'm dreaming."

He tipped her chin up so he could gaze into her eyes. "I feel the same thing, but it's all real and I can't wait to begin our life here together. I won't move in until after we're married. I want to begin living here together."

The kiss he gave her was gentle and so sweet that Roxie felt a little dizzy from it. Then it became more urgent and she embraced him tightly as passion flared between them. His kisses always set her on fire and this time was no exception. She delved her hands into his long, silky hair, reveling in the way it slid through her fingers.

His mouth left hers and he nuzzled her neck, making her shiver. Roxie became bolder. She didn't know where the idea came from, but she bit his earlobe. Wild Wind let out a growl and, in a move so fast that it left her a little dazed, he had her on her back before she knew it. The fierce look on his face was thrilling to her and she met his lips eagerly.

Wild Wind's control was slipping as he kissed and held her. Realizing it, he suddenly rolled away from her, gaining his feet and putting distance between them.

Roxie sat up, breathing heavily and smiling devilishly at him. "What's wrong?"

He grinned at her. "You know exactly what's wrong. Don't tempt me so much."

"You mean like this?" she said, undoing a couple of buttons of her blouse.

"Roxie, I'm warning you. Don't do that. It's been a long time and you're the most beautiful woman I've ever seen. I'm not sure how much I can resist you."

Her hands stilled. "You've been with other women?"

"Yes. While women are expected to be virgins when they marry, there is nothing wrong with widows or divorced women taking lovers. A lot of times, they share their sleeping robes with the younger men who aren't married. It can keep a brave from violating a maiden before she's married and it also shows him the proper way to make love to a woman so that when he marries he can please his wife."

The thought of him being with other women made her intensely jealous, but on the other hand she thought it was good that he knew what he was doing since she didn't know how that part of things went. Although she loved kissing and caressing him, she had never been past a certain point and it made her a little nervous. However, what he'd just told her gave Roxie confidence that when the time came, she would have nothing to worry about.

She giggled and said, "I look forward to benefiting from the wisdom of the women who educated you in that department."

He found her scandalous remark hilarious and let out a shout of laughter that echoed in the large lodge. Roxie's laughter joined his and he came to her, pulling her to her feet.

"I want to get married here," she said. "It's so beautiful and I feel as though it would bring us luck to have our wedding here."

His eyes widened in surprise. "You don't want a church wedding?"

"I did until I saw this. Would that be all right with you?"

A smile curved his mouth upwards. "Yes. I think it would be lucky, too."

She hugged him and then they started going around the tipi, talking about things they wanted to do with it. She inspected the bedroom and kitchen more. Wild Wind was amused and pleased by her excitement over everything and he told her that since the tipi was technically hers she could do anything she wanted to with it.

Once they'd discussed the wedding more and finished looking around, he took her home, but she would come out to Lucky's farm that night to spend more time with him and whoever was around. As they rode into town, everything still felt magical and dreamlike to Roxie. Wild Wind kept looking at his woman, thinking how lucky he was to have found her.

He walked her to the door, stole another kiss, and reluctantly left her. Riding back home, Wild Wind envisioned their future together and he had to stifle his impatience to begin it. Arriving back home, his joy grew to such a high that he threw up his arms, let out a whoop, and shouted a prayer of thanks to the Great Spirit.

Chapter Twenty-One

Andi didn't know what to do. She had a moral dilemma and had no idea how to solve it. She had talked to Bea about it, but her best friend didn't have an answer for her, either. One night after a council meeting, she took Edna off to the side.

"You're a very wise woman," Andi said. "I need some advice."

Edna smiled. "Well, thank you. I'll do my best."

Andi said, "I don't know if you're aware, but Arliss and I are seeing each other."

"Yes, I know," Edna said. "He's halfway in love with you, from what I gather."

Blushing, Andi said, "He's always telling me that he's crazy about me. But I'm in a very strange situation. You know about his other personalities."

Over the last couple of weeks, Arliss had been "introducing" R.J. around to his friends so they could get to know him. His transformations were amazing to watch and people came to believe that the two personalities were in fact separate entities who each knew what the controlling personality was doing.

"Yes, I do, and I've been curious about how you're handling it, but I didn't want to pry."

"Well, I haven't met the third personality, but the two I know I'm very taken with, which leads me to my question," Andi said, fidgeting a little.

"Ok," Edna said. "Go ahead."

"Is it cheating to see two different personalities? And you know that they are completely different," Andi said.

Edna couldn't control the laughter that bubbled up. "I'm so sorry, but you have to admit that it's sort of funny."

"I know," Andi said, smiling. "The really funny thing is that I can't make up my mind which one I like best."

"I can understand that. They both have such good qualities and each of them is very entertaining in his own way."

"Yes, and even their sense of humors are different. R.J. tends to have a drier wit while Arliss is more boisterous."

Edna pressed her fingers to her mouth for a moment as she considered the situation. "No. I don't believe it's cheating because they're all sides of the same man. They're just in different compartments in his brain, but they're in the same body. Therefore, you're not cheating."

Relief made Andi a little giddy and she and Edna had a good laugh over it.

"I would never cheat and I wanted to make sure this didn't fall into that category," she said.

Edna gave her a curious look. "If you don't want to answer this, I won't be offended, but do they kiss differently?" she asked in a voice barely above a whisper.

Andi's face turned pink. "Yes, but I still can feel the other one there. It doesn't make sense, but that's what it's like." She giggled a little, something she rarely did. "And both of them are very good at it."

Edna let out a laugh just as Evan approached.

"What are you two ladies talking about that's so funny?" he asked.

"None of your business, sonny boy," Edna said. "That's between us women."

Evan smiled. "You must be talking about men. That's what women say when they don't want men to know they're talking about them."

Edna narrowed her eyes at him. "You think you're so smart since you're the sheriff."

"Well, I do have great deductive reasoning," he retorted.

Edna let out a snort. "Andi, you remember what I told you, all right?"

"Thanks, Edna," Andi said.

"You're welcome. Goodnight. Ok, sonny boy, take me home," Edna said.

"See you soon, Andi," Evan said. "Come on, old woman."

Although he and Edna always teased each other, they loved each other very much and Evan doted on his aunt. Andi watched the careful way Evan helped Edna up and suddenly felt power flow through her.

"Edna, may I pray for you a moment?" she asked.

Edna saw the intense expression on Andi's face and thought back to the night of Andi's interview in front of the council. She'd had the same sort of look about her when she'd prayed for Marvin and not long after, they'd discovered that Ronni had conceived Isaac.

"Yes, of course."

Andi smiled, took her hands, and closed her eyes. *Dear Lord, I'm listening and I humbly ask that You lessen this dear woman's affliction. Take away the arthritis that plagues her so. I feel Your power and I know the miracles that only You can work. I pray that You will grant this request to Your lowly servant. In Your holy name, Amen.*

Opening her eyes, Andi smiled at Edna and released her hands. "Thank you," she said.

Edna's hands tingled. "No, thank you. I don't know what you prayed for, but I know whatever it was, it must be something good."

"It is," Andi agreed. "Well, I won't keep you."

As they left the town hall, Edna wondered what Andi had prayed for, but she knew that the pastor never revealed what she called her "special prayers". Deciding that she would know all in due time, she put it out of her mind for the moment and concentrated on heckling Evan as he drove them home.

The next day, Andi had a meeting with Wild Wind and Roxie to discuss their wedding. She'd been a little uneasy about the meeting because of her past with Wild Wind, but she was determined to be professional.

As they came in and sat down in her office, Wild Wind gave her a friendly smile.

"It's good to see you, Andi. I haven't much lately," he said.

She glanced at Roxie, who didn't appear upset by his remark at all. "It's nice to see you, too. I'm so glad you're feeling better now."

"Thanks."

Roxie could tell that Andi was nervous. "Andi, please don't think that I'm jealous or angry with you in any way. I don't want this to be awkward. All of that is in the past, and I think everything is working out the way it was intended to, don't you?"

Andi smiled and sat back against her chair. "I'm so relieved that you feel that way. I've been worried about how this would go."

"There's no need to be worried," Roxie assured her.

After that, the rest of their meeting went very smoothly and they had fun planning the wedding, which would be held the first Saturday of May. As they left her office, Andi was ashamed that she felt a little jealous of them. When would *she* be the one getting married?

"Shame on you, Andi," she said, rummaging around in a drawer for something.

"Have you been a bad girl, Pastor Andi?" R.J. asked from the doorway.

Startled by his sudden appearance, Andi banged her knee on the drawer. "Ow!"

"I'm sorry, love. Would you like me to rub it?" He flashed a roguish smile.

"No," she said, rubbing it herself. "I'm managing quite fine."

He chuckled and sat down in one of the chairs. "Other than a bruised knee, how are you this fine day?"

"I'm fine. What trouble have you been causing?" she asked.

"Nothing much. I robbed the bank, broke some windows, and roughed up a few people. Other than that, it's been a remarkably boring day."

"Oh, is that all?"

He nodded. "Are you free for lunch?"

"Yes, actually," she said, standing up.

"Good. However, before we go, both Arliss and I feel it's time to introduce you to Blake. You see, our feelings for you are becoming stronger, but in order for you to completely accept us, you must know him, too," R.J. said.

Although she was curious and excited about meeting Blake, she was also leery. "He won't hurt me, will he?"

R.J. smiled reassuringly. "No. We promise he won't."

"All right. Go ahead."

R.J. got up and closed the office door. Coming back to the desk, he took a small piece of paper from his jeans pocket, and handed it to her. Taking it from him, she read, *Tag! You're it!*

"This is the key to bring out Blake?"

"Yes, and you're the only one who knows it. We've decided that a couple of other people should know it since it might come in handy, but we haven't given it to them yet. We wanted you to be the first to have it."

She was getting used to both personalities talking about themselves in the plural fashion.

Her brown eyes met his. "And you're sure he won't hurt me."

"Positive."

"All right. Here goes. Tag, you're it," she said.

R.J.'s body posture changed and his facial features took on a harder look. His jaw seemed to square and the gaze that settled on her was completely different. She took a step back from him, ready to give the other signal to get R.J. or Arliss back if needed.

"H-hello, Blake," she stammered.

"Hi, Andi. Good to finally meet you," he said, moving closer to her.

His voice was rougher with no discernible accent.

"It's nice to meet you, too," she said hesitantly, backing up again.

"You don't sound too sure about that," Blake said.

Andi didn't want to show fear, but the predatory gleam in his eye and the way he approached her made her uneasy.

"I'm not at the moment," she said, honestly.

He smiled. "You'll get used to me."

She backpedaled until she was in the corner behind her desk and he kept coming on until they stood only inches apart. He ran a hand down her arm.

"I'm not gonna hurt you, honey," he said. "Don't be scared. I'd never hurt you. Other people? Well, as long as they don't upset me off, they'll be fine. But if they try to hurt us or you, I'll make them sorry."

"Please don't hurt other people," she said.

"I won't as long as they behave themselves," he said.

Andi decided to change the subject. "R.J. and Arliss have certain skills. What are yours?"

"Brute force. You see, I don't feel pain at all. You could hit me with a two-by-four and I'd never feel it. You might knock me down, but I'll always get back up. I've been shot three times and all three of those men are dead because I got to them before they could shoot me again. The boys, as I call them, don't let me out much for that reason, which makes me mad. I behave just fine as long as no one causes us trouble," Blake explained.

This information wasn't exactly reassuring to Andi. "But you won't hurt *me*."

He looked intently into her eyes. "Never. You could hit me, punch me, kick me, or slap me, and I'd never raise a hand to you. I wouldn't hurt any woman or a child."

The honesty she saw in his eyes and the slight softening of his face convinced her. His gaze roamed down over her and then back up. "We sure have ourself a good-lookin' lady. I'm jealous."

"Why?"

"Because they've gotten to kiss you a little, but I haven't yet."

"Oh, well, um, maybe later. I don't know you well enough yet," she said, realizing how silly that sounded since they were all a part of the same man.

"It's time we fix that then," he said, cupping the back of her head and bringing his mouth down on hers in a demanding kiss.

She pushed against his chest, but it did no good. He hooked an arm around her waist and pulled her closer. Despite his slightly rough treatment, she began responding to him. He growled low in his throat and the sound excited her. Then she remembered who and what she was and pushed against him in earnest.

He heeded her signal this time and lifted his head from hers, giving her a cocky smile. "Now don't tell me you didn't enjoy that. I know I sure did."

"Be that as it may, it's not proper. I'm a pastor, Blake. You need to be able to respect that if you want to spend time with me. Do you understand that?"

To her surprise, he looked a little chagrined. "Yeah. I get it. Hands off. Sorry," he said, moving away. "Ok. Send me back."

"What? Why?"

"Because R.J. said I should only stay for a little while. I guess I've used up my time," Blake said.

Andi had to stifle a smile at his dejected expression. He suddenly reminded her of a little boy who'd been scolded.

"If you promise to behave, you can have lunch with me," she said, firmly. "And if you don't keep your word, I won't spend any more time with you."

Even his smile was different from R.J. and Arliss'. "I promise."

She put on her light coat and said, "All right. Let's go eat."

"I'll say one more thing and then behave," Blake said.

"Which is?"

"Arliss is right; you wear those pants really good."

She laughed. "That's it, now."

"Ok," Blake said, following her out the door.

Chapter Twenty-Two

As spring came on with a vengeance, love was indeed in Echo's air. Wild Wind and Roxie had been enjoying getting their tipi set up. Their friends had given them a few presents early, such as bed linens and some cooking supplies. However, Roxie had a very nice hope chest and Ross and Wild Wind carefully moved it into the tipi.

Wild Wind had never seen a hope chest before and he was very curious about it. Normally, Roxie's girlfriends would have helped her put the things in it away, but he wanted to do it. She had to explain to him what a few things were and the perplexed expression on his face made her laugh.

"Are you sure you want to help me do this?" she asked him.

"Yes. It's good for me to learn what they are. I've seen Leah cook, but I didn't really pay much attention."

"Ok. Just be careful with the china. I don't want it to get chipped or broken," Roxie said. "It was my grandmother's."

"I'll be very careful," he said, inspecting the pretty blue-and-white design on a saucer. "It's beautiful."

"Thank you. Grandmother had very good taste," Roxie said as they took the china into the kitchen, sitting it on the table.

"So do you, since you're going to marry me."

She smiled at his cocky remark. "Well, you're marrying me, so you have good taste, too."

"I know," he said, coming closer.

"No, no. We have to put these away and then I have to get back to help out with the store since Callie's on bed rest," Roxie said.

"Just one small kiss," Wild Wind coaxed.

"No, because one turns into another and another," Roxie said even though she wanted to kiss him very badly.

"I promise. Only one," he said.

"Ok. Just one."

He gave her a very chaste kiss on the mouth and then moved towards the table again.

"What was that?" Roxie asked.

"What do you mean? I kept my promise, that's all," he said.

"Yes, but that was barely even a kiss," she said.

Keeping a straight face, he said, "You didn't say what kind of kiss it was supposed to be."

"Like the kind you normally give me."

"Oh, well, if you want one like that, you'll have to come and get it," he said, leaving the kitchen.

"Where are you going?" she asked, going after him.

"There are other things to unload from the wagon," he said, quickening his pace.

"Come back here."

Just as she reached him, he sped up again, forcing her to trot after him. He increased his speed yet again and the chase was on. Around and around the fire pit they went, sometimes her chasing him and sometimes him chasing her. They laughed and played until Roxie was out of breath and flopped down on one of the soft cushions on the floor. Wild Wind dropped down by her and took her in his arms, kissing her soundly.

As he broke the kiss, she said, "That's better. Now I really do have to go."

"Ok. We'll get the rest of the stuff unloaded and we'll go back to town. We can put it away later," he said.

Once this was accomplished, they went out to the wagon. Six big dogs of various breeds swarmed them. In Cheyenne, Wild Wind said, "Guard!" The dogs all instantly took on protective stances, one of them lying in front of the tipi entrance. Wild Wind had bought five of the dogs from a trapper passing through the area who was now light on hides after finding out that the man had often traded with the Cheyenne and had trained the animals using the language. The trapper had been happy to get rid of the dogs, using the money Wild Wind paid him to purchase a pack mule that could carry his possessions.

The dogs were an excellent deterrent of trespassers and would also alert them to visitors. Rafe was the sixth dog and he'd made it clear that he was in charge and that the others had better watch their step around him. He'd taken a liking to one of the female dogs, though, and Wild Wind had a hunch that they'd have a litter of pups before too long.

There hadn't been any more trouble for Wild Wind since the sheriff and his deputies had caught two more of those who'd attacked him and sent them to prison. Wild Wind knew that there were still people in town who didn't like him living there, but he felt confident that no one would attempt to do him any more harm. If they were foolhardy enough to try it, he'd be ready for them.

"I can't believe yer not nervous," Lucky said on Roxie and Wild Wind's wedding day.

Wild Wind said, "I don't see any reason to be. I love Roxie and want to be married to her. Why would I be nervous? I've never understood why white men get so nervous about it. Is there something to fear?"

Billy lay on the floor of the spare bedroom in the tipi that would be used as a nursery when the time came. "No, well, not exactly fear, but there's always the chance you'll end up hating each other or that something will go wrong."

Wild Wind grunted. "Yes, that sometimes happens, but it won't with Roxie and me. We know each other very well now and we know how to compromise. Besides, even unexpected marriages can work out," he said, kicking Billy's moccasin-clad foot. "Right?"

Billy grinned and sat up. "Touché. I couldn't be happier. I guess the Great Spirit knew what he was doing when he brought Nina and me together."

"Aye, He did."

Billy looked at Lucky's hair. "I can't believe you let your hair grow."

Lucky's wheat-blond hair was now a little past his shoulders. He smiled. "It's not as long as it was at one time, but it's on its way."

"You look like a Viking with it that long, not an Indian," Billy said.

Wild Wind laughed. "A Viking in Cheyenne clothing."

"No worse than a Cheyenne brave in a white man's suit, which ye've been known to wear," Lucky said.

"Never again," Wild Wind said, adjusting his bone breast plate over his ceremonial shirt. "I mean no offense, but I'm going to stay much more true to myself. I've made some compromises for Roxie's sake, but that's it."

Billy said, "It's hard being a part of two different cultures, but I think you're doing well at it."

"Thanks."

Someone scratched on the hide wall.

"Come," Wild Wind said.

The hide was pulled back and Nina entered the room carrying Tommy. "You all look very handsome," she said in Cheyenne. "Your bride will be very pleased with her groom, Wild Wind."

He smiled as Billy took his son from her. The little fellow with his mother's green eyes looked at all of the men and smiled. "Hi," he said.

Lucky smiled. "If he were Lakota, he'd say something fairly close to that in greeting."

"Don't tell me you know another language," Billy said. "If you do that means you're up to eight."

Wild Wind gave him a doubtful look. "Eight? How do you figure?"

LYNDA BRIDEY

Billy said, "He knows American English, Irish, which we call Gaelic, Irish English, Cheyenne, Chinese, Indian sign, and American Sign Language. Lakota would make eight."

"I know it, but I'm not fluent. I can get by pretty well, though," Lucky said.

"Eight it is," Billy said. "So how do they say hello?"

"*Hau.*"

"Yeah, that's what I asked. How?"

Lucky smiled. "No, it sounds like 'how', but it's spelled differently. H-a-u. *Hau.* Only the men say that though. The women say *han.* I'll teach ya more sometime."

Wild Wind said, "Nina and I know it, too, since the Cheyenne are allies with the Lakota and some bands are intermarried with each other. We trade a lot with the Lakota, too."

"Showoffs," Billy complained.

Tommy squirmed to get down and Billy set him on his little feet. He ran to the hide flap and peeked out of it, letting out a squeal. There were a couple of yells sent back in response from a few of the children and the sounds reverberated in the tipi.

Nina laughed and then pulled Tommy away from flap. He giggled and let out another squeal. All of them covered their ears and Billy scolded Tommy.

"You have to be quiet, mostly because I don't want my ears to bleed, buddy. I swear you and Mia are competing for who can be the loudest." When he looked over at Lucky and Wild Wind, he was startled to see them scowling at him. "Hey, that coddling thing might be how you raise kids, but I was raised by white people and I turned out just fine."

Nina laughed and Billy glared at her. "This from the woman who scolded him for feeding Sugar all her pancakes while her back was turned."

Now Wild Wind and Lucky turned their disapproving frowns on Nina. She picked up Tommy, gave Billy a hard stare, and left the room.

Lucky and Wild Wind laughed.

"Looks like someone is in the dog house," Lucky said.

184

Wild Wind said, "Let that be a lesson to you: never tell on your wife. It will cause more harm than good."

Billy said, "I hate you guys."

———⌒———

Smoothing down the white buckskin dress she wore, Roxie asked Nina, "Are you sure I look all right?" as she entered the bedroom her and her groom would soon share.

Nina nodded. "You look beautiful. I can't wait to see Wild Wind's face. He's still expecting you to be wearing a dress from your culture."

Roxie had asked Nina to be her maid of honor since Callie couldn't and she'd asked Erin to be her bridesmaid. Nina had helped her make a Cheyenne wedding dress and one for Erin, too. Her golden blonde hair had been done up in two braids and she wore silver-and-turquoise earrings that matched the design on her dress.

She wasn't used to wearing so little clothing and felt naked without her petticoats even though her dress reached mid-calf. Erin, who often wore pants, didn't mind it, however. She liked the feel of the soft buckskin garment.

Erin said, "Win has no idea that I'm wearing a Cheyenne dress, either. It should be fun seeing his reaction."

"I made Billy swear not to tell anyone about the dresses and he kept his mouth shut," Nina said.

"That's good or you'd be a widow soon," Roxie said, smiling.

Nina said, "Humph. That sounds good right about now."

Erin said, "Uh oh. What did he do now?"

"Told Yelling Bear and Wild Wind that I scolded Tommy for feeding Sugar my pancakes. You know how they are about that. So then they were upset with me," she said.

Erin and Roxie laughed.

"It's not funny," Nina insisted. "You have no idea what it's like when they gang up on you like that. You just wait, Roxie. They'll do it to you, too, when you have children."

Roxie stopped laughing. "That's how Wild Wind expects our children to be raised?"

"Of course, he does," Erin said. "He's Cheyenne after all."

"Well, I guess we're going to have to discuss that later on, but first we have to make some," Roxie said with a wicked little smile.

"Hello in there," Ross called from outside the hide flap.

Roxie said, "You're supposed to scratch. You should know that by now."

"I keep forgetting," he said. "Is it safe to come in?"

"Yes," Roxie replied.

His eyes rounded when he saw her. "What are you wearing?"

"Shh! Not so loud!" she said.

"You didn't tell me you were wearing a Cheyenne outfit," he said more quietly. "I should be wearing one, too."

Roxie said, "I didn't want you to because it would have given it away that I was wearing a Cheyenne wedding dress. I wanted to surprise Wild Wind."

"Well, you sure surprised me. You look beautiful though," he said, kissing her cheek. "They're ready out there, are you?"

"Yes," she said, suddenly more excited than nervous. "I'm ready to marry my brave."

Ross stuck his arm out of the room and waved. In a few moments, music began to play. Josie played her guitar while Arliss played fiddle. Porter's buddy, Henley Remington, who was a musical prodigy, played flute, which lent an ethereal quality to the Wedding March.

Otto had begged to be the ring bearer, and even though Wild Wind and Roxie had been going to pick him anyway, they'd told him he could only if he did his Cheyenne dance like he had at Keith and Molly's wedding. He'd immediately agreed. Now, properly attired in Cheyenne regalia, he performed his dance while the flower girl, Julie Taft, was guided along by her father since she was more interested in talking with the guests than following Otto.

However, Wild Wind let out a birdcall and her head whipped around.

He sent her the Indian sign for "come here" and she went running after Otto.

Evan mumbled, "I'm gonna have to start doing that with her, I guess."

Wild Wind hugged his niece and nephew before Evan guided them away to sit down. Then the brave and his two best friends stood at the altar area that had been set up and watched Erin exit the bedroom and walk down the aisle that separated the chairs arranged around the tipi. Wild Wind was surprised to see Erin's Cheyenne outfit and looked at Win. However, the veterinarian only had eyes for his wife as she walked to the altar.

Wild Wind sent a quizzical glance her way, but Erin just smiled enigmatically at him. Next came Nina, and Billy watched her with appreciation as she walked towards them. He smiled at her, but she ignored him, which amused Lucky and Wild Wind. Nina took her place by Erin and Wild Wind's attention returned to the bedroom area. While the flap was held back by Shadow, Ross came out the bedroom with Roxie on his arm.

Wild Wind felt a shockwave of surprise and desire when he saw Roxie in the dazzling white buckskin dress with the loose, long-fringed sleeves and matching moccasins. Long, golden braids hung down the front of it and her luminous blue eyes looked bigger to him. She was stunningly gorgeous and he was even prouder than before to be marrying such a beautiful woman.

Roxie had never seen Wild Wind in his ceremonial clothing and she thought he looked regal in the ornate bone breastplate and beautifully decorated leggings and breechcloth. His ceremonial shirt was decorated with dyed porcupine quills and beads that denoted his status as a warrior. His plaited hair was adorned with eagle feathers and red feather earrings hung from his earlobes.

More than ever, Roxie was glad that he'd gone back to wearing the clothing of his people. She'd never seen a handsomer man and it seemed to her that he exuded virility. His eyes never left hers as she came to stand before him and she saw his appreciation of her in them. As Ross gave her hand to Wild Wind, he and the brave exchanged a look before he moved away to sit with the Deckers.

As Andi performed a slightly altered version of a Christian service to include a Cheyenne prayer given by Lucky, Wild Wind held Roxie's hands tightly, saying his vows with the utmost seriousness. Roxie did the same, her love for him showing in her eyes. He had agreed to wear a wedding ring since he knew how important it was to Roxie and he was willing to do anything to please her.

As she slid it onto his finger, Wild Wind found that he liked seeing it there. It was a symbol of their undying love and it let the world know that he belonged to the wonderful woman before him. By the same token, he was proud to put yet another ring on her finger that proclaimed to all that she was his for all time.

He wasn't used to kissing women in public, but he'd seen his friends do it often enough that he felt fairly comfortable with it. Once Andi gave them permission, Wild Wind embraced his new wife and kissed her tenderly. Roxie's heart sang with joy and desire as they kissed. Parting, they smiled into each other's eyes before turning to the congregation so Andi could present them.

As the guests clapped and cheered for them, the couple beamed. Wild Wind wasn't fond of having his picture taken, but he endured it while Dan took some photographs of him and Roxie. Then the wedding guests followed the newlyweds outside to the wedding feast. The chairs were brought outside for seating under the shade of the maple trees that stood near the tipi.

The newlyweds stood waving goodbye to the last of their guests as the sun descended in the sky. The dogs came back to them after following the last wagon to the property line. The night became quiet and they went inside their new home. A low fire burned in the fire pit.

Roxie motioned to a cushion. "Sit down, husband. Would you like some tea?"

He sat and smiled up at her. "Yes."

She'd been taking Cheyenne cooking lessons from Nina and Lucky and she could cook several dishes now. She put stones in the fire to heat and went to the kitchen to get water. Coming back, she put it in a cooking container and then left him again, going into their bedroom. Wild Wind wondered what she was doing, but didn't say anything.

Returning, she knelt behind him and began undoing his braids. Carefully, she unwound his hair from around the eagle feathers in his hair and laid them to the side. She ran a comb through the silky, black locks, enjoying the way his hair felt against her fingers. Wild Wind was touched that she would honor him this way. He closed his eyes, relaxing as she worked.

When she'd finished, she put the hot stones in the cooking container so the tea could steep. When she would have gone to put the comb away, Wild Wind snagged her wrist, halting her.

"Your turn," he said.

She smiled and sat down in front of him. He performed the same affectionate gesture for her, relishing the softness of her sunny hair as he worked the comb through it, making sure not to pull it. Moving her hair to the side, he pressed a kiss to the nape of her neck. Roxie gasped and shivered. He did it again and she abruptly turned around, startling him by kissing him with a fiery passion that brought his own desire rapidly to a boil.

He wrapped his arms around her and pulled her onto his lap as they demanded and coaxed each other along. One of the quills from her dress jabbed his shoulder and he broke the kiss.

Easing her from his lap, he said, "Come with me, wife."

"But the tea," she said.

His smile was suggestive as they walked to the bedroom. "We can drink tea later."

Roxie's heart beat faster as he crouched and tapped each of her ankles so that she would lift them, allowing him to remove her moccasins. She exhaled rapidly when she felt his hand trace her calves and come slowly upwards over her thighs and hips, lifting her dress up over her that way.

The fire cast enough light into the bedroom for them to see by and Wild Wind was entranced by her beautiful body. His eyes barely left her as he neatly folded her dress and sat it on the hope chest. He brought her hands to his waist, urging her to do the same thing.

Encouraged by his patient smile, Roxie lifted his shirt, skimming her fingers over his warm, smooth skin. He helped her since he was so much taller than her, but she took the shirt from him, folding it and putting with her dress. Then he taught her how to untie his leggings and breechcloth.

Her hands trembled a little as she folded them and laid them on the hope chest. She used the task to steady her nerves, but when she was done, Wild Wind took her hands and brought them back to his chest. He saw her anxious expression.

"Roxie, I know you're scared, but I won't hurt you. I'm nervous, too."

"You are? Why? You've done this before."

"Yes, but not on a bed," he said, smiling. "I'm sure it will feel different than a sleeping pallet."

She giggled at the idea of him being nervous for that reason. He was glad to be able to relieve some of her tension and slid his arms around her, holding her close.

"You are so beautiful," he said in Cheyenne. "I want to make you mine in every way and I promise to bring you as much pleasure as you will bring me."

Roxie understood enough of his words to get the gist of what he was saying as he caressed her back. Then she looked at her pale hands pressed against his much darker chest and was fascinated by the contrast. Soon her hands moved over his bronzed skin and he captured her mouth in a heated kiss.

She responded to him, drawing confidence from the loving words he spoke to her and his reassurances that he found her beautiful and exciting. He lay down on the bed and motioned for her to join him. Lying beside him, she surrendered herself to the man she'd loved for so long, completely placing her trust in him.

Their embraces and kisses grew more urgent and soon desire replaced fear. It was a magical night for the two people as they became one in every sense of the word and shared in a joy that surpassed anything they'd ever known. The fire in the tipi died down as time passed, but the flames of their love and passion took much longer to fade.

Chapter Twenty-Three

At the last town council meeting of May, Adam waited until Jerry asked for new business to say, "I have some new business to discuss. I know someone who'd be perfect for the permanent teacher's position."

"Who's that, son?" Spike asked.

Sitting straighter, Adam said, "Me."

Jerry said, "We're all grateful to you for filling in for the rest of the year, Adam, but I think we need—"

"Me," Adam interjected. "I know there are teachers out there who have more experience than me, but I have more to offer than that. All I ask is that you hear me out."

"Ok, go ahead," Jerry said.

Molly had printed copies of a report that Adam had created and he handed them out to the rest of the council members.

"I've listed the grades of each student at the time of Hank's passing, although I've only labeled each of them with a letter to preserve their privacy. As of the end of last week, these are the scores they'll end up with for the year.

"As you can see, most of their scores have improved. I had Pastor Andi sit in on a few classes so she could see my teaching methods and she also verified these scores for me as well."

Marvin said, "These improvements are quite impressive, Adam."

"Thank you. Hank was a good teacher, but over the last year, I noticed that he'd gotten a little complacent. Our kids deserve better than that and I've improved the curriculum. This is the first time I've taught professionally, but I've been helping Hank for a long time, so I'm somewhat experienced.

"I also have the heart and determination to help educate our children in a way that will help them prepare for college, and even for those who don't, they'll have skills and knowledge that will help them in their everyday lives. These kids know me and trust me. After what happened with Hank, I think that's one of the biggest benefits of me teaching them. If you hire me permanently, I promise to work like a dog to make sure Echo's kids have the best education possible." Finished, Adam sat back in his chair to await their decision.

"Andi, since you've observed Adam, what do you think?" Jerry asked.

Andi said, "Adam encouraged all of the children and never made them feel inferior if they had trouble learning something. He gave them a lot of personal attention and rewarded them when they worked hard and improved. He also goes outside at recess and plays with them, which I thought was very nice. He doesn't make them call him Mr. Harris and it seems to make them feel comfortable with him.

"I saw him share his lunch with a child who had forgotten their lunch, which shows his kindness towards them. He makes up little games that the kids enjoy and that help them learn. In my opinion, Adam is an excellent teacher and he gets my vote."

Marvin said, "I, too, had the opportunity to observe Adam, and I agree with Andi's assessment of his performance and abilities. Ronni and I are confident that our children will receive an excellent education should Adam be the teacher when they begin attending school. I also vote yes to Adam being our new teacher."

Spike said, "That's good enough for me. I vote yes."

Edna said, "How about we put it to an official vote, folks? All in favor of hiring Adam as Echo Canyon's permanent teacher, say aye."

Everyone said "aye" and there were no opposing votes.

"Congratulations, Adam. You're our permanent teacher," Jerry said.

Adam grinned. "I can't thank you enough. I won't let you down. Feel free to stop by the school at any time to see what we're doing."

Edna said, "We have complete confidence in you. I only hope you'll be able to handle Julia when she starts school."

The council members chuckled at her remark.

When the meeting ended, Adam left the town hall with elation coursing through him. He couldn't stop smiling as he rode home. Charlene was thrilled with his good news.

She hugged him, saying, "I'm so proud of you. I knew you could do it. You did such a good job with those kids. You deserve the job."

"Thanks, Ma. Now that I have a steady job, I can propose to Allie." His heart swelled with love for his girl. "I just hope she says yes."

Charlene said, "Of course she will. She loves you and she knows what a good man you are. I just can't believe you're old enough to get married. Just yesterday you were a little boy and now look at you—all grown up and a teacher!"

Adam laughed. "That's what happens with kids: they grow up."

"So how are you going to propose to Allie?"

A gleam entered his brown eyes. "Don't worry. I have that all planned out. I'll let you know how it goes."

The next evening, Adam came to the McIntyre household to pick up Allie to take her to dinner. Although he was anxious inside, he did a good job of hiding it. He went into the Everything Room to wait for her to come downstairs.

"Well there's our new teacher," Jessie said.

She sat in her usual chair with her feet up on the ottoman. Thad sat in a chair close to her, holding T.J. in the crook of his arm while he read the

Express. He hadn't had a chance in the morning, so he was catching up on all the news.

Adam wore a pleased smile. "I still sort of can't believe it."

Thad said, "I can. You worked your ass off, just like you said you would. We're proud of you, son."

"Thanks," he said. "Can I hold T.J.?"

"Sure," Thad said, handing over the baby.

Having a baby was such a great joy that Thad found himself wishing that he would have had one earlier in life, but only if it had been with Jessie. He'd teased her about having another one and she'd just glared at him, which had made him laugh.

Adam looked into the baby's face. "I don't know who he looks more like. He has your brown eyes, Thad, but I think he has Jessie's nose."

Jessie said, "It's going to be interesting to see who he looks more like, but I wish he would stay little like that."

Thad got a mischievous smile on his face and Jessie said, "No. I'm not having any more babies."

"I didn't say anything," Thad said.

"You didn't have to," she said.

He raised his hands in surrender as Allie came into the room. Adam thought she was the prettiest girl in the world in her pale blue muslin dress.

"Hi. You look beautiful," he said.

"Thank you," she said, as he quickly kissed her cheek.

"All set?" he asked.

"Yes." Allie kissed her little brother before Adam handed him back to Thad.

Adam bid Thad and Jessie goodnight and he and Allie left.

When Adam had picked her up, Allie assumed that they were going to the diner, but he took her to a secluded place down by the river where they liked to go and talk while watching the water and listening to the wildlife around them. Adam helped her down from the buggy and they walked hand-in-hand through the short trail that opened up to the water's edge.

Allie saw a garden table and two chairs sitting there and looked at Adam.

He grinned. "I wanted to do something special for you."

"You are so sweet. That's one of the reasons I love you so much. You're so thoughtful and always surprising me with things like this," Allie said. "You're going to spoil me."

"Nah. Nothing's too good for my lady," Adam said. "Come on while the food is hot."

Going to the table, he lit the two tall candles on it. Then he helped seat her. Three silver-covered serving trays sat on the table and a wonderful aroma floated on the slight breeze.

Adam lifted one of the covers, revealing two very nice salads. He placed one in front of each of them.

"I can't believe you did all this," Allie said, picking up her fork.

"I had some help, so I can't take all the credit."

"It's still wonderful. I've never eaten outside like this," she said.

"Really? I've been to a place over in Dickensville that has outdoor dining during the summer. We'll go sometime," he said.

They talked about his new job and her current one as they worked their way through their salad and Italian wedding soup. Then with a flourish, Adam uncovered the main course: lasagna, which was one of Allie's favorite dishes.

"Oh! How did you know I've been so hungry for this?" she asked.

"I didn't, but I know how much you like it," Adam said, serving the delectable food. "Sylvia Terranova was kind enough to make it for me, so you know it's going to be delicious."

Since Adam was so well-liked in Echo, he was friendly with most of the families, including the Terranovas, whose ranch and wealth rivaled the Earnests'. Sylvia and Alfredo Terranova were the heads of the family of six. Their three boys and one girl all helped on their ranch and would inherit it one day.

Sylvia especially liked Adam and she always complied with any request he made of her, much like an aunt might. She was an outspoken, beautiful woman who most definitely ruled the roost when it came to anything domestic. Alfredo knew better than to cross his wife concerning anything in that department.

Through Adam, Allie had also become friendly with the large family and they'd had dinner with them a couple of times, so she knew that Sylvia was a superb cook. Her oldest son, Nick, and she often cooked together, arguing over food preparation and what ingredients worked best.

Taking her first forkful, Allie made an appreciative sound. "There's nothing like Mama T's lasagna," she said, using the nickname that many people in Echo called Sylvia.

Adam agreed. "I don't know what all she puts in it, but I could eat a whole pan of it myself. Keith almost does when he goes over there."

"It's no wonder. He needs more to eat since he's so big." Allie chuckled. "It's so funny to hear him and Molly argue, but you can see that they love each other very much. I had my doubts since Molly is so young, but so far, so good."

Adam said, "Keith fell hard and fast, but he's genuinely in love with Molly. It's too bad about their baby, though."

Allie said, "I know. They were so excited about it. But, they're young and they'll have a baby before too long."

Adam nodded, thinking about the children he wanted to have with Allie.

When their lasagna was finished, Adam unveiled tiramisu, and Allie was surprised again. Even though she was getting full, she attacked the decadent dessert, relishing the sweetness of it. Adam liked watching her eat, knowing that she was enjoying the dinner. He was relieved with how wonderful it was turning out to be.

Once dessert was over, Adam placed a small silver tray before Allie.

"Adam, I can't eat anymore. I'm stuffed as it is," she said.

"Oh, c'mon. It's just one more little thing," he said.

Allie gave him a slightly annoyed look and lifted the lid. A sparkling diamond ring lay in an open ring box. Allie thought she was seeing things and put the lid back down as she stared at Adam with wide eyes. He smiled at her amazed expression.

She raised the lid again and set it to the side. Adam came over, took the ring box, and knelt in front of her.

"I knew the very first time I saw you that I wanted to marry you, and that feeling has only gotten stronger since then. One look in those gorgeous blue eyes of yours was all it took for me to fall in love with you. I never thought I'd meet anyone like you—someone so beautiful, strong, intelligent, and caring. You make me so happy and I want to share my life with you. Allison Leanne Alderman, will you do me the incredible honor of marrying me and becoming my wife?"

Holding back tears, Allie took his handsome face in her hands and said, "I would be honored to be your wife. Yes, I'll marry you."

Smiling, Adam kissed her right palm and then took her left hand as he removed the ring from the box and slipped it onto her ring finger. Allie loved the way it shimmered in the candlelight, but what made it beautiful was the love that had gone into its choosing.

"It's lovely, Adam. I'll cherish it," she said.

Adam was the happiest he'd ever been and he kissed Allie with a passion he'd been holding back until then. He rose to his feet, pulled her with him, and embraced her tightly, savoring the lingering sweetness of dessert on her lips. He was spurred on by the way she wrapped her arms around his neck and kissed him back.

Holding and kissing her like that was the most exciting thing Adam had ever felt and he could have stood there all night, doing nothing more than kissing her. Allie loved how safe she felt in his strong arms and she became very warm as he kissed her possessively. He'd always held back before and she'd wondered from time to time if he found her desirable.

Judging by the way his hands moved over her back and his demanding kisses, he certainly did. He made her feel dizzy and she clung to his shoulders. Adam had never felt such intense desire for a girl and he wanted her fiercely. However, he brought his urges under control and slowed down, ending the embrace with one last soft kiss.

Both of them were breathing heavily by this point and Adam was relieved that his asthma hadn't kicked in.

"Well," Allie said, still a little dazed. "I hope that happens more often."

Adam laughed. "You do?"

"Yes. Don't you?"

"Well, yeah, but I've been afraid to until now."

"Why on Earth would you be afraid?" Allie asked.

"This is so embarrassing."

"Adam, there is nothing you can't tell me," she said.

"You know how sometimes when I get angry or excited about something it aggravates my asthma?"

She nodded.

"I've been afraid that I'd have an attack while we were kissing or, after we're married, making love. Is my face as red as it feels?" he asked.

Allie smiled at how sweet he was. "Well, so far so good and we'll deal with whatever comes."

"I hate it. You realize that probably within the next several days I'm gonna get sick, right?"

His jaw clenched and she wanted to alleviate his frustration. "Maybe you won't. It's later in the season and you're still all right. Or maybe it won't be so bad."

Holding her close, he said, "I hope you're right. I just want to stay right here with you forever."

"I would love that, but I should go home since I have work in the morning."

"Damn work," Adam said, making her laugh. "Yeah, I have to finish up at school, too."

"Let's get everything cleaned up and go tell my family," she said. "Let's stop by your house and tell your mother, though, since it's on the way."

Adam grinned. "Fine by me."

Working together, they soon had all of the dinner things stowed in the buggy and Adam would come back the next day for the table and chairs. As they drove off into the night, the young couple began making their wedding plans, knowing that in each other, they'd found their perfect mate.

Chapter Twenty-Four

Putting her arms around Wild Wind where he knelt as he milked a goat, Roxie bit his earlobe, giggling when he jerked in reaction.

"Let's go make a baby when you're done," she whispered against his ear, making gooseflesh break out over his bare shoulders and back.

It never failed to amaze Wild Wind how playful Roxie was now about lovemaking. There was also no resisting her whenever she bit or played with his ears and she knew it. Her nimble hands moving over his back only made it worse and he couldn't concentrate on what he was doing.

He stood and turned around so fast that he almost knocked her over. He quickly caught her, however, giving her a hard kiss. Then he said, "Hayloft. Now. Be naked when I get there. I just have to put this milk in the container."

Roxie loved it when he was forceful with her and she scampered away to the hayloft ladder while Wild Wind grinned. The past month with Roxie had been a time of great happiness for the both of them. Living together was a joyous, fun experience and he'd been pleased to discover that Roxie was even more skilled at running a household than he'd thought.

She was particular about where things went and was able to efficiently prepare a meal. Much like a Cheyenne woman, when he'd offered to help her clean, she'd nicely refused his offer, saying that she didn't want to have to redo it after he was done. He'd smiled to himself over her answer, but had pretended to be offended. She'd soothed his "hurt" feelings by making him a strawberry pie, which she fed to him in bed.

When he'd asked her where she'd gotten that idea, she'd given him a coy look and said, "Women do talk, you know."

He'd grinned and said, "May the Great Spirit bless whoever you talked to."

They also enjoyed it when their friends came to visit, which was often. Roxie liked showing Lucky that she was now very good at Cheyenne cooking and they'd started a competition to see who could make the best venison stew. Lucky had been at it longer and had the advantage over her, but she was determined to best him one day.

The kids liked playing hide and seek in the huge tipi because they could conceal themselves behind the large hide tapestries and in the spare room. Win was a talented ghost story teller and he liked scaring them with gruesome stories of the macabre as m they sat around the large fire.

Roxie couldn't wait until Christmas because they would be able to put up a huge Christmas tree. Edna had been delighted by that idea. "I can't wait to see a Christmas tree inside an Indian tipi. Make sure you take pictures," she'd said.

Finished stowing the milk, Wild Wind exited the storeroom and froze at the sight of a Cheyenne brave standing not far away. Wild Wind's hand automatically went for his knife, even though the man was from the same tribe as him. Looking closer, Wild Wind was further shocked when he recognized the brave.

"Arrow?" he asked in Cheyenne.

The brave smiled. "It is good to finally see you again, my brother."

Wild Wind let out a laugh and embraced his little brother. "Likewise. I can't believe you're here."

"Wild Wind? Where are you?"

Stepping away from his brother, Wild Wind shouted, "Roxie, put your clothes back on. We have company!"

Arrow's understanding of English was limited since he hadn't been all that good friends with Lucky when he'd been with their tribe. He was considerably younger than Wild Wind, having come to their parents later in life. He wondered who his brother was talking to.

Roxie hurried back into her dress and brushed hay from her hair and clothes before standing up and descending the ladder. Wild Wind helped her down and Roxie squeaked in surprise when she saw a strange Indian standing near them. She was used to Wild Wind, but he had a much more civilized air about him.

This brave, who stood before them in nothing more than a breechcloth, was fierce for all that he was young. He was a little taller than Wild Wind and had slightly sharper facial features, but she could still see the resemblance between them.

"Husband, who is this?" she asked in Cheyenne. Her pronunciations still needed work, but she was learning.

Arrow arched an eyebrow over this white woman knowing how to speak his language, even though it wasn't perfect.

"This is my younger brother, Arrow. Arrow, this is my wife, Roxie," Wild Wind said.

She smiled at him. "It good to meet you, Arrow. Wild Wind told many good things about you."

He looked at her outstretched hand with confusion. Normally men and women didn't grasp arms, but although he questioned his brother's choice in a wife, he didn't want to be rude and anger his brother.

Stepping forward, he grasped her arm, which was very small in his large hand. Roxie had been expecting him to shake hands the way white people did, but then realized that was stupid. Of course he'd shake hands the Cheyenne way. She grasped his forearm, still smiling at him. They released each other and he stepped back again.

"Come into our home and we will eat," Wild Wind said. "You have come a long way and I am sure you would like to rest. Then you can tell us why you are here."

As he followed them to the tipi, Arrow tried to figure out why his brother had a barn and why he was living in a very strange-looking tipi. He also wondered how it was that Wild Wind had come to marry a white woman. He noticed the way they held hands as they walked side by side. To his way of thinking, she should be walking behind her husband so he could protect her. Of course, it didn't seem as though there was much to be afraid of at the moment.

He knew what sheep were, but he didn't know why his brother was tending them like a white man would. As they stepped inside the tipi, his eyes roamed over the beautifully painted panels, the amazing design of the floor mats, and the large central fire. His brother must be very rich to live in such a fine lodge.

Then he saw Roxie go through a doorway into a room he recognized as a kitchen. He'd seen such rooms in the buildings on the reservation, but he'd never gone into one. He avoided the army and the reservation officials if at all possible. In fact, he avoided white people altogether.

He was surprised when she came back and started to steep tea using the Cheyenne method. She also swung a large pot over the fire. Going closer, he saw some sort of stew in it and gave Wild Wind a quizzical look. His big brother smiled at him.

In Indian sign, Wild Wind said, "She is beautiful and knows how to cook. She is a good wife."

Arrow sent back, "Why do you want to be married to a white woman whom you have to coddle? Why does she want to play at being a Cheyenne wife?"

Highly offended, Wild Wind frowned at him. "You know nothing about my life here, so I will remind you to hear what I have to say before you judge me, little brother. This is my home and you will not disrespect me or my wife."

Arrow sighed before signing, "Very well."

Wild Wind nodded and smiled again. "Roxie makes very good stew." He still spoke in Cheyenne.

Roxie smiled a little, nervous because she sensed that Arrow was less than approving of her. However, since she knew he must be confused about the way Wild Wind was living, she let it go.

"Please, sit, make yourself comfortable," she said, sitting down on a cushion.

The men joined her and Wild Wind had Arrow tell them his story. Their father had taken ill and wanted Wild Wind to come home to fulfill his duties. So Arrow had sneaked away from the reservation to find his brother and bring him back home. He'd remembered the name of the place Wild Wind had told him and had remembered that it was in Montana. He'd left right away and had finally arrived in Echo that morning.

Although he didn't know English, he'd asked for Wild Wind and had been lucky enough to run into Billy, who spoke Cheyenne. He'd directed Arrow to Wild Wind's farm.

"That is how I came to be here," Arrow said, finishing his stew. He had to admit that it was tasty. "This stew is very good," he said. "*Néá'eše.*" This meant "thank you."

Roxie smiled and nodded but remained quiet.

"Father wishes you to return home and become chief when he dies," Arrow said.

Roxie picked on the gist of what he was saying. In English, she asked, "Did he just say that you're supposed to be chief?"

Wild Wind grunted. "Yes. Our father is the chief of our tribe. He was elected shortly before I left."

"Why didn't you tell me that you're the son of a chief?" she asked.

"It isn't important anymore," he said. "I don't want to be chief. I don't want to live on the reservation."

Arrow said, "I take it that you did not tell your wife that you are supposed to be chief."

He shook his head, switching back to Cheyenne. "No. Go back and tell Father that he should choose someone else as chief. I do not want to be chief. My life is here now."

"You are duty bound, Wild Wind. You should not have run away in the first place. Your cowardly act caused us to lose face and they almost removed Father as chief. You broke his heart and our mother's! She now walks the next life."

Wild Wind inhaled swiftly at this news and pain filled his breast over his mother's death.

"Why did you leave?" Arrow asked, forcing his grief away.

"I was dying on that reservation and you know it!" Wild Wind said. "My spirit and my heart were withering inside my chest. If I had stayed, I would be dead by now."

"Do you think you are the only one who felt—who feels—that way? You are selfish and I would not have come if it were not that Father asked me to bring you home," Arrow said.

"If that is the case, you go back and become chief! I want no part of it. I tried to convince you to come with me and Yelling Bear. I tried to convince our parents, too, but they would not. It is not my fault if they did not come!"

"So you ran away like a cowardly dog to come here with a white man who is no relation to you and live like a white man and marry a white woman?" Arrow asked, with a look of disdain at Wild Wind and then at Roxie.

She understood some of what was being said and the way Arrow had glanced at her affirmed her suspicions that he did not approve of her. She didn't have to sit there and take that. Proudly, she rose and turned her back on the men, taking their dishes into the kitchen.

Wild Wind wanted to punch his brother. "You will apologize to her. She has done nothing to you. We only married a month ago, so she had nothing to do with me coming here and does not deserve your anger. She is a good, loving woman and I have many good friends here. You would like them if you would get to know them."

"Perhaps she is a good woman, but she will prevent you from coming home. They will not let her onto the reservation since she is white."

"I know that. That is another reason I am not going back. I will not leave my wife. I am deeply grieved over Mother and upset that Father is not well, but he must realize that coming back is impossible for me," Wild Wind said. "It would never work, even if I did not have Roxie."

Seeing that his brother wasn't going to budge on the issue, Arrow sighed. "You should at least go back to tell him this yourself."

Wild Wind shook his head. "No. It is too dangerous to travel; the chances of the military capturing us and putting us on a reservation with an enemy tribe is too great. You should not go back now, either."

"Perhaps you are afraid, but I am not," Arrow said. "I will fight to the death to stay free and if it is my time to walk the spirit world, then so be it. I will die with my conscience clear."

"It is not myself I worry about, Arrow. Even now, my seed may have taken hold in Roxie's womb and I will not leave my wife and child," Wild Wind. "You have a choice; stay here and live a life of much freedom or go back empty handed, possibly dying along the way. Father may be gone by the time you get back anyway. My choice is made and I will not speak of it again. I have spoken."

Arrow made a frustrated noise, rose and walked from the tipi. Wild Wind looked after him for a moment and then went to comfort his wife.

Chapter Twenty-Five

Over the next week, Arrow only went to his brother's lodge whenever no one was around. Lucky had been happy to see him, but after being rebuffed a couple of times by Arrow, he didn't bother the young brave again, which was strange considering that Lucky usually had the patience of Job with people. Billy kept trying to bring Arrow around, though.

Arrow couldn't figure out why he kept coming to his tiny camp.

"What are you getting out of this?" he asked Billy. "You are not even really Cheyenne."

Unoffended, Billy smiled. "I hear that a lot. You have an opportunity here that you may not get again, but you seem to be too stupid to realize it."

"What do you mean? And do not call me stupid if you wish to live."

Billy said, "You do not scare me. Wild Wind and I have shown the people of Echo that we are not just dumb Indians who cannot be taught or learn new ways. I was born to this life, but people have still always thought of me as an Indian. Wild Wind learned to speak English almost perfectly, understands our customs, and has made friends here. And he found a wife. You could do the same if you chose to or were smart enough. Maybe that is the problem. You lack the intelligence needed." His smile took the sting out his words.

"Why would I want to? I am Cheyenne."

Billy sobered. "Because whether or not you like it, the white men are in charge and you can either adapt or die—if not physically, then in your heart. You do not seem like a very happy man. Why is that? Because you cannot hunt as you wish? Because you do not have enough to eat or clean living conditions? You could have all of that here."

Arrow pounded the ground with a fist. "And leave my family, my tribe, there to rot all alone?"

"The best thing you can do for your people is to show the white man that you are not an ignorant savage who is incapable of adapting, but that you are a proud intelligent man who knows his mind and becomes a representative for his people. That is how you can best serve your family and tribe. The question is whether you are willing to accept that or not. Believe me, I had the same issue at one time, and, thanks to Yelling Bear, I rose to the challenge and I now have the life I've always wanted. Again, the choice is yours."

As Arrow lay down to sleep that night, he thought about all Billy had said to him.

Roxie was a nervous wreck whenever Arrow was around and often retreated to their bedroom while he visited with Wild Wind. She knew that Arrow was still trying to convince Wild Wind to go back with him, which grated on her nerves. Somehow, she'd been able to hold her tongue. However, it was getting to her.

When he came to bed that night, he could tell how upset she was because she barely spoke to him. She blew out the lantern and rolled away from him, which was another sign; usually she slept curled around him.

"Roxie, I'm sorry about all this."

"I know he's your brother and you love him, but why can't he just accept your answer and either go away or make a life here?"

"It's not so simple. He's trying to honor our father and he takes that very seriously, as do I, but I won't be a good chief. Maybe at one time I would've been, but not anymore. My heart isn't in it and that would be very bad for the people. My life is here," he said.

"Are you sure? I don't want to stand in your way from doing your duty," she said.

Putting an arm around her, he turned her to face him. "I'm positive. You're my wife and I want to be with you. You wouldn't be allowed on the reservation even if I did want to go back."

"I don't want you to regret not going back," she said.

"I won't."

Reassured, she let him hold her while they slept.

Roxie was fixing breakfast a few days later when Arrow silently appeared, scaring her.

"I am sorry, sister," he said, smiling. "I did not mean to frighten you. I came to thank you."

"For what?"

"For telling my brother that it is all right to go back to the reservation to see our father one last time," he said. "It is very generous of you."

Roxie couldn't breathe for a moment. "I said no such thing."

He gave her a puzzled look. "Why would he say you did then?"

"Wild Wind would not play games like that. I think you are lying. I do not want him to go. I know your father is sick and I am very sorry for that, but he is my husband—"

"Why are you keeping him from seeing our father one last time before he dies? *Your* father is not well. What if your mother called you to his side because he was dying? Would you go?"

With a start, she realized that Arrow was right. If her mother sent for her and Ross, she would go to their father. She was being selfish in denying Wild Wind the same opportunity.

"Yes, I would," she said.

"So only white people can travel to see their dying loved ones? Would Wild Wind be welcomed in your father's big camp? Would your parents approve? Do they even know that you have married a Cheyenne brave?" Arrow asked.

"Yes, they know, and they were concerned at first, but they have accepted it now."

"But they really do not like it, do they?" he asked.

She couldn't deny that. "No."

"So you would not take my brother with you then."

"Yes, I would, and they would see what a good man he is, Cheyenne or not. I would go to the reservation, but I am not allowed there," she said.

"I doubt you would. Either way, you are keeping him from seeing our father, but then that is what white people are: selfish and greedy." He gave her an insolent glare and left the tipi.

Roxie pulled out a chair and sat down. The encounter had left her shaking. As much as she didn't like it, Arrow had a valid point. She was keeping Wild Wind from his dying father.

When Wild Wind came in that evening, Roxie went out and put out cross sticks so they weren't disturbed. When she came back in, she said, "You should go with Arrow to see your father before he dies. If my father were dying, I would go see him, so you should go see yours. It's unfair of me to try to keep you from him."

"No, I'm not going. It's my decision and I don't want to go. It's too dangerous. I may not come back because I could die or someone would tell the military that I had escaped and come back. They would punish me. Kill me."

Roxie said, "You're a very smart man. You could slip in, see your father, and get out again before anyone was the wiser. It's not right for me to interfere with you seeing your father. I won't be responsible for you not seeing him one last time."

"You're not," his black eyes never wavered from hers. "I won't go."

"If I wasn't in the picture, would you go?"

He pursed his lips and didn't answer her.

"See? I *am* holding you back! Go see your father or I'll always feel guilty," Roxie said.

"No! You aren't holding me back. You *are* in my life. I love you and I won't leave you!"

Roxie was furious. "Either you go or I'll divorce you because I can't live with that kind of guilt. If we're divorced and you don't go, it's not on my head. Make up your mind!"

He recoiled, her words like physical blows to his heart. "You said you would never divorce me."

"That was before all of this came up. I wish he hadn't come here, but he did and now you have a choice. Go see your father or we're divorced," she said.

He saw her conviction in her eyes. Even as his heart shriveled in his chest, he went to their bedroom, averting his eyes from the bed where they'd made love so often as he packed a few things in his buckskin bag. Exiting their bedroom, he walked past Roxie without looking at her and left the tipi.

Arrow saw him leaving and trotted from his camp over to his brother. "Where are you going? I will go with you."

Without warning, Wild Wind, whirled and slammed a fist into his brother's face, knocking Arrow backwards. "I do not want you to go with me. Do not bother me any longer. Because of you, my wife has divorced me."

"Divorced you?" Arrow said, bending over so the blood from his nose dripped onto the ground instead of onto his clothing. "Why?"

"Because she said that I should go see Father since she felt like she was holding me back, and that if I did not, she would divorce me," Wild Wind said.

Arrow hadn't expected this sort of outcome. As much as he didn't understand his brother's marriage to a white woman, he had come to realize how much his brother loved Roxie and hadn't wished to cause them to break up.

"Why do you not just come with me and then she will take you back? It sounds like she is just looking out for you," Arrow said.

Wild Wind wanted to hit Arrow again. "Because it is a fool's mission to go and I may be many things, but I am not foolish. I am not going no matter what you say or what she says! I do not understand why no one can respect my decision! It is mine to make! Not yours and not hers. Now leave me alone and do not follow me."

So saying, he stomped off into the night.

The next morning, Arrow was startled when someone hauled him up off his sleeping robes and he found himself staring into the face of a very angry Irishman.

Lucky's gray eyes were alight with fury and his strong jaw was clenched. "I do not know what you did to cause this divorce, but you will fix it. I do not know what happened because Wild Wind will not tell me, but I know you are responsible. Ever since you came here, you have tried to drive a wedge between your brother and all of his loved ones. You have done your duty to your father. Unless you are going to kidnap your brother, he will not go with you and you need to accept that.

"But before you go, you will fix this terrible thing you have done and you will watch over your sister-in-law since you drove her husband away because you could not let well enough alone. If you do not, I will hunt you down and kill you myself. I am capable of that and much more. If you do not believe me, ask my brother. *Our* brother."

Arrow shoved Lucky away from him. "You have no authority over me. I am not some sniveling coward who shrinks from the big, white Yelling Bear."

Lucky's smile was cold and malevolent—a far cry from the warm, winsome ones he was known for. "You are not smart enough to be afraid, but you will not do these things out of fear. You will do them out of honor. Do you think your father, the chief, would be proud of your actions here? Do you think he would be proud of how you schemed and tore a wonderful marriage apart? Do you forget that I know Spotted Frog well? You were only a youth when I was with your tribe, but I spent much time with him and fought beside him. I know that he would not have wanted to you to do this. You should be ashamed of yourself; I know he would be." So saying, Lucky took his leave.

Chapter Twenty-Six

After encountering Wild Wind that day when he was coming to milk the goats and do some other work, Roxie took to either leaving for town very early in the mornings or waiting until she knew he'd be gone before going. Both of them had stared at each other for a moment before going their separate ways.

She hadn't expected Wild Wind to really leave. She'd thought that he'd just go see his father and come back. It had been a bluff on her part that had horribly backfired. Wild Wind had taken her at her word, however, and now she was utterly miserable. She heard the same thing about Wild Wind, but she didn't know how to reconcile with him.

Legally they were still married, but by Cheyenne standards, they weren't. Would he even take her back? She didn't know, but what she did know was that her heart longed for her husband. The beautiful home he'd built for them now felt empty and ugly because they were no longer sharing it. Some days, she had to force herself out of bed even though she couldn't sleep. Roxie was depressed and withdrawn when she was helping Ross in the shop.

Callie was still recovering from the birth of their son, John, so Roxie was filling in for her. Ross had tried to talk to both parties, but he hadn't gotten anywhere with them. It was the same for anyone else who attempted to discuss it with them.

Much to his aggravation, Arrow had seen the wisdom in Lucky's words and he knew that in his zeal to convince Wild Wind to come with him, he'd acted rashly and without honor. He looked into his heart and saw that his motives had also been selfish. His mother was gone, his father might already be, and his only brother lived halfway across the country. His choices for a wife were limited and some of his friends had died from disease or at the army's hands when they'd opposed them about something. He had thought that at least if he had Wild Wind, he wouldn't be so lonely.

Roxie didn't know it, but he'd taken to sleeping in the space in between the door and tipi flap, guarding her at night. A woman living alone was vulnerable and even though Roxie was a white woman, he felt that she deserved some protection. Since he'd helped run off her protection, he decided that Lucky was right; he should make sure she was safe.

One night, he looked at the rabbit he'd killed that was roasting over a spit and then thought about the stew Roxie made. He would much rather have had some of that. He saw that there was firelight in the tipi. Why would she feed him when he'd been so mean to her? He shouldn't even think about going in there. She'd probably throw him out anyway.

Then an idea occurred to him. If he could become friends with her, maybe he could convince her that she should talk to Wild Wind about coming back home. And if he could get back into Wild Wind's good graces, maybe he could convince his brother to be receptive to Roxie. Smiling, he jogged over to the tipi, went to the interior flap, and scratched.

"Come in," Roxie called out.

Ducking inside, he smiled uncertainly at her. "I came to see if you needed anything."

Roxie said, "No. I need nothing." *Nothing except my husband.*

Coming closer, he asked, "May I sit down?"

"Yes."

As he did, she asked, "Why have you not gone back to your tribe? Wild Wind is not going to go with you, so what is the point of you staying here?"

"I want to apologize to you for causing trouble between you and him. It was wrong of me and very selfish," he said. "I have greatly offended you and I need to make restitution for that. So I will stay and make sure that you have enough to eat and that you are protected. You have the dogs, but they cannot shoot bow and arrows or a gun. Please allow me to do this so that I can earn back some honor and perhaps get to know my sister-in-law."

Arrow's sincerity surprised her. "You can stay, but you should sleep inside."

His eyes grew wide. "No, sister. I cannot do that. It would not be proper without your husband living here. I am fine where I am."

"How will you guard me from so far away?"

He frowned at her question. "I will sleep in that little room outside the flap then. No one will get by me there."

"What if I need to go out and you are lying there?" she asked.

He rolled his eyes. His brother's wife was a smart woman. Getting up, he went outside, over to his little camp, and kicked dirt over the fire. He packed up his meager belongings and brought them inside the tipi and put them in a spot off to the right side of the inner flap.

"I will sleep here and no closer to your sleeping room," he said, firmly.

Roxie hid her smile. "That will be fine. Would you like some roast beef and mashed potatoes?"

"What are 'mashed potatoes?'" he asked, trying out the two English words she'd intermixed with her stilted Cheyenne.

She did smile then. "I will show you. Come with me."

When they entered the kitchen, she pulled out a chair. "Sit."

Arrow had never sat on a chair before and wasn't sure about doing it now. Gingerly he rested his behind on the seat in case the chair collapsed on him. He wiggled on it experimentally and found that it was sturdy. He pulled it in closer to the table and looked around. Roxie sat a steaming plate of food in front of him and the aroma made his stomach growl.

When he would have begun eating with his hands, Roxie batted his hand away and handed him a fork. He'd seen soldiers eating with them and knew how it was done, but he'd never eaten with one. Giving Roxie an irritated glance, he stabbed the fork into the fluffy white potatoes with brown gravy drizzled over them and stuffed a big mound into his mouth.

Roxie almost laughed when his expression changed from one of anger to one of surprised enjoyment. He swallowed and proceeded to eat the rest of the food with relish—it reminded Roxie of the way Billy ate.

"See what happens when you are nice to people?" she asked.

He smirked at her and then smiled to show her he wasn't angry. "Yes. You are right. I have been very rude and I am sorry. You speak pretty good Cheyenne."

"There have been several people teaching me," she said, not mentioning Wild Wind's name out loud.

Seeing the sheen of tears in her eyes, Arrow felt even guiltier. Obviously she loved his brother very much if she was that sad. Also if she was willing to live in a tipi—even if it had some modifications to it. He noticed that she wore moccasins a lot and that she often cooked over the fire pit. To distract her from her sorrow, he began telling her funny stories about him and his friends, thinking that he needed to start earning his honor back right away.

Mid-June came and with it a bout of rain. Arrow was still staying with Roxie and he felt that they were indeed friends now. He saw why his brother had married her and thought that Wild Wind could have done much worse in picking a wife, white or Cheyenne. She had many fine qualities that any man would want in his mate.

One evening, he asked, "How long are you going to stay apart from Wild Wind?"

She jerked at little at his question. "We are divorced."

He shook his head. "Not in your heart, and Billy says that in your culture you are still married, so you are not really divorced. Both of you are just being stupid. I know you still love him and I know he still loves you. You should still be together. It is only because I came here and caused trouble that you are not." He looked at her with tears in his eyes, feeling terrible about what he'd done.

"Please do not let your love be lost because I was stupid and did some very stupid things." He didn't want to cry in front of her so he left the tipi. Braves were not supposed to show so much emotion, but he found that the strain of everything was becoming overwhelming and couldn't help it.

He didn't know it, but Roxie took his words to heart and decided that she needed to be courageous and try to reconcile with Wild Wind. It was time to stop wallowing and do something about it.

The next night, Wild Wind lay in his old tipi on Lucky's farm listening to the thunderstorm that raged outside. He had a big beautiful tipi on his own farm with a gorgeous, fun, kind woman in it, and yet here he was alone in this tipi that had seen better days. The thunder crashed so loudly that he didn't hear someone scratching on the tipi flap until the sound had died down to a low growl.

"Come," he said, half sitting up. His shock over seeing a bedraggled Roxie enter the dwelling couldn't have been greater. "Why are you out in this?" he asked, his first thought being for her welfare.

"I couldn't stay away from you anymore. Arrow made me see how stupid I've been, not coming to talk to you sooner," she said, dropping to her knees by him.

His stomach tightened as desire consumed him. She looked even more beautiful than ever to him, even though her hair was plastered to her head and drops of rain ran down her face. One trailed over her full lips and he barely suppressed the urge to kiss it from them.

"We are divorced; there is nothing more to talk about," he said.

"Do you still love me?" she asked. "I still love you. I'm not divorced from you in here where it counts the most." She placed her hand over her heart. "Do you still love me?"

In the low firelight, her eyes were beautiful deep blue pools, and in them he saw sorrow, pleading, and love. He tried to harden his heart to her and he looked away. She further surprised him by grabbing his face and making her face him again.

"Answer me! Do you still love me?"

"Yes! Yes, I still love you!"

"Then if we love still love each other, why are we still apart?" she asked.

Pride. Anger. Stupidity. "There are no good reasons," he said. "You are right."

Roxie began taking off her soaked gingham dress.

"What are you doing?" he asked.

"I'm getting out of these so they can dry and so you can make love with me. We'll do that and then talk later. You lying there in only your breechcloth like that is making it too hard for me to think."

He laughed and felt lighter than he had since they'd split up. The dress and a couple of petticoats were sticking to her, so he ended up helping her out of them. Her damp skin heated under his caresses and their mouths met hungrily. He bore her to his sleeping pallet and they reunited in a blaze of passion that was stunning in its intensity.

As she lay in his arms afterwards, she kissed his shoulder and said, "I'm so sorry. I never thought you'd actually leave. I was only trying to get you to go see your father so that you wouldn't resent me someday because you hadn't had that opportunity to talk with him one last time. You would want me to go if it was my father, wouldn't you?"

"Yes, but it's different. Traveling for me is extremely dangerous and I won't take the chance of getting trapped on the reservation again. I'll admit that it's for selfish reasons. I don't want to be without you, and you could be pregnant. I would be stuck there not knowing if I'd ever see you or our baby again. I saw what that did to Lucky and how much Avasa hurt when they were separated. I don't want that to happen to us. It almost did, but in a different way.

"I became so angry because it was my decision to make and neither you nor Arrow were respecting it, as if I didn't know my own mind. So when you said that you would divorce me if I didn't go to see Father, I took you at your word and left," Wild Wind said. "I'm sorry that I let anger and pride cloud my judgment."

Roxie sighed. "I'm just as guilty. I did treat you as though you were being foolish. I thought I was being selfish by asking you not to go and that it was wrong of me to hold you back. I shouldn't have said that I would divorce you. It was cruel and stupid. I'm so sorry."

He felt her sob against him and her wet tears dampened his chest. Pulling her closer, he whispered soothing words to her and kissed her tears away even as a few of his own fell. They held each other until close to dawn, falling into a contented sleep, secure once again in their love for one another.

Epilogue

"I don't know how you lads did it," Lucky said as he came out of his and Leah's bedroom and walked into the parlor holding a blanket-wrapped baby. "It's a girl. We have a daughter. Please hold her, Evan. I'm shakin' so bad I'm afraid I'll drop her."

The sheriff took the baby and smiled down at her. "She's a pretty little girl, too."

"Aye, she is," Lucky said as he sat down on the sofa by Billy.

Billy put a hand on his arm. "Jeez, you're shaking like a leaf. It's ok, Lucky. She's all right. How's Leah?"

"Tired, of course. Happy. Laughin' at me. All of that. Oh God. I think I'm gonna be sick," Lucky said.

"Take some deep breaths," Josie, who sat on the other side of Lucky, said. She hugged him. "It's ok. You did great."

Thad came into the room, holding out a shot glass. When he saw how much Lucky's hand trembled, he said, "Tell you what: just open your big trap and I'll dump it in."

Lucky complied and Thad poured the whiskey into his mouth.

Josie said, "It's like watching a baby bird being fed."

They all laughed at that.

"More," Lucky said and Thad fed him another shot. "That's better." He closed his eyes, took a deep breath, and reopened them. "All right, Evan. I'm ready to hold her now."

Evan gave the baby to her father and Lucky smiled at her. "Well, now, let me look at ya properly. Yes, yer a bonnie lass. Ya look like yer ma. Ya have her dark hair, too."

Josie and Billy crowded in close so they could look at her, too.

Billy said, "Yep. She does look like Leah. Hi, I'm your Uncle Billy. What's her name?"

"Lillian Ann Quinn. Lily for short, of course," Lucky said.

Thad passed around drinks to everyone but Josie and Otto, to whom he gave shot glasses of milk. "To Lillian Ann Quinn," he said, holding his glass aloft.

"Hear, hear!"

A few months after the birth of Lily Quinn in July, Andi and Arliss stood in her office.

"I don't want you to go. Please don't go," she pleaded.

Arliss smoothed back Andi's hair from her face as he looked into her brown-sugar-hued eyes. "Darlin', we've put this off as long as we can. It's almost the beginning of October. We should have gone months ago, but I just couldn't bear to leave you. The sooner we get it done, the sooner we can get back. I can't offer you anything without having this off our back."

"You won't even tell me anything," she said.

"We'll tell you all about it when we get back, but until then it's best that you don't know," he said. "And don't you go reading our mind."

Andi gave him a small smile. "I've been tempted to, but I haven't."

"Good girl. Believe me, we wouldn't go if we didn't have to. Will you wait for us and not go runnin' into someone else's arms?" he asked.

Tears filled her eyes and she shook her head. "How can I do that when I love you all so much?" It was the first time she'd told her three-men-rolled-into-one how she felt, but just in case something happened to them, she wanted them to know.

Arliss pulled her into his arms, his heart singing with joy upon hearing those sweet words. "We love you, too. So much it hurts sometimes. We'll do everything we can to come back to you. Besides, we're not goin' alone. Marvin and Win are tough, and between us all, we'll be just fine."

She took a shuddering breath as she tried to bring her emotions under control. "I know. You can't blame me for being worried, though."

"I know." Arliss and his two counterparts would have liked to stand in her office holding her all day, but they had to go meet Win and Marvin at the sheriff's office, where they would leave from. "Ok, time for us to get going. Are you gonna kiss us goodbye?"

Pulling back she said, "Yes, and I'm going to make it count. Just in case."

Arliss grinned. "I like the sound of that."

Andi pressed her lips firmly to his, pouring her love into the kiss. If this was the last time she might ever kiss her men, then she would do so with abandon and not feel guilty. Arliss had never wanted to make love to a woman more than he did Andi and right at that moment, he would have gladly done so right there. However, he couldn't and wouldn't.

He and Andi chose the same moment to end the kiss. She surprised him by saying, "Come out come out, wherever you are."

She watched Arliss fall back and R.J. come forward. "Don't look so sad, love. We know what we're doing. We'll be back before you know it."

"You're full of crap," she said.

He grinned. "Are preachers supposed to say crap?"

"Not really," she said, laughing.

"Well, I'm sure God will forgive you. Is it time for my kiss?"

"Yes."

He kissed her soundly and her body temperature rose higher. Ever so slowly, he ended the kiss, smiling into her eyes.

"You do realize this is not making it easy for us to leave," R.J. said.

"It's not easy for me, either," she said.

"I know, but we'll be as quickly as we can," he said. "Goodbye, love."

"Goodbye. Tag you're it."

No sooner had she said the words than Blake crushed her to him and kissed her fiercely. By the time he was done, Andi felt like she was on fire and was out of breath when he released her quickly. Then he grinned at her. "Don't worry, I'll keep the other two safe—maybe even the rich boy and the Chinaman, too."

She laughed and wagged a finger at him. "Remember what we've been working on and behave."

He said, "I'll do my best, but no promises." Pulling her to him again, he smacked her rear end lightly.

"That is *not* behaving."

"I couldn't resist because you're wearing those pants. I love you. See you soon."

"I love you, too. Come out, come out, wherever you are," she said and Arliss was back.

"Ok. We really gotta go now," he said. "We'll send you a postcard, ok?"

She nodded. "Go before I latch onto you again."

He gave her a naughty smile. "When we get back, you can latch on to us all you want."

"Get going," she said, turning him around and pushing him towards the door.

He laughed and left, giving her a wink on the way out.

She went back into her office, shutting and locking the door. Then she sat behind her desk, praying for forgiveness and for her men's safety while she cried her eyes out.

Wild Wind and Roxie had moved Arrow into the spare room of their tipi. The young man had decided to stay on after learning in June that their father had passed away. Lucky had written a letter inquiring as to the chief's health and had been informed of his death. The young brave had disappeared for days after they'd received the distressing news, preferring to deal with his grief in private.

When he'd come back, Wild Wind and Roxie hadn't drawn attention to the fact that he'd been gone, just saying that it was good to see him again. Since then, he'd continued to be withdrawn and he rarely ever went to town. His spirit was restless and he often walked alone along trails for hours. They never pressed him about where he'd been or what he'd been doing, knowing that he couldn't be pressured into learning a new way of life.

Roxy and Wild Wind's relationship deepened with each passing day and they had learned some valuable lessons about compromise and saying only what they really meant. Their hearts were more in tune with each other and they could sometimes read each other's thoughts. Their life together was a rich, happy one, filled with days spent working their farm together and nights in each other's arms as they worked on making a baby.

As autumn began in Echo, there was virtually no heart that wasn't dealing with something. Some were filled with love and the joy of new births while others were filled with grief. Still others were crowded with worry and anxiety over their loved ones who couldn't be with them. Even as all of those hearts were filled with a myriad of emotions, all of them had one thing in common: they held out hope that the future held only good things and that all of their hearts' desires would be fulfilled.

The End

Thank you for reading and supporting my book and I hope you enjoyed it.

Please will you do me a favor and review "Montana Hearts" so I'll know whether you liked it or not, it would be very much appreciated, thank you.

Linda's Other Books

Echo Canyon Brides Series

Montana Rescue
  (Echo Canyon brides Book 1)
Montana Bargain
  (Echo Canyon brides Book 2)
Montana Adventure
  (Echo Canyon brides Book 3)
Montana Luck
  (Echo Canyon brides Book 4)
Montana Fire
  (Echo Canyon brides Book 5)
Montana Hearts
  (Echo Canyon brides Book 6)

Montana Mail Order Brides Series

Westward Winds
  (Montana Mail Order brides Book 1)

Westward Dance
  (Montana Mail Order brides Book 2)
Westward Bound
  (Montana Mail Order brides Book 3)
Westward Destiny
  (Montana Mail Order brides Book 4)
Westward Fortune
  (Montana Mail Order brides Book 5)
Westward Justice
  (Montana Mail Order brides Book 6)
Westward Dreams
  (Montana Mail Order brides Book 7)
Westward Holiday
  (Montana Mail Order brides Book 8)

Westward Sunrise
(Montana Mail Order brides
Book 9)

Westward Moon
(Montana Mail Order brides
Book 10)

Westward Christmas
(Montana Mail Order brides
Book 11)

Westward Visions
(Montana Mail Order brides
Book 12)

Westward Secrets
(Montana Mail Order brides
Book 13)

Westward Changes
(Montana Mail Order brides
Book 14)

Westward Heartbeat
(Montana Mail Order brides
Book 15)

Westward Joy
(Montana Mail Order brides
Book 16)

Westward Courage
(Montana Mail Order brides
Book 17)

Westward Spirit
(Montana Mail Order brides
Book 18)

Westward Fate
(Montana Mail Order brides
Book 19)

Westward Hope
(Montana Mail Order brides
Book 20)

Westward Wild
(Montana Mail Order brides
Book 21)

Westward Sight
(Montana Mail Order brides
Book 22)

Westward Horizons
(Montana Mail Order brides
Book 23)

Connect With Linda

Visit my website at **www.lindabridey.com** to view my other books and to sign up to my mailing list so that you are notified about my new releases.

About Linda Bridey

LINDA BRIDEY lives in New Mexico with her three dogs; a German shepherd, chocolate Labrador retriever, and a black Pug. She became fascinated with Montana and decided to combine that fascination with her fictional romance writing. Linda chose to write about mail-order-brides because of the bravery of these women who left everything and everyone to take a trek into the unknown. The Westward series books are her first publications.

Made in the USA
Monee, IL
22 August 2020

38943737R00142